ARMS AND THE WOMAN

A Romance

HAROLD MacGRATH

1st WORLD
LIBRARY
Literary Society

Arms and the Woman

Harold MacGrath

© 1st World Library, 2007
PO Box 2211
Fairfield, IA 52556
www.1stworldlibrary.com
First Edition

LCCN: 2007927832

Softcover ISBN: 978-1-4218-4545-6
Hardcover ISBN: 978-1-4218-4461-9
eBook ISBN: 978-1-4218-4629-3

Purchase *"Arms and the Woman"*
as a traditional bound book at:
www.1stWorldLibrary.com/purchase.asp?ISBN=978-1-4218-4545-6

1st World Library is a literary, educational organization
dedicated to:

- Creating a free internet library of downloadable ebooks

- Hosting writing competitions and offering book
publishing scholarships.

Interested in more 1st World Library books?
contact: literacy@1stworldlibrary.com
Check us out at: www.1stworldlibrary.com

1st World Library Literary Society

Giving Back to the World

"If you want to work on the core problem, it's early school literacy."

- James Barksdale, former CEO of Netscape

"No skill is more crucial to the future of a child, or to a democratic and prosperous society, than literacy."

- Los Angeles Times

"Literacy... means far more than learning how to read and write... The aim is to transmit... knowledge and promote social participation."

- UNESCO

"Literacy is not a luxury, it is a right and a responsibility. If our world is to meet the challenges of the twenty-first century we must harness the energy and creativity of all our citizens."

- President Bill Clinton

"Parents should be encouraged to read to their children, and teachers should be equipped with all available techniques for teaching literacy, so the varying needs and capacities of individual kids can be taken into account."

- Hugh Mackay

To her, that is to say, to the hand that rocked the cradle.

CHAPTER I

The first time I met her I was a reporter in the embryonic state and she was a girl in short dresses. It was in a garden, surrounded by high red brick walls which were half hidden by clusters of green vines, and at the base of which nestled earth-beds, radiant with roses and poppies and peonies and bushes of lavender lilacs, all spilling their delicate ambrosia on the mild air of passing May. I stood, straw hat in hand, wondering if I had not stumbled into some sweet prison of flowers which, having run disobedient ways in the past, had been placed here by Flora, and forever denied their native meadows and wildernesses. And this vision of fresh youth in my path, perhaps she was some guardian nymph. I was only twenty-two—a most impressionable age. Her hair was like that rare October brown, half dun, half gold; her eyes were cool and restful, like the brown pools one sees in the heart of the forests, and her lips and cheeks cozened the warm vermilion of the rose which lay ever so lightly on the bosom of her white dress. Close at hand was a table upon which stood a pitcher of lemonade. She was holding in her hand an empty glass. As my eyes encountered her calm, inquiring gaze, my courage fled precipitately, likewise the object of my errand. There was a pause; diffidence and embarrassment on my side, placidity on hers.

"Well, sir?" said she, in a voice the tone of which implied

that she could readily understand her presence in the garden, but not mine.

As I remember it, I was suddenly seized with a great thirst.

"I should like a glass of your lemonade," I answered, bravely laying down the only piece of money I possessed.

Her stern lips parted in a smile, and my courage came back cautiously, that is to say, by degrees. She filled a glass for me, and as I gulped it down I could almost detect the flavor of lemon and sugar.

"It is very good," I volunteered, passing back the glass. I held out my hand, smiling.

"There isn't any change," coolly.

I flushed painfully. It was fully four miles to Newspaper Row. I was conscious of a sullen pride. Presently the object of my errand returned. Somewhat down the path I saw a gentleman reclining in a canvas swing.

"Is that Mr. Wentworth?" I asked.

"Yes. Do you wish to speak to him? Uncle Bob, here is a gentleman who desires to speak to you."

I approached. "Mr. Wentworth," I began, cracking the straw in my hat, "my name is John Winthrop. I am a reporter. I have called to see if it is true that you have declined the Italian portfolio."

"It is true," he replied kindly. "There are any number of reasons for my declining it, but I cannot make them public. Is that all?"

"Yes, sir; thank you;" and I backed away.

"Are you a reporter?" asked the girl, as I was about to pass by her.

"Yes, I am."

"Do you draw pictures?"

"No, I do not."

"Do you write novels?"

"No," with a nervous laugh.

There is nothing like the process of interrogation to make one person lose interest in another.

"Oh; I thought perhaps you did," she said, and turned her back to me.

I passed through the darkened halls of the house and into the street.

I never expected to see her again, but it was otherwise ordained. We came together three years later at Block Island. She was eighteen now, gathering the rosy flowers of her first season. She remembered the incident in the garden, and we laughed over it. A few dances, two or three evenings on the verandas, watching the sea, moonlit, as it sprawled among the rocks below us, and the even tenor of my way ceased to be. I appreciated how far she was above me; so I worshipped her silently and from afar. I told her my ambitions, confidences so welcome to feminine ears, and she rewarded me with a small exchange. She, too, was an orphan, and lived with her uncle, a rich banker, who, as a diversion, consented to represent his country at foreign courts. Her given name was Phyllis. I had seen the name a thousand times in print; the poets had idealised it, and the novelists had embalmed it in tender phrases. It was the first time I had ever met a woman by the name of Phyllis. It appealed to my poetic instinct. Perhaps that was the cause of it all. And then, she was very beautiful. In the autumn of that year we became great friends; and through her influence I began to see beyond the portals of the mansions of the rich. Matthew Prior's Chloes and Sir John Suckling's Euphelias lost their charms. Henceforth my muse's name became Phyllis. I took her to the opera when I didn't know where I was going to breakfast on the morrow. I sent her roses and went without tobacco, a privation of which woman knows nothing.

Often I was plunged into despair at my distressed circumstances. Money to her meant something to spend; to me it meant something to get. Her income bothered her because she could not spend it; my income was mortgaged a week in advance, and did not bother me at all. This was the barrier at my lips. But her woman's intuition must have told her that she was a part and parcel of my existence.

I had what is called a forlorn hope: a rich uncle who was a planter in Louisiana. His son and I were his only heirs. But this old planter had a mortal antipathy to my side of the family. When my mother, his sister, married Alfred Winthrop in 1859, at the time when the North and South were approaching the precipice of a civil war, he considered all family ties obliterated. We never worried much about it. When mother died he softened to the extent of being present at the funeral. He took small notice of my father, but offered to adopt me if I would assume his name. I clasped my father's hand in mine and said nothing. The old man stared at me for a moment, then left the house. That was the first and last time I ever

Harold MacGrath

saw him. Sometimes I wondered if he would remember me in his will. This, of course, was only when I had taken Phyllis somewhere, or when some creditor had lost patience. One morning in January, five years after my second meeting with Phyllis, I sat at my desk in the office. It was raining; a cold thin rain. The window was blurred. The water in the steam-pipes went banging away. I was composing an editorial which treated the diplomatic relations between this country and England. The roar of Park Row distracted me. Now and then I would go to the window and peer down on the living stream below. A dense cloud of steam hung over all the city. I swore some when the copy boy came in and said that there was yet a column and a half to fill, and that the foreman wanted to "close up the page early." The true cause of my indis-position was due to the rumors rife in the office that morning. Rumors which emanate from the managing editor's room are usually of the sort which burden the subordinate ones with anxiety. The London correspondent was "going to pieces." He had cabled that he was suffering from nervous prostration, supplementing a request for a two months' leave of absence. For "nervous prostration" we read "drink." Our London correspondent was a brilliant journalist; he had written one or two clever books; he had a broad knowledge of men and affairs; and his pen was one of those which flashed and burned at frequent intervals; but he drank. Dan's father had been a victim of the habit. I remember meeting the elder Hillars. He was a picturesque individual, an accomplished scholar, a wide traveller, a diplomatist, and a noted war correspondent. His work during the Franco-Prussian war had placed him in the front rank. After sending his son Dan to college he took no further notice of him. He was killed while serving his paper at the siege of Alexandria, Egypt. Dan naturally followed his father's footsteps both in profession and in habits. He had been my classmate at college, and no one knew him better than I, except it was himself. The love of adventure and drink had ended the life of the one; it might end the life of the other.

The foreman in the composing room waited some time for that required column and a half of editorial copy. I lit my pipe; and my thoughts ran back to the old days, to the many times Dan had paid my debts and to the many times I had paid his. Ah, me! those were days when love and fame and riches were elusive and we went in quest of them. The crust is hyssop when the heart is young. The garret is a palace when hope flies unfettered. The most wonderful dreams imaginable are dreamt close to the eaves. And when a man leaves behind him the garret, he also leaves behind the fondest illusions. But who—who would stay in the garret!

And as my thoughts ran on, the question rose, Whom would they send in his place—Dan's? I knew London. It was familiar ground. Perhaps they might send me. It was this thought which unsettled me. I was perfectly satisfied with New York. Phyllis lived in New York. There would be time enough for London when we were married. Then I began to build air castles. A newspaper man is the architect of some splendid structures, but he thoughtlessly builds on the sand when the tide is out. Yes, foreign corresponding would be all well enough, I mused, with Phyllis at my side. With her as my wife I should have the envy of all my fellow craftsmen. We should dine at the embassies and the attaches would flutter about us, and all London would talk of the beautiful "Mrs. Winthrop." Then the fire in my pipe-bowl went out. The copy boy was at my elbow again.

"Hang you!" said I.

"The foreman says he's coming down with an axe," replied the boy.

It was like churning, but I did manage to grind the copy. I was satisfied that the United States and Great Britain would not go to war over it.

The late afternoon mail brought two letters. I opened the one from Phyllis first. It said:

"DEAR JACK—Uncle Bob has a box for the opera to-night, but he has been suddenly called to Washington; politics, possibly, but he would not say. Aunty and I want you to go with us in his stead. Ethel and her fiance, Mr. Holland, will be together, which means that Aunty and I will have no one to talk to unless you come. Carmen is to be sung. Please do not fail me.

"PHYLLIS."

Fail her! I thought not.

Then I read the second letter. I read it three or four times, and even then I was not sure that I was not dreaming. I caught up my pipe again, filled it and lit it. I read the letter once more. I was solemnly informed that my uncle was dead and that I was mentioned in the will, and that if I would kindly call at the Hoffman House the following morning a certain sum of money would be given to me. I regretted that I had reached that age when a man's actions must be dignified, although alone; otherwise I dare say I should have danced the pas seul. Whatever my uncle's bequest might be, I believed that it would make me independently rich. I am ashamed to admit that I did not feel sorry at the news of his sudden departure from this life. It is better to be rich than to be ambitious. It is better to have at hand what you want than to work for it, and then not get it. Phyllis was scarcely an arm's length away now. I whistled as I locked up my desk, and proceeded down stairs and sang a siren song into the waxen ears of the cashier.

"You have only twenty coming this week, Mr. Winthrop," said he.

"Never mind," I replied; "I'll manage to get along next week." It was only on very rare occasions that I drew my full pay at the end of the week.

I dined at a fashionable restaurant. As I sipped my wine I built one of my castles, and Phyllis reigned therein. There would be a trip to Europe every summer, and I should devote my time to writing novels. My picture would be the frontispiece in the book reviews, and wayside paragraphs would tell of the enormous royalties my publishers were paying me. I took some old envelopes from my pocket and began figuring on the backs of them as to what purposes the money should be put. It could not be less than $50,000, perhaps more. Of course my uncle had given a harbor to a grudge against me and mine, but such things are always forgotten on the death bed. It occurred to me that I never had known before what a fine world it was, and I regretted having spoken ill of it. I glanced across the way. The sky had cleared, and the last beams of the sun flamed in the windows of the tall buildings. Fortune, having buffeted me, was now going to make me one of her favorite children. I had reached the end of the long lane.

As I left the restaurant I decided to acquaint Phyllis with my good luck and also my desire that she should share of it. I turned into a florist's and had a dozen roses sent up to her. They were American Beauties. I could afford it now.

I found Phyllis thrumming on the piano. She was singing in a low voice the aria from "Lucia." I stood on the threshold of the drawing-room and waited till she had done. I believed her to be unaware of my presence. She was what we poets call a "dream of loveliness," a tangible dream. Her neck and shoulders were like satin, and the head above them reminded me of Sappho's which we see in marble. From where I stood I could catch a glimpse of the profile, the nose and firm chin, the exquisite mouth, to kiss which I would gladly have given up any number of fortunes. The cheek had that delicate curve of a rose leaf, and when the warm blood surged into it there was a color as matchless as that of a jack-rose. Ah, but I loved her. Suddenly the music ceased.

"There is a mirror over the piano, Jack," she said, without turning her head.

So I crossed the room and sat down in the chair nearest her. I vaguely wondered if, at the distance, she had seen the love in my eyes when I thought myself unobserved.

"I thank you for those lovely roses," she said, smiling and permitting me to press her hand.

"Don't mention it," I replied. It is so difficult for a man to say original things in the presence of the woman he loves! "I have great news for you. It reads like a fairy tale, you know; happy ever afterward, and all that."

"Ah!"

"Yes. Do you remember my telling you of a rich uncle who lived in the South?"

"Is it possible that he has left you a fortune?" she cried, her eyes shining.

"You have guessed it."

"I am very glad for your sake, Jack. I was beginning to worry about you."

"Worry about me?"

"Yes. I do not understand how a newspaper man can afford to buy roses four or five times a week—and exist." She had the habit of being blunt and frank to her intimate friends. I secretly considered it an honor when she talked to me like this. "I have told you repeatedly to send me flowers only once a week. I'd rather not have them at all. Last week you spent as much as $30 on roses alone. Mr. Holland does not do that for Ethel, and he has a million."

"I'm not Holland," I said. "He doesn't—that is—I do not think he—." Then I foundered. I had almost said: "He doesn't care as much for Ethel as I do for you."

Phyllis pretended not to note my embarrassment. The others came in then, and conversation streamed into safer channels.

When we entered the box at the opera the curtain had risen. Phyllis and I took the rear chairs. They were just out of the glare of the lights.

"You are looking very beautiful to-night," I whispered lowly. I was beginning business early. There was no barrier at my lips.

"Thank you," she replied. Then with a smile: "Supposing I were to say that you are looking very handsome?"

"Oh," said I, somewhat disconcerted, "that would be rather embarrassing."

"I do not doubt it."

Harold MacGrath

"And then it would not be true. The duty we men owe to a beautiful woman is constantly to keep telling her of it."

"And the duty we women owe to a fine-looking man?" a rogue of a dimple in her cheeks.

"Is to explicitly believe all he says regarding your beauty," I answered, evading the question. "A man may tell a woman that she is beautiful, but a woman may not tell a man that he is fine-looking, that is, in public."

"The terms are not fair."

"That may be true, but they make the wheels of the social organization run smoother. For instance, if I met a strange woman and she told me that I was handsome, I shouldn't be able to speak again the whole evening. On the other hand, a beautiful woman, after you say that you are delighted to meet her, expects the very next remark to concern her good looks."

"Your insight is truly remarkable," she said, the dimple continuing its elusive manoeuvres. "Hush; here comes Carmen."

And our voices grew faint in the swell of melody. Mrs. Wentworth was entranced; her daughter was fondly gazing at the back of her fiance's head; Phyllis had turned her face from me to the stage. As for myself, I was not particularly interested in the cigarette girl. It was running through my head that the hour had arrived. I patted my gloves for a moment, then I drew a long breath.

"Phyllis!" said I. There was a quaver in my voice. Perhaps I had not spoken loud enough. "Phyllis!" said I again.

She turned quickly and gave me an inquiring and at the

same time nervous glance.

"What is it?"

"I want to tell you something I have never dared to tell you till now," I said earnestly. The voice on the stage soared heavenward. "I love you. Will you be my wife?"

Ah, me! where were those drooping eyelids, that flush, that shy, sweet glance of which I had so often dreamt? Phyllis was frowning.

"Jack, I have been afraid of this," she said. "I am so sorry, but it cannot be."

"Oh, do not say that now," I cried, crushing my gloves. "Wait awhile; perhaps you may learn to love me."

"Jack, I have always been frank to you because I like you. Do you suppose it will take me five years to find out what my heart says to any man? No. Had I loved you I should not have asked you to wait; I should have said yes. I do not love you in the way you wish. Indeed, I like you better than any man I know, but that is all I can offer you. I should be unkind if I held out any false hopes. I have often asked myself why I do not love you, but there is something lacking in you, something I cannot define. Some other woman will find what I have failed to find in you to love."

I was twisting my gloves out of all recognition. There was a singing in my ears which did not come from the stage.

"Look at it as I do, Jack. There is a man in this world whom I shall love, and who will love me. We may never meet. Then he shall be an ideal to me, and I to him. You

Harold MacGrath

believe you love me, but the love you offer is not complete."

"Not complete?" I echoed.

"No. It would be if I returned it. Do you understand? There is in this world a woman you will truly love and who will return your love in its fulness. Will you meet? That is in the hands of your destinies. Shall I meet my ideal? Who knows? But till I do, I shall remain an old maid."

I nodded wearily. A dissertation on affinities seemed ill-timed.

"And now," she said, "this beautiful friendship of ours must come to an end." And there were tears in her eyes.

"Yes," said I, twisting and untwisting the shreds of my gloves. It seemed as though the world had slipped from under my feet and I was whirling into nothingness. "My heart is very heavy."

"Jack, if you talk like that," hastily, "you will have me crying before all these people."

Unfortunately Ethel turned and saw the tears in her cousin's eyes.

"Mercy! what is the matter?" she asked.

"Jack has been telling me a very pathetic story," said Phyllis, with a pity in her eyes.

"Yes; something that happened to-night," said I, staring at the programme, but seeing nothing, nothing.

"Well," said Ethel, "this is not the place for them," turning her eyes to the stage again.

The concluding acts of the opera were a jangle of chords and discords, and the hum of voices was like the murmur of a far-off sea. My eyes remained fixed upon the stage. It was like looking through a broken kaleidoscope. I wanted to be alone, alone with my pipe. I was glad when we at last entered the carriage. Mrs. Wentworth immediately began to extol the singers, and Phyllis, with that tact which is given only to kind-hearted women, answered most of the indirect questions put to me. She was giving me time to recover. The direct questions I could not avoid. Occasionally I looked out of the window. It had begun to rain again. It was very dreary.

"And what a finale, Mr. Winthrop!" cried Mrs. Wentworth,

"Yes, indeed," I replied. To have loved and lost, and such a woman, was my thought.

"The new tenor is an improvement. Do you not think so?"

"Yes, indeed." No more to touch her hand, to hear her voice, to wait upon her wishes.

"It was the most brilliant audience of the season."

"Yes, indeed," I murmured. Those were the only words I could articulate.

The carriage rumbled on.

"Does Patti return in the fall?"

"Yes." Five years of dreaming, and then to awake!

And then the carriage mercifully stopped.

Mrs. Wentworth insisted that I should enter and have some coffee. I had so few words at my command that I could not invent even a flimsy excuse. So I went in. The coffee was tasteless. I put in four lumps of sugar. I stirred and stirred and stirred. Finally, I swallowed the contents of the cup. It was very hot. When the agony was past I rose and made my adieu.

Phyllis came to the door with me.

"Forget what I have said," I began, fumbling the door-knob. "I suppose I was an ass to think that you might love me. They say that it is a malady. Very well. With a few prescribed remedies I shall recover."

"You are very bitter."

"Can you blame me," clicking the latch back and forth, "when all the world has suddenly grown dark?"

"There are other eyes than mine," gently.

"Yes; but they will light other paths than those I shall follow."

"Jack, you are too manly to make threats."

"That was not a threat," said I. "Well, I shall go and laugh at myself for my presumption. To laugh at yourself is to cure. There is no more wine in the cup, nothing but the lees. I'll have to drink them. A wry face, and then it will all be over. Yes, I am bitter. To have dreamed as I have dreamed, and to awake as I have! Ah, well; I must go on loving you till—"

"Till she comes," supplemented Phyllis.

"You wrong me. It is only in letters that I am versatile. Forgive my bitterness and forget my folly."

"Oh, Jack, if you knew how sorry I am! I shall forgive the bitterness, but I will not forget what you term folly. It's something any woman might be proud of, the love of an honest, dear, good fellow. Good night." She held her hand toward me.

"Good night," I said, "and God bless you!" I kissed the palm of her hand, opened the door, and then stumbled down the steps.

I do not remember how I reached home.

It was all over.

My beautiful castle had fallen in ruins about my ears.

CHAPTER II

In my bedroom the next morning there was a sad and heavy heart. The owner woke up, stared at the ceiling, then at the sun-baked bricks beyond his window. He saw not the glory of the sun and the heavens. To his eyes there was nothing poetic in the flash of the distant church-spires against the billowy cloudbanks. The gray doves, circling about the chimneys, did not inspire him, nor the twittering of the sparrows on the window ledge. There was nothing at all in the world but a long stretch of barren, lonely years. And he wondered how, without her at his side, he ever could traverse them. He was driftwood again. He had built upon sands as usual, and the tide had come in; his castle was flotsam and jetsam. He was drifting, and he didn't care where. He was very sorry for himself, and he had the blue devils the worst kind of way. Finally he crawled out of bed and dressed because it had to be done. He was not particularly painstaking with the procedure. It mattered not what collar became him best, and he picked up a tie at random. A man generally dresses for a certain woman's approval, and when that is no longer to be gained he grows indifferent. The other women do not count.

My breakfast consisted of a cup of coffee; and as the generous nectar warmed my veins my thoughts took a philosophical turn. It is fate who writes the was, the is, and the shall be. We have a proverb for every joy and misfortune. It is the only consolation fate gives us. It is like a conqueror asking the vanquished to witness the looting. All roads lead to Rome, and all proverbs are merely sign posts by which we pursue our destinies. And how was I to get to Rome? I knew not. Hope is better than clairvoyance.

Was Phyllis right when she said that I did not truly love her? I believed not. Should I go on loving her all my life? Undoubtedly I should. As to affinities, I had met mine, but it had proved a one-sided affair.

It was after ten by the clock when I remembered that I was to meet the lawyer, the arbiter of my new fortunes. Money is a balm for most things, and coupled with travel it might lead me to forget.

He was the family lawyer, and he had come all the way North to see that I received my uncle's bequest. He was bent, gray and partially bald. He must have been close to seventy, but for all that there was a youthful twinkle in his eyes as he took my card and looked up into my face.

"So you are John Winthrop?" he said in way of preliminary. You may hand a card case full of your name to a lawyer, and still he will insist upon a verbal admission.

"I have always been led to believe so," I answered smartly, placing my hat beside the chair in which I sat down. "How did you manage to locate me in this big city?"

"Your uncle had seen some of your signed articles in New York papers, and said that in all probability I should find you here. A few inquiries set me on your track." Here he pulled out a lengthy document from his handbag. "I confess, however," he added, "that I am somewhat disappointed in your looks."

"Disappointed in my looks!" was my cry. "What sort of a duffer were you expecting to see?"

He laughed. "Well, your uncle gave me the idea that I should find a good-for-nothing hack-writer, a dweller in some obscure garret."

"If that is the case, what under the sun did he send you up here for?"

The merriment went out of the old man's face and his eyes became grave. "Of that anon. Let me proceed with my business and read the will to you. You will find it rather a remarkable document."

I settled back in my chair in a waiting attitude. To tell the truth, I was somewhat confused by all this preamble. To his son my uncle left the bulk of his property, which amounted to more than a million. I was listless. The head overseer received the munificent sum of $50,000; to the butler, the housekeeper and the cook he gave $10,000 each. I began to grow interested. He was very liberal to his servants. Several other names were read, and my interest assumed the color of anxiety. When the lawyer stopped to unfold the last flap, I spoke.

"And where in the world do I come in?"

"In the sense you understand, you do not come in."

I stared at him in amazement. "I don't come in?" I repeated vaguely. "Ah," reaching down for my hat, "then I go out, as it were;" as brilliant as a London yellow fog. "What the devil does all this mean?" I started to rise.

"Wait!" he commanded. "'To my nephew, John Winthrop, I bequeath the sum of $1,000 to be presented to him in person immediately after this will is probated, and with the understanding that he shall make no further demand upon my son and heir in the future.' That is all," concluded the lawyer, folding the document. "I have the check in my pocket."

"Keep it," said I, rising. A hot flush of indignation swept over me. I understood. It was his revenge. To have a man make sport of you after he is dead and gone, leaving you impotent and with never a chance to retaliate! "Keep it," I said again; "throw it away, or burn it. I understand. He has satisfied a petty revenge. It is an insult not only to me, but to my dead parents. You are, of course, acquainted with the circumstances of my mother's marriage. She married the man she loved, disregarding her brother's wishes."

"I knew your mother," said the lawyer, going to the window and looking out and beyond all that met his gaze.

"To think," I went on, cooling none, "that my mother's brother should die in this manner, nourishing so small and petty a spite! When he did this he knew that I should understand his motive. In the first place, I never dreamed that he would remember me in his will; never entertained the least idea of it. I am independent; I am earning a livelihood, small, but enough and to spare. I'll bid you good morning." I took a step toward the door.

"Young man, sit down," said the old man, coming back to his chair. "I want to talk to you for a few minutes. Your uncle was a peculiarly vindictive man. What he considered a wrong he neither forgot nor forgave. His son pleaded with him not to put in that final clause. He offered even to share with you. Your uncle swore he would leave it all to the stablemen first. This journey was forced upon me, or I should not have taken it. This is my advice to you: Accept the check, in the privacy of your room tear it up, or light a cigar with it; that's about all it's worth. You will feel no little satisfaction in lighting a cigar with it, that is, if you are anything like me. Think of it! a thousand dollars to light your cigar. It is an opportunity not to be missed. When you grow old you will say to your grandchildren: 'Once I lit a cigar with a thousand-dollar check.' The oldest inhabitant will be silenced forever; it may become history. And then, too, if there are spirits, as Scripture says there are, your uncle's will writhe at the performance. I trust that you will forgive me my part in the matter. I have taken a fancy to you, and if you will accept my friendship I shall be happy to accept yours. Your uncle's revenge will not be a marker to the restitution his son will make."

"Restitution?—his son?"

"Yes. To my sincere regret he is an invalid who may or may not live the year out. He has already made a will, in which he leaves all to you. The will is in my safe at home. I return to-night, so I may not see you again in this world of sin and tribulation." The merry twinkle had returned to his eyes. "I am very old."

"It is worth all the trouble to have met you," said I. "You should have made the jolt very easy."

So we shook hands, and he gave me a cigar, around which was wrapped the check. He winked. Then he laughed, and I joined him, though my laughter resembled mirth less than it did the cackle of a hen which was disturbed over the future of her brood.

I left him and went down into the wine room and ordered

a stiff brandy and soda. When that disappeared I ordered another. I rattled the ice in the glass. "Ha, ha, ha!" I roared, as the events of the past twenty-four hours recurred to me. There must have been a suicidal accent to my laughter, for the bartender looked at me with some concern. I called for another brandy and shot the soda into it myself. I watched the foam evaporate, "Ha, ha, ha!"

"Hard luck?" the bartender asked sympathetically.

"Yes," said I. I seemed to be speaking to several bartenders who looked at me with several varieties of compassion.

"Have another on me," said the bartender.

I had another, and went out into the street. I walked down Broadway, chuckling to myself. What a glorious farce it all was! My fortune! Phyllis my wife! What if she had accepted me? I laughed aloud, and people turned and stared at me. Oh, yes! I was to travel and write novels and have my pictures in book reviews, and all that! When I arrived at the office I was on the verge of total insanity. I was obliged to ask the paragrapher to write my next day's leader. It was night before I became rational, and once that, the whole world donned cap and bells and began capering for my express benefit. The more I thought of it, the more I laughed. What a whimsical world it was! And was there anything in it so grotesque as my part? I took the check from my pocket and cracked it between my fingers. A cigar was in my mouth. Should I light it with the check? It was for $1,000. After all, it was more than I had ever before held in my hand at once. But what was a paltry thousand, aye a paltry ten thousand, to a man's pride? I bit off the end of my cigar, creased the check into a taper, and struck a match. I watched it burn and burn. I struck another. I held it within an inch of the check, but for the life of me I could not light it.

"The devil take it!" I cried. I flung the cigar out of the window and laid the check on my desk. Courage? Why, it needed the courage of a millionaire to light a cigar with a $1,000 check!

The office boy, who came in then, was salvation. The managing editor wanted to see me. I sprang up with alacrity; anything but the sight of that figure 1 and the three demon eyes of that $1,000 check!

"Winthrop," said the managing editor to me as I entered his office, "you've got to go to London. Hillars has gone under—"

"Not dead!" I cried.

"No, no! He has had to give up work temporarily on account of drink. If it was any other man I'd throw him over in short order. But I feel sorry for Hillars, and I am going to give him another chance. I want you to go over and take care of him if possible. The London work is not new to you. You can handle that and Hillars too. If you can keep him in check—"

I shuddered. The word "check" jarred on my nerves.

"What's the matter?" asked the editor.

"A temporary chill," I said. "Go on."

"Well, if you can manage to keep him in check for a month or so he'll be able to get on his feet again. And it will be like a vacation to you. If anything happens to Hillars you will be expected to remain permanently abroad. Hillars suggested you in his letter. Will you be ready to go next Monday?"

"To-morrow if you like," I answered readily enough. Here was an opportunity not to be missed. To see new scenes and faces is partially to forget old ones.

"Very well. I'll give you some letters which will help you. Our office is in the Strand. Hillars will find you lodgings. He has bachelor quarters in the west end of the town, where congenial spirits congregate. Come in to-morrow and we'll talk it over."

I was much pleased with the turn of events. If I could get away from New York I might forget Phyllis—no, not forget her; I loved her too well ever to forget her; but the prolonged absence would cure me of my malady.

Before going to bed that night I lit a cigar, but not with the check. On sober second thought I calculated that the sum would pay up all my debts and leave me a comfortable margin. A man can well pocket his pride when he pockets a thousand dollars with it. And why not? I was about to start life anew and might as well begin on a philosophical basis. Who knew but my uncle had foreseen the result of his bequest; my rage, my pride, and finally lighting a cigar with his check? It really might make his spirit writhe to better effect if I became benefited. Sober second thought is more or less a profitable investment.

On the morrow everything was arranged for my departure. I was to leave Saturday morning.

It was a beautiful day, crisp and clear, with a bare ground which rang to the heel. In the afternoon I wandered over to the Park and sat down on a bench, and watched the skaters as they glided to and fro. I caught myself wishing that I was a boy again, with an hour's romp on the sheeny crust in view. Gradually the mantle of peace fell upon me, and there was a sense of rest. I was going to forgive the world the wrong it had done me; perhaps it would feel ashamed of itself and reward me for my patience. So Hillars was "going to pieces." It is strange how we men love another who has shared and spent with us our late patrimonies. Hillars and I had been friends since our youth, and we had lived together till a few years back. Then he went to Washington, from there to Paris, thence to London. He was a better newspaper man than I. I liked to dream too well, while he was always for a little action. Liquor was getting the best of him. I wondered why. It might be a woman. There is always one around some-where when a man's breath smells of whisky. A good deal of this woman's temperance business is caused by remorse. I was drawing aimless pictures in the frozen gravel, when I became aware that two skaters had stopped in front of me. I glanced up and saw Phyllis and Ethel, their eyes like stars and their cheeks like roses.

"I was wondering if it was you," said Ethel. "Phyllis, where is my cavalier?"

"I believe he has forsaken us," said the voice of the woman I loved.

"Will you not accept part of the bench?" I asked, moving along.

The girls dropped easily beside me.

"I was just wishing I was a boy again and was in for a game of hockey," said I. "I am going to London on Saturday. Our foreign correspondent has had to give up work on account of ill health."

"You haven't—" Phyllis stopped suddenly.

"Oh, no," said I intuitively. "I am growing rusty, and they think I need a vacation." I was glad Ethel was there with her voluble chatter.

"Oh, a foreign correspondent!'" she cried.

"Yes."

"You will have a glorious time. Papa will probably return to B—when the next administration comes in. It is sure to be Republican." There are a few women who pose as Democrats; I never met one of them. "You know papa was there twenty years ago. I suppose you will be hob-nobbing with dukes and princes."

"It cannot be avoided," I said gravely. "I do not expect to remain long in London. When my work is done perhaps I shall travel and complete my foreign polish."

"Oh, yes!" said Phyllis. "I forgot to tell you, Ethel, that a fortune has been left to Jack, and he need not work but for the love of it."

I laughed, but they thought it a self-conscious laugh. Somehow I was not equal to the task of enlightening them.

"It is jolly to be rich," said Ethel, clicking her skates together. "It's a bother at times, however, to know what to do with the money. I buy so many things I do not need just because I feel compelled to spend my allowance."

"It must be very inconvenient," I observed.

"And now that you are a man of leisure," said Phyllis, "you will write that book you have always been telling me about?"

"Do you wish it?" I asked.

"I do. What I have always found lacking in you is application. You start out to accomplish something, you find an obstacle in your path and you do not surmount it; you do not persevere."

My pulse beat quickly. Was there a double meaning to what she said? I could not tell, for her eyes remained averted.

I sighed. "It would be nice to become a successful author, but when a man is as rich as I am fame tarnishes." I took out an envelope from my pocket.

"What is that?" asked Phyllis.

I turned over the back and showed it to her.

"Figures!" she laughed. "What do they mean?"

"It is what I am going to do with my fortune," said I. I was holding out my vanity at arm's length and laughing at it silently.

"Your air castles will be realized now," said Phyllis.

"I shall build no more," said I. "The last one gave me a very bad fall."

Phyllis looked away again. A vague perfume from her hair wafted past my nostrils, and for a space I was overwhelmed with sadness. Soon I discerned Mr. Holland speeding toward us.

"I shall not see you again," I said, "so I'll bid you good-bye now. If you should chance to come abroad this summer, do not fail to look me up."

"Good luck to you," said Ethel, shaking my hand. "You must bring home a Princess or a Duchess." Then she moved off a way, thoughtfully.

"You must write to me occasionally, Jack," said Phyllis, "if only once a month. I shall always be interested in your career."

The smile faltered as she put out her gloved hand.

"You will make some man happy, Phyllis," I said.

"Good-bye."

"Good-bye."

And then—and then they sped away, and I followed them with dimming gaze till I could see them no more. I trudged home. . . .

I stood on the upper deck. The spires and domes of the city faded on my sight till all merged into a gray smoky patch on the horizon. With a dead cigar clenched between my teeth I watched and watched with a callous air, as though there had been no wrench, as though I had not left behind all I loved in the world. And yet I gazed, the keen salt air singing past my ears, till there was nothing but the sea as far as the eye could scan.

Thus I began the quest of the elusive, which is a little of love, a little of adventure, and a little of all things.

CHAPTER III

Hillars hadn't been down to the office in two days, so the assistant said.

"Is he ill?" I asked, as I carried a chair to the window.

"Ill?" The young man coughed affectedly.

"Do you believe it possible for him to come in this afternoon?"

"It is quite possible. One does not use the word impossible in regard to Hillars. It is possible that he may be in St. Petersburg by this time, for all I know. You see," with an explanatory wave of the hand, "he's very uncertain in his movements. For the last six months he has been playing all over the table, to use the parlance of the roulette player. I have had to do most of the work, and take care of him into the bargain. If I may take you into my confidence—," with some hesitancy.

"Certainly," said I. "I want you to tell me all about him. He was my roommate at college. Perhaps I can straighten him up."

"The truth is, the trouble began last September. He came back from the Continent, where he had been on an errand, a changed man. Hillars always drank, but never to an alarming extent. On his return, however, he was in a bad shape. It was nearly November before I got him sobered up; and then he went under on an average of three times a week. I asked him bluntly what he meant by it, and he frankly replied that if he wanted to drink himself to death, that was his business. When he isn't half-seas over he is gloomy and morose. From the first I knew that something had gone wrong on the mainland; but I couldn't trap him for a farthing. No man at his age drinks himself to death without cause; I told him so, but he only laughed at me. I'd give a good deal to know what the truth is; not from curiosity, mind you, but to find the disease in order to apply a remedy. Dan's father died of drink."

"No," said I coldly; "he was shot."

"Oh, I know that," was the reply; "but give a conditioned man the same wound and he will recover, nine times out of ten. The elder Hillars was so enervated by drink that he had no strength to fight the fever which came on top of the bullet-hole. Something happened over there; and it's pounds to pence there's a woman back of the curtain. It is some one worth while. Hillars is not a man to fall in love with a barmaid."

I began to respect the young man's wisdom.

"So you believe it to be a woman?"

"Yes. The wind blows from one point at a time. There are four points to the vane of destiny; there is ambition for glory, ambition for power, ambition for wealth, and ambition for love. In Hillars's case, since the wind does not blow from the first three, it must necessarily blow from the fourth. You know him better than I do; so you must certainly know that Hillars is not a man to drink because glory or power or wealth refused to visit him."

"You are a very discerning young man," said I, whereat he laughed. "Did he get my cable?"

"No. I thought that it was some order from headquarters and opened it myself. I put it in his desk. I spoke to him, but he was too drunk to pay any heed to what I said. Well, I must be going. I am getting out a symposium of editorials from the morning papers on the possibility of a Franco-Russian alliance. It must be at the cable office in half an hour. If you are going to wait, you'll find the Berlin and Paris files in the next room. I'll see you later," and he departed.

It was five of the clock. The Strand was choked. Here and there I saw the color of martial attire. Save for this, and that the buildings were low and solid, and that most of the people walked slower, I might have been looking down upon Broadway for all the change of place I saw. There is not much difference between New York and London, except in the matter of locomotion. The American gets around with more rapidity than does his English cousin, but in the long run he accomplishes no more. It is only when one steps onto the Continent that the real difference in the human races is discerned. Strange as this may seem, it is not distinguishable in a cosmopolitan city. My eyes were greeted with the same huge wearisome signs of the merchants; the same sad-eyed "sandwich men;" the same newsboys yelling and scampering back and forth; the same rumble of the omnibuses, the roar of the drays, and the rattle of the cabs. I was not much interested in all I saw. Suddenly my roving eyes rested upon a familiar face. It was Hillars, and he was pushing rapidly across the street. Any one would have instantly marked him for an American by the nervous stride, the impatience at being obstructed. I went into the fire-room, intending to give him a little surprise. I did not have long to wait. The door to the main office opened and he came in, singing a snatch from a drinking song we used to sing at college. The rich baritone that had once made the old glee club famous was a bit husky and throaty. I heard him unlock his desk and roll back the lid. There was a quiet for a moment.

"Dick!" he called. "Hi, Dick! Well, I'm hanged!"

Evidently he had discovered my cable.

"Dick isn't in," said I, crossing the threshold.

In a moment our hands were welded together, and we were gazing into each other's eyes.

"You old reprobate!" I cried; "not to have met me at the station, even."

"Bless my soul, Jack, this cable was the first intimation that you were within 3,000 miles of London. But it does my heart good to see you!" pumping my hand again. "Come out to dinner with me. Now don't begin to talk till we've had something to eat; I'm almost famished. I know all the questions you want to ask, but not now. There's a Bohemian joint a block above that'll do your heart good to see. We'll have chops and ale, just like we did in the old days, the green and salad days, I would they were back again"—soberly. "Oh, I've a long story to tell you, my son; time enough when we get to my rooms; but not a word of it now—not a word. It will all be forgotten in ten minutes with you. We'll rake up the old days and live 'em over for an hour or so. I'm glad that I suggested you in my letter. What did the old man say about my nervous prostration?"—with half a laugh.

Harold MacGrath

"He put quotation marks around it," I answered. "I wanted to see you particularly. They told me that you were rolling downhill so fast that if some one did not put a fulcrum under you, you'd be at the bottom in no time at all. I'm going to be the lever by which you are to be rolled uphill again."

He smiled grimly. "If any one could do that—well, here we are;" and we entered the chop house and took a table in one of the side rooms. "Woods," he said to the waiter, "chops for two, chipped potatoes, and fill up those steins of mine with ale. That will be all. I brought those steins from across, Jack; you'll go crazy over them, for they are beauties."

A college-bred bachelor, nine times out of ten, has a mania for collecting pipes or steins, or both. Dan and I had been affected this way. During the year I had studied at Heidelberg I had gathered together some fifty odd pipes and steins. I have them yet, and many a pleasant memory they beget me. As for the steins of Dan, they were beyond compare.

"I'll tell you a story about them," said Dan, after he had taken a deep swallow of the amber ale. "Few men can boast of steins like these. Not many months ago there was a party of men and women, belonging to the capital of a certain kingdom, who attended a dinner. It was one of those times when exalted personages divest themselves of the dignity and pomp of court and become free and informal. There were twenty of these steins made especially for the occasion. By a circumstance, over which I had no control, I was the only alien at this dinner. The steins were souvenirs. How I came by two was due to the lady whom I took down to dinner, and who presented hers to me after having—after having—well, kissed the rim. Do you see the crest?" pointing to the exquisite inlaid work.

"Why," I said eagerly, "it is the crest of—"

"Yes, a noted King," Dan completed. "And these were made by his express command. But never mind," he broke off. "It's merely a part of the story I am going to tell you when we get to my rooms. I am always thinking of it, night and day, day and night. Talk to me, or I'll be drinking again. This is the first time I've been sober in a month. It's drink or morphine or something like. Do you ever see anything of the old glee boys?"

"Once in a while. You know," said I, lighting a cigarette, "all the fellows but you and I had money. Most of them are carrying on the business of their paters and ornamenting dinner parties and cotillions."

"I thought that you had a rich uncle," said Dan.

"I did have, but he is no more," and I told him all about the bequest.

He laughed so long and heartily over it that I was glad for his sake that it had happened. Already I was beginning to look wholly upon the humorous side of the affair.

"It is almost too good not to be printed," he said. "But his son may square matters when he dies."

"I do not want matters squared," I growled. "I can earn a living for a few years to come. I shan't worry."

"By the way, is that Miss Landors whom you used to rave about in your letters married yet?"

"No." Miss Landors was Phyllis only to her intimate

friends. I called the waiter and ordered him to replenish my stein, Dan watching me curiously the while. "No, Miss Landors is not married yet."

"I have often wondered what she looked like," he mused.

"When do you go on your vacation?" I asked irrelevantly.

"In a week or ten days; may be to-morrow. It's according to how long I stay sober."

I was sorry that he had recalled to me the name of Phyllis. It dampened my sociability. I was not yet prepared to take him into my confidence. The ale, however, loosened our tongues, and though we did not talk about our present affairs we had a pleasant time recounting the days when we were young in the sense that we had no real trouble. Those were the times when we were earning fifteen and twenty the week; when our watches were always in durance vile; when we lied to the poor washerwoman and to the landlady; when we would always be "around to-morrow" and "settle up" with our creditors.

"There was no ennui those days," laughed Hillars.

"True. Do you remember the day you stayed in bed because it was cheaper to sleep than work on an empty stomach?"

"And do you remember the time I saved you from jail by giving the Sheriff my new spring overcoat to pay a washerwoman's bill of six months' standing?"

"I hung around Jersey City that day," said I. And then there was more ale; and so on. It was nine when at last we rose.

"Well, we'll go back to the office and get your case," said Dan. "Where's your trunk?"

"At the Victoria."

"All your luggage must be sent to my rooms. I will not hear of your going elsewhere for lodging while in town. I have a floor, and you shall share it. It's a bachelor's ranch from basement to garret, inhabited by artists, journalists, one or two magazine men, a clever novelist, and three of our New York men. There is no small fry save myself. We have little banquets every Friday night, and they sometimes last till Saturday noon. I've taught the Frenchman who represents the Paris *Temps* how to play poker, and he threatens to become my Frankenstein, who will eventually devour me." Hillars laughed, and it sounded like the laughter of other days. "Jack, I think you will do me good. Stay with me and keep me away from the bottle if you can. No man drinks for pure love of liquor. My father never loved it, and God knows what he was trying to forget. For that's the substance of it all, to forget. When you start out to the point of forgetfulness, you must keep it up; regret comes back threefold with soberness. It seems silly and weak for a man who has been buffeted as I have, who is supposed to gather wisdom and philosophy as a snowball gathers snow as it rolls down hill, to try to drown regret and disappointment in liquor. A man never knows how weak he is till he meets the one woman and she will have none of him."

And somehow I got closer to Hillars, spiritually. There were two of us, so it seemed, only I was stronger, or else my passion did not burn so furiously as his.

The apartments occupied by Dan were all a bachelor could wish for. The walls were covered with photographs, original drawings, beer steins, pipes, a slipper here, a fan there, and books and books and books. I felt at home at once.

I watched Hillars as he moved about the room, tidying up things a bit, and I noticed now more than ever how changed he was. His face had grown thin, his hair was slightly worn at the crown and temples, and there were dark circles under his eyes. Yet, for all these signs of dissipation, he was still a remarkably handsome man. Though not so robust as when I last saw him, his form was yet elegant. In the old days we had called him Adonis, and Donie had clung to him long after the Cambridge time.

"Now," said he, when we had lighted our pipes, "I'll tell you why I'm going to the dogs. I've got to tell it to some one or go daft; and I can't say that I'm not daft as it is."

"It is a woman," said I, after reflection, "who causes a man to drink, to lose all ambition."

"It is."

"It is a woman," I went on, holding the amber stem of my pipe before the light which gleamed golden through the transparent gum, "who causes a man to pull up stakes and prospect for new claims, to leave the new country for the old."

"It is a woman indeed," he replied. He was gazing at me with a new interest. "If the woman had accepted him, he would not have been here."

"No, he would not," said I.

"In either case, yours or mine."

"In either case. Go on with your story; there's nothing more to add to mine."

Some time passed, and nothing but the breathing of the pipes was heard. Now and then I would poke away at the ashes in my pipe bowl, and Dan would do the same.

"Have you a picture of her?" I asked, reaching for some fresh tobacco.

"No; I am afraid to keep one."

To me this was a new phase in the matter of grand passions.

"A likeness which never changes its expression means nothing to me," he explained. "Her face in all its moods is graven in my mind; I have but to shut my eyes, and she stands before me in all her loveliness. Do you know why I wanted this vacation? Rest?" His shoulders went up and his lips closed tighter. "My son, I want no rest. It is rest which is killing me. I am going across. I am going to see her again, if only from the curb as she rolls past in her carriage, looking at me but not recognizing me, telling her footman to brush me aside should I attempt to speak to her. Yet I would suffer this humiliation to see that glorious face once more, to hear again that voice, though it were keyed to scorn. I am a fool, Jack. What! have I gone all these years free-heart to love a chimera in the end? Verily I am an ass. She is a Princess; she has riches; she has a principality; she is the ward of a King. What has she to do with such as I? Three months in the year she dwells in her petty palace; the other months find her here and there; Paris, St. Petersburg, or Rome, as fancy wills. And I, I love her! Is it not rich? What am I? A grub burrowing at the root of the tree in which she, like a bird of paradise, displays her royal plumage. 'Masters, remember that I am an ass; though it be not written down, yet forget not that I am an ass.' The father of this Princess once rendered the present King's father a great service, and in return the King turned over to his care a principality whose lineal descendants had died out. It was with the understanding that so long as he retained the King's goodwill, just so long he might possess the principality, and that when he died the sovereignty would pass to his children. The old King died, and his son sat upon his father's throne. The father of the Princess also died. The King of to-day made the same terms as his father before him. The Princess Hildegarde accepted them, not counting the cost. Last spring she was coronated. Shortly before the coronation, Prince Ernst of Wortumborg became a suitor for her hand. The King was very much pleased. Prince Ernst was a cousin of the Princess Hildegarde's father, and had striven for the principality in the days gone by. The King, thinking to repair the imaginary wrongs of the Prince, forced the suit. He impressed upon the Princess that it was marry the Prince or give up her principality. She gave her consent, not knowing what to do under the circumstances. Prince Ernst is a Prince without principality or revenues. In marrying the Princess he acquires both. I shall tell you how I became concerned."

Hillars laid his smoking pipe in the ash pan. He got up and roamed about the room, stopped at the window and stared at the inken sky, then returned to his chair.

CHAPTER IV

I shall tell Hillars's story as he told it. He said:

Last August I went to B—. My mission was important and took me to the British Legation, where I am well known. I was most cordially invited to attend a ball to be given the next evening. The notables of the court were there. For a few moments the King let his sun shine on the assemblage. It was a brilliant spectacle. At midnight I saw for the first time a remarkably beautiful woman. I was looking well myself that night. All women like to see broad shoulders in a man. It suggests strength—something they have not. Several times this young woman's eyes met mine. Somehow, mine were always first to fall. There was a magnetism in hers mine could not withstand. Later, an attache came to me and said that he wished to present me to her Serene Highness the Princess Hildegarde of—let us call it Hohenphalia. He whispered that she had commanded the introduction. I expected to see some red-faced dowager who wanted to ask me about my country and bore me with her guttural accents. To my intense pleasure, I found myself at the side of the beauty whom I had been admiring. There was a humorous light in her eyes as she put some questions to me.

"Do you speak German?" she asked in that language.

"Poorly, your Highness," I answered.

"Perhaps, then, you speak French?"

"As I do my mother tongue," said I.

"I am interested in Americans," she said.

"Collectively or individually?" I tried to say this with perfect innocence, but the smile on her lips told me that I had failed.

"Yes, I was sure that you would interest me."

She tapped the palm of her hand with the fan she held. "Shall I tell you why I desired to meet you?"

I nodded.

"I have heard it said that the American bows down before a title; and I am a woman, and curious."

Said I, laughing: "Your Highness has been misinformed. We never bow down to a title; it is to the wearers that we bow."

This time her eyes fell.

"This sort of conversation is altogether new to me," she said, opening the fan.

"I hope that I have not offended your Highness," I said.

"Indeed, no. But it seems so strange to have any one talk to me with such frankness and deliberation. Have you no fear?"

"There is seldom fear where there is admiration. If you had used the word awe, now—"

Soft laughter rippled over the fan. She had the most wonderful eyes.

"Are all Americans brave like yourself?" she next asked.

"Brave? What do you call brave?"

"Your utter lack of fear in my presence, in the first place: I am called dangerous. And then, your exploits in the Balkistan, in the second place. Are you not the M. Hillars whose bravery not so long ago was an interesting topic in the newspapers? I know you."

"This is truly remarkable," said I. "The only thing I did was to lead a regiment out of danger."

"The danger was annihilation. If a Captain or a Colonel had done it, we should have thought nothing of it; but an utter stranger, who had nothing in common with either cause—ah, believe me, it was a very gallant thing to do."

"This is positively the first time I was ever glad that I did the thing." I placed my hand over my heart. "But, after all, that is not half so brave as what I am doing now."

"I do not understand," said she puzzled.

"Why, it is simple. Here I am talking to you, occupying your time and keeping those fierce Generals at bay. See how they are gnawing their mustaches and biting their lips and asking one another who I am. There are as many as five challenges waiting for me the moment I depart from your side."

There was mischief in her eye.

"Then you shall stay with me, find me an ice and waltz once with me, for if anything happened to you I should always have myself to blame."

I waltzed with her, and the perfume of her hair got into my head, and I grew dizzy. When the dance came to an end, I went into the smoking room. Suddenly it went through my brain that the world had changed in an incredibly short time. I tried to smoke, and for the first time in my life, tobacco was tasteless, I was falling in love with a Princess. I confess that it did not horrify me; on the contrary, I grew thrilled and excited. There was a spice here which hitherto had been denied me. The cost was unspelled. I fell as far as I could fall. The uncertainty of the affair was in itself an enchantment.

Well, the next day I strolled up the Avenue of Legations and saw her on horseback. She was accompanied by an elderly man with a face like an eagle's. There were various decorations on his breast. As the Princess saw me, she bent her head. She remembered me. That was all that was necessary for my transportation. Later, I was informed that her escort was Prince Ernst of Wortumborg, who was destined to become her lord and master. I did not care who he was; I knew that I hated him.

For a week I lingered on. I met her time and again; alone on horseback, at the various embassies and at the opera. At these meetings I learned a great deal about her. She was known to be the most capricious woman at court, and that she was as courageous as she was daring; and that the Prince might consider himself lucky if he got her, King's will or no King's will. She had little liking for her intended. She treated him contemptuously and held his desires in utter disregard. One fine morning I was told that the Prince was beginning to notice my attentions, that he was one of the most noted pistol shots and swordsmen on the Continent, and that if I had any particular regard for my epidermis I would cease my attendance on the Princess at once. This, of course, made me more attentive than ever; for I can hold my own with any man when it comes to pistols, and I can handle the rapier with some success.

It was one night at the opera that the climax was brought about. I sat in one of the stalls diagonally across from the royal box, where she sat. She saw me and gave me the barest nod of recognition. Perhaps she did not wish to attract the attention of the royal personages who sat with her; for the nod struck me as clandestine. Between the first and second acts a note was handed to me. It was not addressed, neither was it signed. But it was for me; the bearer spoke my name. As near as I can remember, the note contained these words:

"A carriage will await you two blocks south; it will be without lights. You will enter it exactly ten minutes after the opera is ended."

That was all, but it was enough. When I returned to my seat I found the Princess gazing intently at me. I made an affirmative gesture and was rewarded with a smile which set my blood to rushing. I made little out of the last act. I could not dream what the anonymous note had behind it. I suspicioned an intrigue, but what use had she for me, an American, a very nobody? Something unusual was about to take place and I was to be a witness or a participant of it. That was as far as my talent for logical deduction went. Promptly at the stated time I stood at the side of the carriage. It was the plainest sort of an affair. Evidently it had been hired for the occasion. The door opened.

"Step in, monsieur," said a low voice in French. I obeyed. The horse started. As we spun along the pavement a light flashed into the window. The Princess sat before me. There was a ringing in my ears, and I breathed quickly. But I said no word; it was for her to speak first.

"Monsieur is an American," she began. "The American is of a chivalric race."

"That should be the aim of all men," I replied.

"But it is not so. Monsieur, I have been studying you for the past week. To-night I place my honor and my fame in your hands; it is for you to prove that you are a knight. I trust you. When I have said what I shall say to you, you may withdraw or give me your aid, as you please."

"I am grateful for your confidence, your Highness," said I. "What is it that you wish me to do?"

"Have patience, monsieur, till the ride is done," she said. "Do not speak again till I permit you. I must think."

The journey was accomplished in half an hour.

"It is here, monsieur, that we alight," she said as the carriage stopped.

I was glad that her opera cloak was of dark material and that she wore a veil.

The building before which we stood was on the outskirts of the city. Far away to my left I could see the flickering lights of the palaces; a yellowish haze hung over all. Once within the building I noted with surprise the luxurious appointments. Plainly it was no common inn, a resort for the middle and traveling classes; whether it was patronized by the nobility I could only surmise.

"We shall continue to speak in French," she said, as she threw back her cloak and lifted her veil. "Monsieur has probably heard that the Princess Hildegarde is a creature of extravagant caprices; and he expects an escapade."

"Your Highness wrongs me," I protested. "I am an obscure American; your Highness does not share your— that is—"

I stopped, not wishing to give the term escapade to anything she might do. As a matter of fact she has caused her royal guardian, the King, no end of trouble. She went to Paris once unattended; at another time she roamed around Heidelberg and slashed a fencing master; she had donned a student's garb. She is said to be the finest swordswoman on the Continent. Yet, notwithstanding her caprices, she is a noble-minded woman. She does all these things called social vagaries because she has a fine scorn for the innate hypocrisy of the social organization of this country. She loves freedom not wisely but too well. To go on:

"Monsieur wrongs me also," she said. "In what are termed my escapades I am alone. You appealed to me," with a directness which amazed me, "because of your handsome face, your elegant form, your bright eyes. You are a man who loves adventure which has the spice of danger in it. My countrymen—." She crooked one of her bare shoulders, which shone like yellow ivory in the subdued light. This rank flattery cooled me. A woman who has any regard for a man is not likely to flatter him in respect to his looks on so short and slight an acquaintance. "Monsieur," she proceeded, "this is to be no escapade, no caprice. I ask your aid as a desperate woman. At court I can find no one to succor me, save at the peril of that which is dearer to me than my life. Among the commoners, who would dare? An Englishman? It is too much trouble. A Frenchman? I would trust him not quite so far as the door. You are the first American, not connected with the legation, 1 have ever met. Will you help me?"

"If what you ask me to do is within my capabilities, I am yours to command."

"The reward will be small," as if to try me. I laughed. I was so insanely happy, I suppose. "There will be danger," she persisted; "secret danger: there will be scandal."

"The more danger, the merrier," I cried.

"Ah, yes," smiling; "it is the man of Balkistan."

I leaned over the table and inhaled the ineffable perfumes which emanated from her person. "Tell me, from what must I succor the Princess? Is she a prisoner in a castle over which some ogre rules? Well, then, I'll be Sir Galahad."

My jesting tone jarred on her nerves. She straightened in her chair.

"Monsieur is amused," she said coldly.

"And he asks a thousand pardons!" I cried contritely. "Command me," and I grew chilled and serious.

"You have heard that I am to wed Prince Ernst of Wortumborg?"

"Yes." I gnawed the ends of my mustache.

"Monsieur, it is against my will, my whole being. I have no desire to contribute a principality and a wife to a man who is not worthy of one or the other. I refuse to become the King's puppet, notwithstanding his power to take away my principality and leave me comparatively without resources. I detest this man so thoroughly that I cannot hate him. I abhor him. It is you who must save me from him; it is you who must also save me my principality. Oh, they envy me, these poor people, because I am a Princess, because I dwell in the tinsel glitter of the court. Could they but know how I envy their lives, their homes, their humble ambitions! Believe me, monsieur, as yet I love no man; but that is no reason why I should link my life to that of a man to whom virtue in a woman means nothing. He caused my mother great sorrow. He came between her and my father. He spoiled her life, now he wishes to spoil mine. But I will not have it so. I will give up my principality rather. But first let me try to see if I cannot retain the one and rid myself of the other. Listen. To-morrow night there will be a dinner here. The King and the inner court will hold forth. But they will cast aside their pomp and become, for the time being, ordinary people. The Prince will be in Brussels, and therefore unable to attend. You are to come in his stead."

"I?" in astonishment.

"Even so," she smiled. "While the festivities are at their height you and I will secretly leave and return to the city. We shall go immediately to the station, thence to France."

I looked at her as one in a dream. "I!—You!—thence to France?"

CHAPTER V

Hillars went to the sideboard and emptied half a glass of brandy. Coming back to his chair he remained in a reverie for a short time. Then he resumed his narrative.

The Princess looked up into my face and smiled.

"Yes; thence to France. Ah, I could go alone. But listen, monsieur. Above all things there must be a scandal. A Princess elopes with an American adventurer. The Prince will withdraw his suit. The King may or may not forgive me; but I will risk it. He is still somewhat fond of me, notwithstanding the worry I have caused him. This way is the only method by which I may convince him how detestable this engagement is to me. Yet, my freedom is more to me than my principality. Let the King bestow it upon whom he will. I shall become a teacher of languages, or something of that sort. I shall be free and happy. Oh, you will have a merry tale to tell, a merry adventure. You will return to your country. You will be the envy of your compatriots. You will recount at your clubs a story such as men read, but never hear told!" She was growing a bit hysterical. As she looked at me she saw that my face was grave.

"Is there no other way?" I asked. "Can it not be accomplished without scandal?"

"No. There must be scandal. Otherwise I should be brought back and forgiven, and no one would know. In a certain sense, I am valuable. The Hohenphalians love me; I am something of an idol to them. The King appreciates my rule. It gives him a knowledge that there will be no internal troubles in Hohenphalia so long as matters stand as they now do. Still, there are limits to the King's patience; and I am about to try them severely. But monsieur hesitates; he will withdraw his promise."

"No, your Highness," said I, "I have given my word. As for the scandal, it is not for myself that I care. It will be a jolly adventure for me; and then, I shall have such a clever story to tell my friends at the clubs."

She saw that I was offended. "Forgive me, monsieur; I know that you would do no such thing. But let me explain to you. At the station we will be intercepted by two trusted and high officials at court."

"What!" I exclaimed; "do they know?"

"No; but I shall write to them anonymously, the note to be placed in their hands immediately we leave the premises."

I looked at the woman in wonder.

"But this is madness!" I cried.

"Directly you will see the method in the madness. Without their knowing there could be no scandal. They will try to stop us. You will over-power and bind them. There will also be several other witnesses who will not be participants. Through them it will become known that I have eloped with an American. Oh, it is a well-laid plan."

"But, supposing I am overpowered myself, thrown into

jail and I know not what?" All this was more than I had bargained for.

"Nothing of the kind will happen. Monsieur will hold a pistol in each hand when the carriage door is opened. You will say: 'I am a desperate man; one of you bind the other, or I fire!' It will be done. You will spring upon the remaining one and I will help you to bind him likewise. Oh, you will accomplish it well; you are a strong man; moreover, you are rapid."

I sat in my chair, speechless. Here was a woman of details. I had never met one before.

"Well, does monsieur accept the adventure or does he politely decline?" There was a subtle taunt in her tones. That decided me.

"Your Highness, I should be happy to meet a thousand Uhlans to do you service. What you ask me to do is quite simple." I knew that I should lose my head in case of failure. I rose and bowed as unconcernedly as though she had but asked me to join her with a cup of tea.

"Ah, monsieur, you are a man!" And she laughed softly as she saw me throw back my shoulders. There was unmistakable admiration in her eyes. "And yet," with a sudden frown, "there will be danger. You may slip; you may become injured. Yes, there is danger."

"Your Highness," said I lowly, compelling her eyes to meet mine, "it is not the danger of the adventure or its results that I most fear." I was honest enough to make my meaning clear.

She blushed. "I said that I trusted monsieur's honor," was her rejoinder. "Come," with a return of her imperiousness;

"it is time that we were gone!" She drew on her cloak and dropped the veil. "I might add," she said, "that we will remain in France one hour. From there you may go your way, and I shall go secretly to my palace."

And the glamour fell away like the last leaves of the year.

I had to wake up the driver, who had fallen asleep.

"Where shall I say?" I asked.

"To your hotel. I shall give the driver the remaining instructions."

"But you haven't told me," said I, as I took my place in the carriage, "how I am to become a guest at the dinner to-morrow evening."

"I spoke to the King this morning. I said that I had a caprice. He replied that if I would promise it to be my last he would grant it. I promised. I said that it was my desire to bring to the dinner a person who, though without rank, was a gentleman—one who would grace any gathering, kingly or otherwise. My word was sufficient. I knew before I asked you that you would come. Twenty-four hours from now we, that is, you and I, will be on the way to the French frontier. I shall be ever in your debt."

Silence fell upon us. I knew that I loved her with a love that was burning me up, consuming me. And the adventure was all so unheard of for these prosaic times! And so full of the charm of mystery was she that I had not been a man not to have fallen a victim. What possibilities suggested themselves to me as on we rode! Once across the frontier I should be free to confess my love for her. A Princess? What of that? She would be only a woman—the woman I loved. I trembled. Something might happen so that she would have to turn to me. If the King refused to forgive her, she was mine! Ah, that plain carriage held a wonderful dream that night. At length—too shortly for me—the vehicle drew up in front of my hotel. As I was about to alight her hand stretched toward me. But instead of kissing it, I pressed my lips on her round white arm. As though my lips burned, she drew back.

"Have a care, monsieur; have a care," she said, icily. "Such a kiss has to be won."

I stammered an apology and stepped out. Then I heard a low laugh.

"Good night, Mr. Hillars; you are a brave gentleman!"

The door closed and the vehicle sped away into the darkness.

I stood looking after it, bewildered. Her last words were spoken in pure English.

With the following evening came the dinner; and I as a guest, a nervous, self-conscious guest, who started at every footstep. I was presented to the King, who eyed me curiously. Seeing that I wore a medal such as his Chancellor gives to men who sometimes do his country service, he spoke to me and inquired how I had obtained it. It was an affair similar to the Balkistan; only there was not an army, but a mob. The Princess was enchanting. I grew reckless, and let her read my eyes more than once; but she pretended not to see what was in them. At dinner a toast was given to his Majesty. It was made with those steins I showed you, Jack.

The Princess said softly to me, kissing the rim of the stein she held: "My toast is not to the King, but to the gentleman!" I had both steins bundled up and left with the host, together with my address.

It was not long after that the eventful moment for our flight arrived. I knew that I was basely to abuse the hospitality of the King. But what is a King to a man in love? Presently we two were alone in the garden, the Princess and myself. She was whispering instructions, telling me that I was a man of courage.

"It is not too late to back out," she said.

"I would face a thousand kings rather," I replied.

We could see at the gate the carriage which was to take us to the station. Now came the moment when I was tried by the crucible and found to be dross. I committed the most foolish blunder of my life. My love suddenly overleapt its bounds. In a moment my arms were around her lithe body; my lips met hers squarely. After it was done she stood very still, as if incapable of understanding my offence. But I understood. I was overwhelmed with remorse, love, and regret. I had made impossible what might have been.

"Your Highness," I cried, "I could not help it! Before God I could not! It is because I love you better than anything in the world—you cannot be of it!—and all this is impossible, this going away together."

Her bosom heaved, and her eyes flashed like a heated summer sky.

"I will give you one minute to leave this place," she said, her tones as even and as cold as sudden repression of wrath could make them. "I trusted you, and you have dared to take advantage of what seemed my helplessness.

It is well indeed for you that you committed this outrage before it is too late. I should have killed you then. I might have known. Could ever a woman trust a man?" She laughed contemptuously. "You would have made me a thing of scorn; and I trusted you!"

"As God is my judge," I cried, "my respect for you is as high as heaven itself. I love you; is there nothing in that? I am but human. I am not a stone image. And you have tempted me beyond all control. Pardon what I have done; it was not the want of respect—."

"Spare me your protestations. I believe your minute is nearly gone," she interrupted.

And then—there was a crunch on the gravel behind us. The Princess and I turned in dismay. We had forgotten all about the anonymous note. Two officers were approaching us, and rapidly. The elder of the two came straight to me. I knew him to be as inexorable as his former master, the victor of Sedan. The Princess looked on mechanically.

"Come," said the Count, in broken English; "I believe your carriage is at the gate."

I glanced at the Princess. She might have been of stone, for all the life she exhibited.

"Come; the comedy is a poor one," said the Count.

I followed him out of the garden. My indifference to personal safety was due to a numbness which had taken hold of me.

"Get in," he said, when we reached the carriage. I did so, and he got in after me. The driver appeared confused. It was not his fare, according to the agreement. "To the city," he was briefly told. "Your hotel?" turning to me. I named it. "Do you understand German?"

"But indifferently," I answered listlessly.

"It appears that you understand neither the language nor the people. Who are you?"

"That is my concern," I retorted. I was coming about, and not unnaturally became vicious.

"It concerns me also," was the gruff reply.

"Have your own way about it."

"How came you by that medal?" pointing to my breast.

"Honestly," said I.

"Honestly or dishonestly, it is all the same." He made a move to detach it, and I caught his hand.

"Please don't do that. I am extremely irritable; and I might throw you out of the window. I can get back to my hotel without guidance."

"I am going to see you to your lodgings," asserted the Count, rubbing his wrist, for I had put some power into my grasp.

"Still, I might take it into my head to throw you out."

"You'd better not try."

"Are you afraid?"

"Yes. There would be a scandal. Not that I would care about the death of a miserable adventurer, but it might possibly reflect upon the virtue of her Highness the Princess Hildegarde."

"What do you want?" I growled.

"I want to see if your passports are proper so that you will have no difficulty in passing over the frontier."

"Perhaps it would be just as well to wake the American Minister?" I suggested.

"Not at all. If you were found dead there might be a possibility of that. But I should explain to him, and he would understand that it was a case without diplomatic precedent."

"Well?"

"You are to leave this country at once, sir; that is, if you place any value upon your life."

"Oh; then it is really serious?"

"Very. It is a matter of life and death—to you. Moreover, you must never enter this country again. If you do, I will not give a pfennig for your life."

He found my passports in good order. I permitted him to rummage through some of my papers.

"Ach! a damned scribbler, too!" coming across some of my notes.

"Quite right, Herr General," said I. I submitted because I didn't care.

My luggage was packed off to the station, where he saw that my ticket was for Paris.

"Good morning," he said, as I entered the carriage compartment. "The devil will soon come to his own; ach!"

"My compliments to him when you see him!" I called back, not to be outdone in the matter of courtesy.

"And that is all, Jack," concluded Hillars. "For all these months not an hour has passed in which I have not cursed the folly of that moment. Instead of healing under the balm of philosophy, the wound grows more painful every day. She did not love me, I know, but she would have been near me. And if the King had taken away her principality, she would have needed me in a thousand ways. And it is not less than possible that in time she might have learned the lesson of love. But now—if she is the woman I believe her to be, she never could love me after what has happened. And knowing this, I can't leave liquor alone, and don't want to. In my cups I do not care."

"I feel sorry for you both," said I. "Has the Prince married her yet?"

"No. It has been postponed. Next Monday I am going back. I am going in hopes of getting into trouble. I may never see her again, perhaps. To-morrow, to-morrow! Who knows? Well, I'm off to bed. Good night."

And I was left alone with my thoughts. They weren't very good company. To-morrow indeed, I thought. I sat and smoked till my tongue smarted. I had troubles of my own, and wondered how they would end. Poor Hillars! As I look back to-day, I marvel that we could not see the end.

Harold MacGrath

The mystery of life seems simple to us who have lived most of it, and can look down through the long years.

CHAPTER VI

During the first year of my residence in London there happened few events worth chronicling. Shortly after my arrival Hillars disappeared. His two months' vacation stretched into twelve, and I was directed to remain in London. As I knew that Hillars did not wish to be found I made no inquiries. He was somewhere on the Continent, but where no one knew. At one time a letter dated at St. Petersburg reached me, and at another time I was informed of his presence at Monte Carlo. In neither letter was there any mention of her Serene Highness, the Princess Hildegarde of Hohenphalia. Since the night he recounted the adventure the wayward Princess had never become the topic of conversation. I grew hopeful enough to believe that he had forgotten her. Occasionally I received a long letter from Phyllis. I always promptly answered it. To any one but me her letters would have proved interesting reading. It was not for what she wrote that I cared, it was the mere fact that she wrote. A man cannot find much pleasure in letters which begin with "Dear friend," and end with "Yours sincerely," when they come from the woman he loves.

In the preceding autumn I completed my first novel. I carried it around to publishers till I grew to hate it as one hates a Nemesis, and when finally I did place it, it was with a publisher who had just started in business and was

Harold MacGrath

necessarily obscure. I bowed politely to my dreams of literary fame and became wholly absorbed in my journalistic work. When the book came out I could not but admire the excellence of the bookmaking, but as I looked through the reviews and found no mention save in "books received," I threw the book aside and vowed that it should be my last. The publisher wrote me that he was surprised that the book had not caught on, as he considered the story unusually clever. "Merit is one thing," he said, "but luck is another." I have found this to be true, not only in literature, but in all walks of life where fame and money are the goals. Phyllis wrote me that she thought the book "just splendid"; but I took her praise with a grain of salt, it being likely that she was partial to the author, and that the real worth of the book was little in comparison with the fact that it was I who wrote it.

One morning in early June I found three letters on my desk. The first was from Hillars. He was in Vienna.

"MY DEAR SON," it ran, "there is another rumpus. The Princess disappeared on the 20th of last month. They are hunting high and low for her, and incidentally for me. Why me, is more than I can understand. But I received a letter from Rockwell of the American Legation warning me that if I remained in Austria I should be apprehended, put in jail, hanged and quartered for no other reason on earth than that they suspect me having something to do with her disappearance. Due, I suppose, to that other miserable affair. Though I have hunted all over the Continent, I have never seen the Princess Hildegarde since that night at B—. Where shall I find her? I haven't the least idea. But as a last throw, I am going to the principality of Hohenphalia, where she was born and over which she rules with infinite wisdom. The King is determined that she shall wed Prince Ernst. He would take away her principality but for the fact that there would be a wholesale disturbance to follow any such act. If I ever meet that watch dog of hers, the Count von Walden, the duffer who gave me my conge, there will be trouble. The world isn't large enough for two such men as we are. By the way, I played roulette at the Casino last night and won 3,000 francs. Well, au revoir or adieu as the case may be. They sell the worst whiskey here you ever heard of. It's terrible to have an educated palate.

"HILLARS."

So he was still desiring for something he could never have! I got out of patience with the fellow. Even if she loved him, what chance had he against the legions of the King? Hillars was a wild-headed fellow, and, if at liberty, was not incapable of creating a disturbance. It might land him in jail, or on the gallows. The phlegmatic German is not particular whom he hangs. In that wide domain there is always some petty revolution going on. In each of those petty kingdoms, or principalities, or duchies, there are miniature Rousseaus and Voltaires who shout liberty and equality in beer halls and rouse the otherwise peaceful citizens to warfare; short, it is true, but none the less warfare. Military despotism is the tocsin. When the King presses an unwilling subject into the army, upon his discharge the unwilling subject, usually a peasant, becomes a socialist. These Rousseaus and Voltaires have a certain amount of education, but they lack daring. If a man like Hillars, who had not only brains but daring, should get mixed up in one of these embroglios, some blood would be spilled before the trouble became adjusted. Still, Hillars, with all his love of adventure, was not ordinarily reckless. Yet, if he met the Princess, she would find a willing tool in him for her slightest caprice. Whatever happened the brunt would fall upon him. My opinion, formed from various stories I had heard of the Princess, was not very flattering to her. The letter and its possibilities disturbed me.

The second letter was from headquarters in New York.

"DEAR WINTHROP—We want a good Sunday special. Her Serene Highness the Princess Hildegarde of Hohenphalia has taken it into her head to disappear again. Go over and see Rockwell in B—; he will give you a good yarn. It has never been in type yet, and I daresay that it will make good reading. London seems particularly dull just now, and you can easily turn over your affairs to the assistant. This woman's life is more full of romance than that of any other woman of the courts of Europe. The most interesting part of it is her reputation is said to be like that of Caesar's wife—above reproach. Get a full history of her life and of the Prince whom she is to marry. If you can get any photographs do so. I know how you dislike this sort of work, prying into private affairs, as you call it, but with all these sensational sheets springing up around us, we must keep in line now and then. Do you know anything about Hillars; is he dead or alive? Take all the time you want for the story and send it by mail."

"The Princess Hildegarde!" I cried aloud. "The deuce take the woman!"

"What's that?" asked my assistant, who had overheard my outburst.

"Oh, I am to go across on a special story," I said with a snarl, "just as I was fixing for a week's fishing. I've got to concern myself with the Princess Hildegarde of Hohenphalia."

"Ah, the Princess Hildegarde?" said the young fellow, pushing back his hat and elevating his feet, a trick he had acquired while being reared in his native land, which was the State of Illinois, in America. "You want to be careful. Every one burns his fingers or singes his wings around that candle."

"What do you know about her?" I asked.

"A little. You see, about six months ago I discovered all regarding Hillars and his fall from grace. It was through the Reuter agency. Hillars got badly singed. An elopement of some sort between him and the Princess was nipped in the bud. He was ordered to leave the country and warned never to return, at the peril of his liberty. A description of him is with every post on the frontier. As for the Princess she is an interesting character. She was educated in this country and France. She speaks several languages. She is headstrong and wilful, and her royal guardian is only too anxious to see her married and settled down. She masquerades in men's clothes when it pleases her, she can ride a horse like a trooper, she fences and shoots, she has fought two duels, and heaven alone knows what she has not done to disturb the tranquility of the Court. For a man she loved she would be a merry comrade. I saw her once in Paris. She is an extraordinarily beautiful woman. A man takes no end of risk when he concerns himself with her affairs, I can tell you. Hillars— Well, I suppose it's none of my business. He must have had an exciting time of it," concluded the young man.

"I'll leave you in charge for a week or so," said I. "What little news there is at the Houses you can cover. I'll take care of anything of importance that occurs abroad. I might as well pack up and get out to-night. A boat leaves Dover early in the morning."

Then I picked up the third and last letter. It was from Phyllis. It contained the enjoyable news that the Wentworths were coming abroad, and that they would remain indefinitely at B—, where Mr. Wentworth had been appointed charge d'affaires under the American Minister. They were to visit the Mediterranean before coming to London. They would be in town in October. The mere thought of seeing Phyllis made my heart throb.

The next morning I put out from Dover. It was a rough passage for that time of the year, and I came near being sea-sick. A day or so in Paris brought me around, and I proceeded. As I passed the frontier I noticed that my passports were eagerly scanned, and that I was closely scrutinized for some reason or other.

A smartly dressed officer occupied half of the carriage compartment with me. I tried to draw him into conversation, but he proved to be untalkative; so I busied myself with the latest issue of the Paris *L'Illustration*. I never glanced in the direction of the officer but what I found him staring intently at me. This irritated me. The incident was repeated so many times that I said:

"I trust Herr will remember me in the days to come."

"Eh?" somewhat startled, I thought.

"I observed that you will possibly remember me in the days to come. Or, perhaps I resemble some one you know."

"Not in the least," was the haughty retort.

I shrugged and relit my pipe. The tobacco I had purchased in Paris, and it was of the customary vileness. Perhaps I could smoke out Mein Herr. But the task resulted in a boomerang. He drew out a huge china pipe and began smoking tobacco which was even viler than mine, if that could be possible. Soon I let down the window.

"Does the smoke disturb Herr?" he asked, puffing forth great clouds of smoke. There was a shade of raillery in his tones.

"It would not," I answered, "if it came from tobacco."

He subsided.

Whenever there was a stop of any length I stepped out and walked the platform. The officer invariably followed my example. I pondered over this each time I re-entered the carriage. At last my irritation turned into wrath.

"Are you aware that your actions are very annoying?"

"How, sir?" proudly.

"You stare me out of countenance, you refrain from entering into conversation, and by the way you follow me in and out of the carriage, one would say that you were watching me. All this is not common politeness."

"Herr jests," he replied with a forced smile. "If I desire not to converse, that is my business. As for getting in and out of the carriage, have I no rights as a passenger?"

It was I who subsided. A minute passed.

"But why do you stare at me?" I asked.

"I do not stare at you, I have no paper and tried to read yours at a distance. I am willing to apologize for that."

"Oh, that is different," I said. I tossed the paper to him. "You are welcome to the paper."

I covertly watched him as he tried to read the French. By

and by he passed the paper back.

"I am not a very good French scholar, and the French are tiresome."

"They would not have been if they had had a General who thought more of fighting than of wearing pretty clothes."

"Oh, it would not have mattered," confidently.

"Prussia was once humbled by a Frenchman." I was irritating him with a purpose in view.

"Bah!"

"The only reason the French were beaten was because they did not think the German race worth troubling about."

He laughed pleasantly. "You Americans have a strange idea of the difference between the German and the Frenchman."

This was just what I wanted.

"And who informed you that I was an American?"

He was disconcerted.

"Why," he said, lamely, "it is easily apparent, the difference between the American and the Englishman." Then, as though a bright idea had come to him, "The English never engage in conversation with strangers while traveling. Americans are more sociable."

"They are? Then I advise them to follow the example set by the Englishman: Never try to get up a conversation while traveling with a German. It is a disagreeable task;" and I settled back behind my paper.

How had he found out that I was an American? Was I known? And for what reason was I known? To my knowledge I had never committed any offence to the extent that I must be watched like a suspect. What his object was and how he came to know that I was an American was a mystery to me. I was glad that the journey would last but an hour or so longer. The train arrived at the capital late at night. As I went to inquire about my luggage I saw my late fellow passenger joined by another officer. The two began talking earnestly, giving me occasional side-long glances. The mystery was deepening. In passing them I caught words which sounded like "under another name" and "positive it is he." This was anything but reassuring to me. At length they disappeared, only to meet me outside the station. It got into my head that I was a marked man. A feeling of discomfort took possession of me. Germans are trouble-some when they get an idea. I was glad to get into the carriage which was to take me to my hotel. The driver seemed to have some difficulty in starting the horse, but I gave this no attention. When the vehicle did start it was with a rapidity which alarmed me. Corner after corner was turned, and the lights went by in flashes. It was taking a long time to reach my hotel, I thought. Suddenly it dawned upon me that the direction we were going was contrary to my instructions. I tried to open the window, but it refused to move. Then I hammered on the pane, but the driver was deaf, or purposely so.

"Hi there!" I thoughtlessly yelled in English, "where the devil are you going?"

No one paid any attention to my cries. It was becoming a serious matter. The lights grew fewer and fewer, and

Harold MacGrath

presently there were no lights at all. We were, I judged, somewhere in the suburbs. I became desperate and smashed a window. The carriage stopped so abruptly that I went sprawling to the bottom. I was in anything but a peaceful frame of mind, as they say, when the door swung open and I beheld, standing at the side of it, the officer who had accompanied me from the frontier.

"What tomfoolery is this?" I demanded. I was thoroughly incensed.

"It means that Herr will act peacefully or be in danger of a broken head," was the mind-easing reply of my quondam fellow passenger. The driver then came down from the box, and I saw that he was the officer who had joined us at the station.

"If it is a frolic," I said, "one of your beer hall frolics, the sooner it is ended the better for you."

The two laughed as if what I had said was one of the funniest things imaginable.

"Get out!"

"With pleasure!" said I.

Directly one of them lay with his back to the ground and the other was locked in my embrace. I had not spent four years on the college campus for intellectual benefits only. And indignation lent me additional strength. My opponent was a powerful man, but I held him in a grip of rage. Truthfully, I began to enjoy the situation. There is something exhilarating in the fighting blood which rises in us now and then. This exhilaration, however, brought about my fall. In the struggle I forgot the other, who meantime had recovered his star-gemmed senses. A crack from the butt of his pistol rendered me remarkably quiet and docile. In fact, all became a vacancy till the next morning, and then I was conscious of a terrible headache, and of a room with a window through which a cat might have climbed without endangering its spine—a very dexterous cat.

"Well," I mused, softly nursing the lump on my head, "here's the devil to pay, and not a cent to pay him with."

It was evident that, without knowing it, I had become a very important personage.

CHAPTER VII

I saw some rye bread, cold meat and a pitcher of water on the table, and I made a sandwich and washed it down with a few swallows of the cool liquid. I had a fever and the water chilled it. There was a lump on the back of my head as large as an egg. With what water remained I dampened my handkerchief and wound it around the injury. Then I made a systematic search through my clothes. Not a single article of my belongings was missing. I was rather sorry, for it lent a deeper significance to my incarceration. After this, I proceeded to take an inventory of my surroundings. Below and beyond the little window I saw a wide expanse of beautiful gardens, fine oaks and firs, velvet lawns and white pebbled roads. Marble fountains made them merry in the roseate hue of early morning. A gardener was busy among some hedges, but beyond the sound of my voice. I was a prisoner in no common jail, then, but in the garret of a private residence. Having satisfied myself that there was no possible escape, I returned to my pallet and lay down. Why I was here a prisoner I knew not. I thought over all I had written the past twelvemonth, but nothing recurred to me which would make me liable to arrest. But, then, I had not been arrested. I had been kidnapped, nothing less. Nothing had been asked of me; I had made no statement. It had been all too sudden. Presently I heard footsteps in the corridor, and the door opened. It was mine enemy. He locked the door and thrust the key into his pocket. One of his eyes was decidedly mouse-colored. The knuckles of my hand were yet sore. I smiled; he saw the smile, his jaws hardening and his eyes threatening.

"I am sorry," I said. "I should have hit you on the point of your chin; but I was in a great hurry. Did you ever try raw meat as a poultice?"

"Enough of this," he snapped, laying a pistol on the table. I was considered dangerous; it was something to know that. "You must answer my questions."

"Must?"

"Must."

"Young man you have no tact. You are not an accomplished villain," said I, pleasantly. "You should begin by asking me how I spent the night, and if there was not something you could do for my material comfort. Perhaps, however, you will first answer a few questions of mine?"

"There are only two men whose questions I answer," he said.

"And who might they be?"

"My commander and the King. I will answer one question—the reason you are here. You are a menace to the tranquility of the State."

"Oh; then I have the honor of being what is called a prisoner of State? Be careful," I cried, suddenly; "that pistol might go off, and then the American Minister might ask you in turn some questions, disagreeable ones, too."

"The American Minister would never know anything about it," said he, gruffly. "But have no fear; I should hesitate to soil an innocent leaden bullet in your carcass."

"Be gentle," I advised, "or when we meet again I shall feel it my duty to dull the lustre of your other eye."

"Pah!" he ejaculated. "We are indebted to the French for the word canaille, which applies to all Americans and Englishmen."

"Now," said I, climbing off the pallet, "I shall certainly do it."

"I warn you not to approach me," he cried, his fingers closing over the pistol.

"Well, I promise not to do it now," I declared, going over to the window. I found some satisfaction in his nervousness; it told me that he feared me. "What place is this; a palace?"

"Answer this question, sir: Why did you cross the frontier when you were expressly forbidden to do so?"

"I forbidden to cross the frontier?" My astonishment was indescribable. "Young man, you have made a blunder of some sort. I am not a Socialist or an Anarchist. I have never been forbidden to cross the frontier of any country. Your Chancellor is one of the best friends I have in the world. I went to school with his son."

He rocked to and fro on the table, laughing honestly and heartily. "You do not lack impudence. Are you, or are you not, the London correspondent of the New York—?"

"I certainly am."

"You admit it?" eagerly.

"I see no earthly reason why I should not."

"When did you last visit this city?"

"Several years ago."

"Several years ago?" incredulously.

"Exactly. Have you ever seen me before?"

"No. But it was a little less than two years ago when you were here."

"It is scarcely polite," said I, "to question the veracity of a man you never saw before and of whom you know positively nothing." Suddenly my head began to throb again and I grew dizzy. "You hit me rather soundly with that pistol. Still, your eye ought to be a recompense."

He replied with a scowl.

"Perhaps your name is—"

"Winthrop, John Winthrop, if that will throw any light on the subject.'"

"One name is as good as another," with a smile of unbelief.

"That is true. What's in a name? There is little difference, after all, between the names of the nobility and the rabble."

"You are determined to irritate me beyond measure," said he. A German is the most sensitive man in the world as regards his title.

"Grant that I have some cause. And perhaps," observing him from the corner of my eye, "it is because you smoke such vile tobacco."

Remembering the incident in the railway carriage, he smiled in spite of the gravity of the situation.

"It was the best I had," he said; "and then, it was done in self-defence. I'll give you credit for being a fearless individual. But you haven't answered my question."

"What question?"

"Why you returned to this country when you were expressly forbidden to do so."

"I answered that," said I. "And now let me tell you that you may go on asking questions till the crack of doom, but no answer will I give you till you have told me why I am here, I, who do not know you or what your business is, or what I am supposed to have done."

He began to look doubtful. He thumped the table with the butt of the pistol.

"Do you persist in affirming that your name is Winthrop?"

"These gardens are very fine. I could see them better," said I, "if the window was larger."

"Perhaps," he cried impatiently, "you do not know where she is?"

"She?" I looked him over carefully. There was a perfectly sane light in his eyes. "Am I crazy, or is it you? She? I know nothing about any she!"

"Do you dare deny that you know of the whereabouts of her Serene Highness the Princess Hildegarde, and that you did not come here with the purpose to aid her to escape the will of his Majesty? And do you mean—Oh, here, read this!" flinging me a cablegram.

The veil of mystery fell away from my eyes. I had been mistaken for Hillars. Truly, things were growing interesting. I bent and picked up the cablegram and read:

"COUNT VON WALDEN: He has left London and is on his way to the capital. Your idea to allow him to cross the frontier is a good one. Undoubtedly he knows where the Princess is in hiding. In trapping him you will ultimately trap her. Keep me informed."

The name signed was that of a well-known military attache at the Embassy in London. I tossed back the cablegram.

"Well?" triumphantly.

"No, it is not well; it is all very bad, and particularly for you. Your London informant is decidedly off the track. The man you are looking for is in Vienna."

"I do not believe you! It is a trick."

"Yes, it is a trick, and I am taking it, and you have lost a point, to say nothing of the time and labor and a black eye. If you had asked all these questions yesterday I should have told you that Mr. Hillars—"

"Yes, that's the name!" he interrupted.

"I should have told you that he is no longer the London representative of my paper. It is true that the description of Hillars and myself tallies somewhat, only my hair is dark, while his is light, what there is left of it, and he is a handsomer man than I. All this I should have told you with pleasure, and you would have been saved no end of trouble. I presume that there is nothing left for you to do but to carry me back to the city. To quell any further doubt, here are my passports, and if these are not satisfactory, why take me before Prince O—, your Chancellor."

He was irresolute, and half inclined to believe me.

"I do not know what to do. You know, then, the gentleman I am seeking?"

"Yes."

"Would he enter this country under an assumed name?"

"No. He is a man who loves excitement. Whatever he does is done openly. Had it been he instead of me, he would have thrown you out of the carriage at the first sign on your part that you were watching him. He is a very strong man."

"If he is stronger than you, I am half glad that I got the wrong man. You strike a pretty hard blow. But, whether you are the man I want, or not, you will have to remain till this afternoon, when the Count will put in appearance. I daresay it is possible that I have made a mistake. But I could not do otherwise in face of my instructions."

"The Princess seems to me more trouble than she is worth."

"It is possible that you have never seen her Highness," he said, hinting a smile. "She is worth all the trouble in the world."

"If a man loved her," I suggested.

"And what man does not who has seen her and talked to her?" he replied, pacing.

"The interest, then, you take in her discovery is not all due to that imposed upon you by Count von Walden?" I could not resist this thrust.

"The subject is one that does not admit discussion," squaring his shoulders.

"Suppose we talk of something that does not concern her? All this is a blunder for which you are partly to blame. I have a bad lump on my head and you have a black eye. But as you did what you believed to be your duty, and as I did what every man does when self-preservation becomes his first thought, let us cry quits. Come, what do you say to a game of cards? Let us play ecarte, or I will teach you the noble game of poker. To tell you the truth, I am becoming dreadfully bored."

"Believe me, I bear you no ill will," he said, "and I am inclined to your side of the story. Whoever you are, you have the bearing of a gentleman; and, now that we have come to an understanding, I shall treat you as such. I have a pack of cards downstairs. I'll go and get them. This is not my house, or I should have placed you in better quarters. I shall leave the door unlocked," a question in his eyes.

"Rest assured that I shall return to the city as I came—in a carriage. And to be honest, I am anxious to see the Count von Walden, who poses as the Princess's watchdog."

And when he came back and found me still sitting on the pallet, his face cleared.

We played for small sums, and the morning passed away rather pleasantly than otherwise. The young officer explained to me that he held an important position at court, and that he was entitled to prefix Baron to his name.

"The King is getting out of all patience with her Highness," he said. "This makes the second time the marriage has been postponed. Such occurrences are extremely annoying to his Majesty, who does not relish having his commands so flagrantly disregarded. I shouldn't be surprised if he forced her into the marriage."

"When he knows how distasteful this marriage is to her, why does he not let the matter go?"

"It is too late now. Royalty, having given its word, never retracts it. Events which the King wills must come to pass, or he loses a part of his royal dignity. And then, a King cannot very well be subservient to the will of a subject."

"But has she no rights as a petty sovereign?" I asked.

"Only those which the King is kind enough to give her. She is but a tenant: the rulers of Hohenphalia are but guests of his Majesty. It is to be regretted, but it cannot be helped."

That afternoon, as I lay on my pallet, it seemed to me that in some unaccountable way I was destined to become concerned in the affairs of her Serene Highness. I had never seen the woman, not even a picture of her. Certainly, she must be worth loving, inasmuch as she was worth trouble. I have always found it to be the troublesome woman who has the largest train of lovers. Troublesome, they are interesting; interesting, they are lovable.

It was more than a year since last I saw Phyllis; yet my love for her knew no diminution. I began to understand why Hillars traveled all over the Continent to get a glimpse of the woman he loved. With the pleasant thought that I should see Phyllis again, I dozed. I was half asleep when I was aroused by loud voices in the corridor.

"But I do not believe him to be the man," I heard my jailer declare.

"Bah! I know there is no mistake," roared a voice which was accustomed to command. "He's been trying to hoodwink you. Watch the surprise in his face when he sees me, the cursed meddler and scribbler. It would be a pleasure to witness his hanging. Come, show him to me."

"Yes; come along, my dear old warhorse," I murmured, turning my face toward the wall. "There is a nice little surprise party in here waiting for you."

The door opened.

"Unlocked!" bawled the Count. "What does this mean, Baron?"

"He gave his word as a gentleman," was the quiet reply.

"Gentleman? Ach! I'll take a look at the gentleman," said the Count, stepping up to the pallet and shaking me roughly by the shoulder. "Wake up!"

I sat up so as not to miss the comedy which was about to set its scenes upon the grim visage of the Count. As his eyes met mine his jaw fell.

"A thousand devils! Who are you?"

"I couldn't swear," said I, meekly. "Everybody hereabouts insists that I am some one else. The situation warrants a complete explanation. Perhaps you can give it?" I should have laughed but for those flashing eyes.

"You are a blockhead," he said to his subaltern.

"He is the man, according to your London correspondent," responded the other with some show of temper. "I cannot see that the fault lies at my door. You told me that he would enter the country under an assumed name."

"I presume the affair is ended so far as I am concerned," I said, shaking the lameness from my legs.

"Of course, of course!" replied the Count, pulling at his gray mustaches, which flared out on either side like the whiskers of a cat.

"I should like to return to the city at once," I added.

"Certainly. I regret that you have been the victim of a blunder for which some one shall suffer. Your compatriot has caused me a deal of trouble."

"I assure you that he is in no wise connected with the present matter. According to his latest advices he is at Vienna."

"I should be most happy to believe that," was the Count's rejoinder, which inferred that he didn't believe it.

"My friend seems to be a dangerous person?"

"All men of brains, coupled with impudence, are dangerous; and I give your friend credit for being as brave as he is impudent. But come, my carriage is at your service. You are a journalist, but you will promise not to make public this unfortunate mistake."

I acquiesced.

When the Count and I parted company I had not the vaguest idea that we should ever hold conversation again.

The result of the adventure was, I sent a very interesting story to New York, omitting my part in it. This done, I wired my assistant in London not to expect me for some time yet.

The truth was, I determined to hunt for Hillars, and incidentally for her Serene Highness the Princess Hildegarde of Hohenphalia.

CHAPTER VIII

As I came along the road, the dust of which had been laid that afternoon by an odorous summer rain, the principal thing which struck my eyes was the quaintness and unquestioned age of the old inn. It was a relic of the days when feudal lords still warred with one another, and the united kingdom was undreamt of. It looked to be 300 years old, and might have been more. From time to time it had undergone various repairs, as shown by the new stone and signs of modern masonry, the slate peeping out among the moss-covered tiles. It sat back from the highway, and was surrounded by thick rows of untrimmed hedges, and was partly concealed from view by oaks and chestnuts. The gardens were full of roses all in bloom, and their perfumes hung heavy on the moist air. And within a stone's throw of the rear the Danube noiselessly slid along its green banks. All I knew about the inn was that it had been by a whim of nature the birthplace of that beautiful, erratic and irresponsible young person, her Serene Highness the Princess Hildegarde. It was here I thought to find Hillars; though it was idle curiosity as much as anything which led me to the place.

The village was five miles below. I could see the turrets of the castle which belonged to the Princess. She was very wealthy, and owned as many as three strongholds in the petty principality of Hohenphalia. Capricious indeed must have been the woman who was ready to relinquish them for freedom.

The innkeeper was a pleasant, ruddy-cheeked old man, who had seen service. He greeted me with some surprise; tourists, he said, seldom made this forgotten, out-of-the-way village an objective point. I received a room which commanded a fine view of the river and a stretch of the broad highway. I was the only guest. This very loneliness pleased me. My travel-stained suit I exchanged for knickerbockers and a belted jacket. I went down to supper; it was a simple affair, and I was made to feel at home. From the dining-room I caught a momentary flash of white skirts in the barroom.

"Ah," I thought; "a barmaid. If she is pretty it will be a diversion."

In the course of my wanderings I had seen few barmaids worth looking at twice.

When the table was cleared I lit a cigar and strolled into the gardens. The evening air was delicious with the smell of flowers, still wet with rain. The spirit of the breeze softly whispered among the branches above me. Far up in the darkening blues a hawk circled. The west was a thread of yellow flame; the moon rose over the hills in the east; Diana on the heels of Apollo! And the river! It was as though Nature had suddenly become lavish in her bounty and had sent a stream of melting silver trailing over all the land. There is nothing more beautiful to see than placid water as it reflects a summer's twilight. The blue Danube! Who has heard that magic name without the remembrance of a face close to your own, an arm, bare, white, dazzling, resting and gleaming like marble on your broadcloth sleeve, and above all, the dreamy, swinging strains of Strauss? There was a face once which had rested near mine. Heigho! I lingered with my cigar and watched the night reveal itself. I lay at the foot of a tree, close to the water's edge, and surrendered to the dream-god. Some of my dreams knew the bitterness of regret. "Men have died and worms have eaten them, but not for love." Yet, no man who has loved and lost can go through his allotted time without the consciousness that he has missed something, something which leaves each triumph empty and incomplete.

And then, right in the midst of my dreams, a small foot planted itself. I turned my head and saw a woman. On seeing the bright end of my cigar, she stopped. She stood so that the light of the moon fell full upon her face.

My cigar trembled and fell.

"Phyllis!" I cried, springing to my feet, almost dumb-founded, my heart nigh suffocating me in its desire to leap forth. "Phyllis!—and here? What does this mean?"

The woman looked at me with a puzzled frown, but did not answer. Then, as I started toward her with outstret-ched arms, she turned and fled into the shadows, leaving with me nothing but the echo of her laughter, the softest, sweetest laughter! I made no effort to follow her, because I was not quite sure that I had seen anything.

"Moonlight!" I laughed discordantly.

Phyllis in this deserted place? I saw how impossible that was. I had been dreaming. The spirit of some wood-nymph had visited me, and for a brief space had borrowed the features of the woman I loved. In vain I searched the grove. The vision was nowhere to be found. I went back to the inn somewhat shaken up.

Several old veterans were seated in the barroom, smoking bad tobacco and drinking a final bout. Their jargon was unintelligible to me.

"Where's your barmaid?" I asked of the inn-keeper.

His faded blue eyes scanned me sharply. I read a question in them and wondered.

"She went into the garden to get a breath of fresh air," he said. "She does not like the smoke."

It annoyed me. I had seen some one, then. What would Phyllis, proud Phyllis, say, I mused, when she heard that a barmaid was her prototype? This thought had scarcely left me when the door in the rear of the bar opened and in came the barmaid herself. No, it was not Phyllis, but the resemblance was so startling that I caught my breath and stared at her with a persistency which bordered on rudeness. The barmaid was blonde, whereas Phyllis was neither blonde nor brunette, but stood between the extremes, and there was a difference in the eyes: I could see that even in the insufficient light.

"Good evening, fraulein," said I, with apparent composure. "And what might your name be?"

"It is Gretchen, if it please you," with a courtesy. I had a vague idea that this courtesy was made mockingly.

"Gretchen? I have heard the name before," said I, "and you remind me of some one I have seen."

"Herr has been to the great city?"

B—is the greatest city in the world to the provincial.

"Yes," said I; "but you remind me of no one I ever saw there."

She plucked a leaf from the rose she wore and began nibbling at it. Her mouth was smaller than the one belonging to Phyllis.

"The person to whom I refer," I went on, "lives in America, where your compatriots brew fine beer and wax rich."

"Ah, Herr is an American? I like Americans," archly. "They are so liberal."

I laughed, but I did not tell her why. All foreigners have a great love of Americans—"They are so liberal."

"So you find Americans liberal? Is it with money or with compliments?"

Said Gretchen: "The one when they haven't the other."

A very bright barmaid, thought I.

Then I said: "Is this your home?"

"Yes," said Gretchen. "I was born here and I have tended the roses for ever so long."

"I have heard of Gretchen of the steins, but I never before heard of a Gretchen of the roses."

"Herr must have a large store of compliments on hand to begin this early."

"It is a part of my capital," said I. "Once in Switzerland I complimented an innkeeper, and when my bill was presented I found that all extras had been crossed off."

Gretchen laughed. It was a low laugh, a laugh which appeared to me as having been aroused not at what I had said, but at something which had recurred to her. I wanted to hear it again.

So I said: "I suppose you have a stein here from which the King has drunk; all taverns and inns have them."

Gretchen only smiled, but the smile was worth something.

"No; the King has never been within five miles of this inn."

"So much the worse for the King."

"And why that?"

"The King has missed seeing Gretchen."

It was then Gretchen laughed.

"I have never heard compliments like Herr's before."

"Why, I have any amount of them. I'll drink half a litre to your health."

She filled one of the old blue earthen steins.

"I haven't seen your roses in the gardens, but I'll drink to those in your cheeks," said I, and I drew back the pewter lid.

"How long does Herr intend to stay?" asked Gretchen.

"To the day is the evil thereof."

"Ah, one must be happy with nothing to do."

"Then you have the ambition common to all; to sit around and let others wait upon you?"

"No, that is not my ambition. I wish only to wait upon my own desires and not those of the—the others."

"It is all the same," said I. "Some must serve, others must be served."

When I went upstairs to my room it was my belief that a week or so at the inn would not hang heavy on my hands. I had forgotten for the moment the Princess, or that I was hunting for Hillars. It is strange how a face may upset one's plans. Gretchen's likeness to Phyllis, whom I loved, upset mine for many days to come.

As I gazed from my window the next morning I beheld the old innkeeper and Gretchen engaged in earnest conversation. He appeared to be pleading, nay, entreating, while she merely shook her head and laughed. Finally the old man lifted his hands to heaven and disappeared around the wing. When I came down Gretchen was in the gardens culling roses. She said they were for the table.

"Very well," said I; "give me one now."

"You may have them all at the table."

"But I shall not want them then."

She gave me an enigmatical glance, then cut a rose for me which was withered and worm-eaten.

"Gretchen is unkind," I observed.

"What matters it whether the rose be fresh or withered? It dies sooner or later. Nothing lasts, not even the world itself. You wish a rose, not because it is a rose, fresh and fragrant, but because I give it to you."

"You wrong me, Gretchen; I love a rose better than I love a woman. It never smiles falsely, the rose, nor plays with the hearts of men. I love a rose because it is sweet, and because it was made for man's pleasure and not for his pain."

"That sounds like a copy-book," laughed Gretchen. "The withered rose should teach you a lesson."

"What lesson?"

"That whatever a woman gives to man withers in the exchange; a rose, a woman's love."

Said I reproachfully: "You are spoiling a very pretty picture. What do you know about philosophy?"

"What does Herr know about roses?" defiantly.

"Much; one cannot pick too many fresh ones. And let me tell you a lesson which you should have learned among these roses. Nature teaches us to love all things fresh and beautiful; a rose, a face, a woman's love."

"Here," holding forth a great red rose.

"No," said I, "I'll keep this one."

She said nothing, but went on snipping a red rose here, a white one there. She wore gloves several sizes too large for her, so I judged that her hands were small and tender, perhaps white. And there was a grace in her movements, dispite the ungainly dress and shoes, which suggested a more intimate knowledge of velvets and silks than of calico. In my mind's eye I placed her at the side of Phyllis. Phyllis reminded me of a Venus whom Nature had whimsically left unfinished. Then she had turned from Venus to Diana, and Gretchen became evolved: a Diana, slim and willowy. A sculptor would have said that Phyllis might have been a goddess, and Gretchen a wood nymph, had not Nature suddenly changed her plans. What I admired in Phyllis was her imperfect beauties. What I admired in Gretchen was her beautiful perfections. And they were so alike and yet so different. Have you ever seen a body of fresh water, ruffled by a sudden gust of wind, the cool blue-green tint which follows? Then you have seen the color of Gretchen's eyes. Have you ever seen ripe wheat in a sun-shower? Then you have seen the color of Gretchen's hair. All in all, I was forced to admit that, from an impartial and artistic view Gretchen the barmaid was far more beautiful than Phyllis. From the standpoint of a lover it was altogether a different matter.

"Gretchen," said I, "you are very good-looking."

"It would not be difficult to tell Herr's nationality."

"Which means—?"

"That the American says in one sentence what it would take a German or a Frenchman several hundred sentences to say."

Gretchen was growing more interesting every minute.

"Then your mirror and I are not the only ones who have told you that you are as beautiful as Hebe herself?"

"I am not Hebe," coldly. "I am a poor barmaid, and I

never spill any wine."

"So you understand mythology?" I cried in wonder.

"Does Herr think that all barmaids are as ignorant as fiction and ill-meaning novelists depict them? I have had a fair education."

"If I ever was guilty of thinking so," said I, answering her question, "I promise never to think so again."

"And now will Herr go to his breakfast and let me attend to my duties?"

"Not without regret," I said gallantly. I bowed to her as they bowed in the days of the beaux, while she looked on suspiciously.

At the breakfast table I proceeded to bombard the innkeeper. I wanted to know more about Gretchen.

"Is Gretchen your daughter?" I began.

"No, I am only her godfather," he said. "Does Herr wish another egg?"

"Thanks. She is very well educated for a barmaid."

"Yes. Does Herr wish Rhine wine?"

"Coffee is plenty. Has Gretchen seen many Americans?"

"Few. Perhaps Herr would like a knoblauch with salt and vinegar?"

It occurred to me that Gretchen was not to be discussed. So I made for another channel.

Harold MacGrath

"I have heard," said I, "that once upon a time a princess was born in this inn?"

The old fellow elevated both eyebrows and shoulders—a deprecating movement.

"They say that of every inn; it has become a trade."

If I had known the old man I might have said that he was sarcastic.

"Then there is no truth in it?" disappointedly.

"Oh, I do not say there is no truth in the statement; if Herr will pardon me, it is something I do not like to talk about."

"Ah, then there is a mystery?" I cried, with lively interest, pushing back my chair.

But the innkeeper shook his head determinedly.

"Very well," I laughed; "I shall ask Gretchen."

He smiled. The smile said: "Much good it will do you."

Gretchen was in the barroom arranging some roses over the fireplace. Her hands were bare; they were small and white, and surprisingly well kept.

"Gretchen," said I, "I want you to tell me the legend of the inn."

"The legend?"

"Yes; about the Princess who was born here."

Gretchen laughed a merry laugh. The laugh said: "You are an amusing person!"

"Ah, the American is always after legends when he has tired of collecting antiquities. Was there a Princess born here? Perhaps. At any rate it is not a legend; history nor peasantry make mention of it. Will Herr be so kind as to carry the ladder to the mantel so I may wind the clock?"

I do so. Even at this early stage I could see that Gretchen had the faculty of making persons forget what they were seeking, and by the mere sound of her voice. And it was I who wound the clock.

"Gretchen," said I, "time lags. Make a servant out of me this morning."

"Herr does the barmaid too much honor," with lowered eyes.

"I, am in the habit of doing anything I please."

"Ah, Herr is one of those millionaires I have read about!"

"Yes, I am very rich." I laughed, but Gretchen did not see the point.

"Come, then, with me, and you shall weed the knoblauch patch."

She was laughing at me, but I was not to be abashed.

"To the patch be it, then!" I cried. "An onion would smell as sweet under any other name."

So Gretchen and I went into the onion patch, and I weeded and hoed and hoed and weeded till my back ached and my hands were the color of the soil. Nothing was done satisfactorily to Gretchen. It was, "There, you have ruined the row back of you!" or "Pull the weeds more gently!" and sometimes, "Ach! could your friends see you now!" I suppose that I did not make a pretty picture. The perspiration would run down my face. I would forget the condition of my hands and push back my hair, which fell like a mop over my brow, whereat she would laugh. Once I took her hand and helped her to jump over a row. I was surprised at the strength of her grasp.

"What does Herr do for a living, he works so badly as a gardener?"

"I am a journalist," I answered, leaning on my hoe and breathing heavily.

"Ach! one of those men who tell such dreadful stories about kings and princes? Who cause men to go to war with each other? Who rouse the ignorant to deeds of violence? One of those men who are more powerful than a king, because they can undo him?" She drew away from me.

"Hold on!" I cried, dropping the hoe; "what do you know about it?"

"Enough," sadly. "I read the papers. I always look with fear upon one of those men who can do so much good, and yet who would do so much evil."

I had never looked at it in that light before.

"It seems to me, Gretchen," I said quietly, "that you are about as much a barmaid as I am a weeder of knoblauches."

The color of excitement fled from Gretchen's cheeks, her eyes grew troubled and she looked away.

"Gretchen has a secret," said I. "It is nothing to me what Gretchen's secret is; I shall respect it, and continue to think of her only as a barmaid with—with a superior education." I shouldered the hoe. "Come, let us go back; I'm thirsty."

"Thank you, Herr," was the soft reply. Then Gretchen became as dumb, and our return to the inn was made in silence. Once there, however, she recovered. "I am sorry to have put you at such a disadvantage," glancing at my clothes, which were covered with brown earth.

"Let that be the least of your troubles!" I cried gayly. Then I hummed in English:

> So, ho! dear Gretchen, winsome lass,
> I want no tricky wine,
> But amber nectar bring to me,
> Whose rich bouquet will cling to me,
> Whose spirit voice will sing to me
> From out the mug divine
> So, here's your toll—a kiss—away,
> You Hebe of the Rhine!
> No goblet's gold means cheer to me,
> Let no cut glass get near to me—
> Go, Gretchen, haste the beer to me,
> And put it in the stein!

I thought I saw a smile on her lips, but it was gone before I was certain.

"Gott in Himmel!" gasped the astonished innkeeper, as I went into the barroom. I still had the hoe over my shoulder.

Harold MacGrath

"Never mind, mein host. I've been weeding your knoblauch patch as a method of killing time."

"But—" He looked at Gretchen in dismay.

"It was I who led him there," said Gretchen, in answer to his inquiring eyes.

A significant glance passed between them. There was a question in his, a command in hers. I pretended to be examining the faded tints in the stein I held in my hand.

I was thinking: "Since when has an innkeeper waited on the wishes of his barmaid?"

There was a mystery after all.

CHAPTER IX

I took my pipe and strolled along the river bank. What had I stumbled into? Here was an old inn, with rather a feudal air; but it was only one in a thousand; a common feature throughout the Continent. And yet, why had the gods, when they cast out Hebe, chosen this particular inn for her mortal residence? The pipe solves many riddles, and then, sometimes, it creates a density. I put my pipe into my pocket and cogitated. Gretchen had brought about a new order of things. A philosophical barmaid was certainly a novelty. That Gretchen was philosophical I had learned in the rose gardens. That she was also used to giving commands I had learned in the onion patch. Hitherto I had held the onion in contempt; already I had begun to respect it. Above all, Gretchen was a mystery, the most alluring kind of mystery—a woman who was not what she seemed. How we men love mysteries, which are given the outward semblance of a Diana or a Venus! By and by, my journalistic instinct awoke. Who are those who fear the newspapers? Certainly it is not the guiltless. Of what was Gretchen guilty? The inn-keeper knew. Was she one of those many conspirators who abound in the kingdom? She was beautiful enough for anything. And whence came the remarkable likeness between her and Phyllis? Here was a mystery indeed. I had a week before me; in that time I might learn something about Gretchen, even if I could solve nothing. I admit that it is true, that had Gretchen been plain, it would not have been worth the trouble. But she had too heavenly a face, too wonderful an eye, too delicious a mouth, not to note her with concern.

I did not see Gretchen again that day; but as I was watching the moon climb up, thinking of her and smoking a few pipes as an incense to her shrine, I heard her voice beneath my window. It was accompanied by the bass voice of the inn-keeper.

"But he is a journalist. Is it safe? Is anything safe from them?" came to my ears in a worried accent, a bass.

So the inn-keeper, too, was a Socialist!

Said an impatient contralto: "So long as I have no fear, why should you?"

"Ach, you will be found out and dragged back!" was the lamentation in a throaty baritone. Anxiety raises a bass voice at least two pitches. "If you would but return to the hills, where there is absolute safety!"

"No; I will not go back there, where everything is so dull and dead. I have lived too long not to read a face at a glance. His eyes are honest."

"Thanks, Gretchen," murmured I from above. I was playing the listener; but, then, she was only a barmaid.

"And it is so long," went on the contralto, "since I have seen a man—a strong one, I wish to see if my power is gone."

"Aha!" thought I; "so you have already laid plans for my capitulation, Gretchen?"

"But," said the bass voice once more, "supposing some of the military should straggle along? There might be one who has seen you before. Alas! I despair! You will not hide yourself; you will stay here till they find you."

I fell to wondering what in the world Gretchen had done.

"I have not been to the village since I was a little girl. Dressed as I am, who would recognize me? No one at the castle, for there is no one there but the steward. Would you send me away?"

"God forbid! But this American? You say you can read faces; how about the other one?"

Silence.

"Yes; how about him?"

Said Gretchen: "We are not infallible. And perhaps I was then much to blame."

"No; we are not infallible; that is the reason why you should take no chance," was the final argument of the innkeeper.

"Hush!" said Gretchen.

"Confound the pipe!" I muttered. It had fallen over the window sill.

Five minutes passed; I heard no sound. Glancing from the side of the window I saw that Gretchen and the innkeeper were gone.

Yes, there wasn't any doubt about it; Gretchen was a conspirator. The police were hunting for her, and she was threatened with discovery. It was beyond my imagination what she could have done. Moreover, she was rather courting danger; the military post was only five miles down the river. The one thing which bothered me was the "him" who had suddenly intruded upon the scene, invisible, but there, like Banquo's ghost. Perhaps her beauty had lured some fellow to follow her fortunes and his over-zeal, or lack of it, had brought ruin to some plot.

"Gretchen," said I, as I jumped into bed, "whoever he was, he must have been a duffer."

Her Serene Highness the Princess Hildegarde was in Jericho, and Hillars along with her, where I had consigned them.

Next morning Gretchen waited upon me at breakfast. She was quiet and answered my questions in monosyllables. Presently she laid something at the side of my plate. It was my pipe. I looked at her, but the leads of my eyes could not plumb the depths in hers.

"Thanks," said I. "It dropped from my window last night, while I was playing the disgraceful part of eavesdropper." I dare say she had expected anything but this candid confession. It was very cunning in me. She knew that I knew she knew. Had I lied I should have committed an irreparable blunder.

As it was she lifted her chin and laughed.

"Will you forgive me?"

"Yes; for you certainly wasted your time."

"Yes, indeed; for I am just as much in the dark as ever."

"And will remain so."

"I hope so. A mystery is charming while it lasts. Really, Gretchen, I did not mean to play the listener, and I promise that from now on—"

"From now on!" cried Gretchen. "Does not Herr leave to-day?"

"No; I am going to spend a whole week here."

There was a mixture of dismay and anger in her gaze.

"But, as I was going to say, I shall make no effort to pry into your affairs. Honestly, I am a gentleman."

"I shall try to believe you," said she, the corners of her mouth broadening into a smile.

She condescended to show me through the rose gardens and tell me what she knew about them. It was an interesting lecture. And in the evening she permitted me to row her about the river. We were getting on very well under the circumstances.

The week was soon gone, and Gretchen and I became very good friends. Often when she had nothing to do we would wander along the river through the forests, always, I noticed, by a route which took us away from the village. Each day I discovered some new accomplishment. Sometimes I would read Heine or Goethe to her, and she would grow rapt and silent. In the midst of some murmurous stanza I would suddenly stop, only to see her start and look at me as though I had committed a sacrilege, in that I had spoiled some dream of hers. Then again I myself would become lost in dreams, to be aroused by a soft voice saying: "Well, why do you not go on?" Two people of the opposite sexes reading poetry in the woods is a solemn matter. This is not appreciated at the time, however. It comes back afterward.

In all the week I had learned nothing except that Gretchen was not what she pretended to be. But I feared to ask questions. They might have spoiled all. And the life was so new to me, so quiet and peaceful, with the glamour of romance over it all, that I believe I could have stayed on forever. And somehow Phyllis was fading away, slowly but surely. The regret with which I had heretofore looked upon her portrait was lessening each day; from active to passive. And yet, was it because Gretchen was Phyllis in the ideal? Was I falling in love with Gretchen because she was Gretchen, or was my love for Phyllis simply renewing itself in Gretchen? Was that the reason why the portrait of Phyllis grew less holding and interesting to me? It was a complex situation; one I frowned over when alone. It was becoming plainer to me every hour that I had a mystery all of my own to solve. And Gretchen was the only one to solve it.

I shall never forget that night under the chestnuts, on the bank of the wide white river. The leaves were gossiping among themselves; they had so much to talk about; and then, they knew so much! Had not they and their ancestors filtered the same moonbeams, century on century? Had not their ancestors heard the tramp of the armies, the clash of the sabre, the roar of the artillery? Had not the hand of autumn and the hand of death marked them with the crimson sign? Ah, the leaves! It is well to press them in books when they themselves have such fine stories to tell.

"Gretchen," said I, echoing my thoughts, "had I been born a hundred years ago I must have been a soldier. Napoleon was a great warrior."

"So was Bluecher, since it was he who helped overcome the little Corsican."

The Germans will never forgive Napoleon.

"But war is a terrible thing," went on Gretchen.

"Yes, but it is a great educator; it teaches the vanquished how little they know."

"War is the offspring of pride; that is what makes it so abhorred."

"It is also the offspring of oppression; that is what makes it so great."

"Yes; when the people take up arms it is well. War is the torch of liberty in the hands of the people. Oh, I envy the people, who are so strong, yet know it not. If I were a man I would teach the people that a king has no divine right, save when it is conferred upon him by them."

"Gretchen, I'm afraid that you're a bit of a Socialist."

"And who is not who has any love for humanity?"

"A beautiful woman who is a Socialist, Gretchen, is a menace to the King. Sometimes he fears her. At large, she is dangerous. He seeks her, and if he finds her, he takes away her liberty." All this was said with a definite purpose. It was to let Gretchen know that I knew her secret. "Gretchen, you are an embryo Socialist; a chrysalis, as it were."

"No, Herr," sadly; "I am a butterfly whose wings have been clipped."

I had not expected this admission,

"Never mind," said I. "Gretchen, I do not want you to call me Herr; call me Jack."

"Jack!" she said. It became an uncommon name now.

"Whatever your true name may be, I shall never call you anything but Gretchen."

"Ah, Jack!" She laughed, and the lurking echoes clasped the music of that laughter in their wanton arms and hurried it across the river.

"Sing to me," said I.

Then imagine my surprise—I, who had heard nothing but German fall from her lips?—when in a heavenly contralto she sang a chanson from "La Fille de Madame Angot," an opera forgotten these ten years!

"*Elle est tellement innocente!*"

She had risen, and she stood there before me with a halo of moonshine above her head. The hot blood rushed to my ears. Barmaid, Socialist, or whatever she might be, she was lovable. In a moment I was kissing her hand, the hand so small, so white, and yet so firm. A thousand inarticulate words came to my lips—from my heart! Did the hand tremble? I thought so. But swiftly she drew it from my clasp, all the joy and gladness gone from her face and eyes.

"No, no!" she cried; "this must not be; it must not be!"

"But I—" I began eagerly.

"You must not say it; I command you. If you speak, Gretchen will be Gretchen no more. Yes, the King seeks Gretchen; but will you drive her away from her only haven?" with a choking sound.

"Gretchen, trust me. Shall I go to-morrow? Shall I leave you in peace?" Somehow I believed myself to be in danger. "Speak!"

There was an interval of stillness, broken only by the beating of hearts. Then:

"Stay. But speak no word of love; it is not for such as I. Stay and be my friend, for I need one. Cannot a woman look with favor upon a man but he must needs become her lover? I shall trust you as I have trusted other men. And though you fail me in the end, as others have done, still I shall trust you. Herr, I conspire against the King. For what? The possession of my heart. All my life I have stood alone, so alone."

"I will be your friend, Gretchen; I will speak no word of love. Will that suffice?"

"It is all I ask, dear friend. And now will you leave me?"

"Leave you?" I cried. "I thought you bade me stay?"

"Ah," putting out her hand; "you men do not understand. Sometimes a woman wishes to be alone when—when she feels that she—she cannot hold back her tears!"

Gravely I bent over her hand and kissed it. It seemed to me as I let the hand fall that I had never kissed a woman on the lips. I turned and went slowly down the path. Once I looked back. I saw something white lying at the foot of the tree. Heaven knows what a struggle it was, but I went on. I wanted to take her in my arms and tell her that I loved her. When I reached the inn I turned again, but I saw nothing. I sat in my room a long time that night, smoking my pipe till the candle gasped feebly and died in the stick, and the room was swallowed in darkness.

I did not know, I was not sure, but I thought that, so long as I might not love Phyllis, it would not be a very hard task to love her image, which was Gretchen. You see, Phyllis was so very far away and Gretchen was so near!

CHAPTER X

I lowered the glasses. I discerned them to be cavalrymen, petty officers. They were mounted on spirited horses.

"Gretchen," said I, "they are cavalrymen. They do not wear the Hohenphalian uniform; so, perhaps, it would be just as well for you to go to your room and remain there till they are gone. Ah," said I, elevating the glasses again; "they wear his Majesty's colors. You had best retire."

"I refuse. They may be thirsty."

"I'll see to that," I laughed.

"But—" she began.

"Oh, Gretchen wishes to see new faces," said I, with chagrin.

"If it pleases you, sir," mischievously.

"What if they are looking for—for—"

"That is the very reason why I wish to see them."

"You are determined?"

"I am."

"Very well," said I; "you had best eat an onion."

"And for what purpose?"

"As a preventive to offensive tactics," looking slyly at her.

Her laugh rang out mockingly.

"Do you not know that aside from dueling, the German lives only for his barmaid, his beer and his knoblauch? Nevertheless, since you wish it I will eat one—for your sake."

"For my sake?" I cried in dismay. "Heaven forfend!"

"Does Herr—"

"Jack," said I.

"Does Herr Jack think," her eyes narrowing till naught but a line of their beautiful blue-green could be seen, "that one of those would dare take a liberty with me?"

"I hope he will not. I should have the unpleasant duty of punching his head." If I could not kiss Gretchen nobody else should.

"You are very strong."

"Yes; and there are some things which add threefold to a man's strength."

"Such as—" She looked at me daringly.

"Yes, such as —" Her eyes fell before my glance, A

delicate veil of rose covered her face for a moment. I wondered if she knew that it was only because I clinched my fists till the nails cut, that I did not do the very thing I feared the stragglers coming down the road might do. "Come," said I, peremptorily; "there is no need of your welcoming them here."

So we entered the inn; and she began furbishing up the utensils, just to tease me more than anything else.

Outside there was a clatter of hoofs, the chink of the spur, intermingled with a few oaths; and then the two representatives of the King came in noisily. They gazed admiringly at Gretchen as she poured out their beer. She saw the rage in my eyes. She was aggravating with her promiscuous smiles. The elder officer noticed my bulldog pipe.

"English?" he inquired, indifferently. The German cannot disassociate an Englishman and a briarwood bulldog pipe.

"English," I answered discourteously. It mattered nothing to me whether he took me for an Englishman or a Zulu; either answered the purpose.

He wore an eyeglass, through which he surveyed me rather contemptuously.

"What is your name, fraulein?" he asked turning to Gretchen.

"Gretchen," sweetly.

"And what is the toll for a kiss?"

"Nothing," said Gretchen, looking at me. The lieutenant started for her, but she waved him off. "Nothing, Herr

Lieutenant, because they are not for sale."

I moved closer to the bar.

"Out for a constitutional?" I asked, blowing the ash from the live coal in my pipe.

"We are on his Majesty's business," with an intonation which implied that the same was none of mine. "Gretchen, we shall return to-night, so you may lay two plates at a separate table," with an eye on me. He couldn't have hated me any more than I hated him. "Then, there is no way of getting a kiss?"

"No," said Gretchen.

"Then I'll blow you one;" and Gretchen made a pretty curtesey.

I nearly bit the amber stem off my pipe. They were soon gone, and I was glad of it.

"Herr Jack is angry," said Gretchen.

"Not at all," I growled. "What right have I to be angry?"

"Does Herr Jack wish Gretchen always to be sad?"

"Certainly not: but sometimes your joy is irritating. You are sad all day, then some strangers come, and you are all smiles. Your smiles do not come in my direction as often as I should like."

"Well, then, look at me," said Gretchen.

The smile would have dazzled an anchorite, let alone a man who didn't know whether he loved her for certain, but who was willing to give odds that he did!

"Gretchen!" I cried, starting toward her.

But with a low laugh she disappeared behind the door. Gretchen was a woman. As a man must have his tobacco, so must a woman have her coquetry. It was rather unfair of Gretchen, after what I had promised. It was like getting one in a cage and then offering sweetmeats at a safe distance.

It now became a question of analysis. So I went to the river and sat down in the grass. A gentle wind was stirring the leaves, and the sunbeams, filtering through the boughs, fell upon the ground in golden snowflakes. What was Gretchen to me that I should grow jealous of her smiles? The night before I could have sworn that I loved her; now I was not so sure. A week ago all the sunshine in the world had come from Phyllis's face; a shadow had come between. Oh, I knew the symptoms. They were not new to me. They had visited me some five years back, and had clung to me with the tenacity of a creditor to a man with expectations. When a man arrives at that point where he wants the society of one woman all to himself, the matter assumes serious proportions. And a man likes to fall in love with one woman and continue to love her all his days; it is more romantic. It annoys him to face the fact that he is about to fall in love with another. In my case I felt that there was some extenuation. Gretchen looked like Phyllis. When I saw Gretchen in the garden and then went to my room and gazed upon the likeness of Phyllis, I was much like the bachelor Heine tells about—I doddered.

The red squirrel in the branches above me looked wisely. He was wondering how long before the green burrs would parch and give him their brown chestnuts. I was contemplating a metaphysical burr. I wanted to remain true to Phyllis, though there wasn't any sense in my doing so. Had Gretchen resembled any one but Phyllis I never should have been in such a predicament. I should have gone away the day after my arrival. Here I was going into my second week. My assistant in London was probably worrying, having heard nothing from me during that time. As matters stood it was evident that I could not be true either to Phyllis or Gretchen, since I did not know positively which I loved. I knew that I loved one. So much was gained. I wanted to throw up a coin, heads for Phyllis, tails for Gretchen, but I couldn't bring myself to gamble on the matter. I threw a stick at his squirrelship, and he scurried into the hole in the crotch of the tree. A moment later he peered at me, and, seeing that nothing was going to follow the stick, crept out on the limb again, his tail bristling with indignation.

"If it hadn't been for Gretchen," said I, "you would have been a potpie long ago."

He must have understood my impotence, for he winked at me jeeringly.

A steamer came along then, puffing importantly, sending a wash almost at my feet. I followed it with my eye till it became lost around the bend. Over there was Austria and beyond, the Orient, a new world to me.

"If I could see them together!" I mused aloud.

The squirrel cocked his head to one side as if to ask: "Austria and Turkey?"

"No," said I, looking around for another stick; "Phyllis and Gretchen. If I could see them together, you know, I could tell positively then which I love. As it is, I'm in doubt. Do you understand?"

The squirrel ran out to the end of the limb and sat down. It was an act of deliberation.

"Well, why don't you answer?"

I was startled to my feet by the laughter which followed my question. A few yards behind me stood Gretchen.

"Can't you find a better confidant?" she asked,

"Yes, but she will not be my confidant," said I. I wondered how much she had heard of the one-sided dialogue. "Will you answer the question I just put to that squirrel of yours?"

"And what was the question?" with innocence not feigned.

"Perhaps it was, Why should Gretchen not revoke the promise to which she holds me?"

"You should know, Herr," said Gretchen, gently.

"But I do not. I only know that a man is human and that a beautiful woman was made to be loved." Everything seemed solved now that Gretchen stood at my side.

But she turned as if to go.

"Gretchen," I called, "do not go. Forgive me; if only you understood!'"

"Perhaps I do understand," she replied with a gentleness new to me. "Do you remember why I asked you to stay?"

"Yes; I was to be your friend."

"This time it is for me to ask whether I go or stay."

"Stay, Gretchen!" But I was a hypocrite when I said it.

"I knew that you would say that," simply.

"Gretchen, sit down and I'll tell you the story of my life, as they say on the stage." I knocked the dead ash from my pipe and stuffed the bowl with fresh weed. I lit it and blew a cloud of smoke into the air. "Do you see that, Gretchen?"

"Yes, Herr," sitting down, the space of a yard between us.

"It is pretty, very; but see how the wind carries it about! As it leaves my throat it looks like a tangible substance. Reach for it and it is gone. That cloud of smoke is my history."

"It disappears," said Gretchen.

"And so shall I at the appointed time. That cloud of smoke was a fortune. I reached for it, and there was nothing but the air in my hand. It was a woman's love. For five years I watched it curl and waver. In it I saw many castles and the castles were fair, indeed. I strove to grasp this love; smoke, smoke. Smoke is nothing, given a color. Thus it is with our dreams. If only we might not wake!"

Gretchen's eyes were following the course of the languid river.

"Once there was a woman I thought I loved; but she would have none of it. She said that the love I gave her was not complete because she did not return it. She brought forth the subject of affinities, and ventured to say that some day I might meet mine. I scoffed inwardly. I have now found what she said to be true. The love I gave her was the bud; the rose—Gretchen," said I, rising, "I love you; I am not a hypocrite; I cannot parade my regard for you under the flimsy guise of friendship."

"Go and give the rose to her to whom you gave the bud," said Gretchen. The half smile struck me as disdainful. "You are a strange wooer."

"I am an honest one." I began plucking at the bark of the tree. "No; I shall let the rose wither and die on the stem. I shall leave to-morrow, Gretchen. I shall feel as Adam did when he went forth from Eden. Whatever your place in this world is it is far above mine. I am, in truth, a penniless adventurer. The gulf between us cannot be bridged."

"No," said Gretchen, the smile leaving her lips, "the gulf cannot be bridged. You are a penniless adventurer, and I am a fugitive from—the law, the King, or what you will. You are a man; man forgets. You have just illustrated the fact. His memory and his promises are like the smoke; they fade away but soon. I shall be sorry to have you go, but it is best so."

"Do you love any one else?"

"I do not; I love no one in the sense you mean. It was not written that I should love any man."

"Gretchen, who are you, and what have you done?"

"What have I done? Nothing! Who am I? Nobody!"

"Is that the only answer you can give?"

Harold MacGrath

"It is the only answer I will give."

There was something in Gretchen's face which awed me. It was power and resolution, two things man seldom sees in a woman's face.

"Supposing, Gretchen, that I should take you in my arms and kiss you?" I was growing reckless because I felt awed, which seems rather a remarkable statement. "I know you only as a barmaid; why, not?"

She never moved to go away. There was no alarm in her eyes, though they narrowed.

"You would never forgive yourself, would you?"

I thought for a moment. "No, Gretchen, I should never forgive myself. But I know that if I ask you to let me kiss your hand before I go, you will grant so small a favor."

"There," and her hand stretched toward me. "And what will your kiss mean?"

"That I love you, but also respect you, and that I shall go."

"I am sorry."

It was dismal packing. I swore a good deal, softly. Gretchen was not in the dining-room when I came down to supper. It was just as well. I wanted to be cool and collected when I made my final adieu. After supper I lit my pipe (I shall be buried with it!) and went for a jaunt up the road. There was a train at six the next morning. I would leave on that. Why hadn't I taken Gretchen in my arms and kissed her? It would have been something to remember in the days to come. I was a man, and stronger; she would have been powerless. Perhaps it was the color of her eyes.

I had not gone up the highway more than 100 yards when I saw the lonely figure of a man tramping indirectly toward me and directly toward the inn. Even in the dusk of twilight there was something familiar about that stride. Presently the man lifted up his voice in song. The "second lead," as they say back of the scenes, was about to appear before the audience.

Evidently Hillars had found "Jericho" distasteful and had returned to protest.

Harold MacGrath

CHAPTER XI

"Hello, there!" he hailed, seeing but not recognizing me; "have you seen any cavalry pass this way?"

"No, I have not," I answered in English.

"Eh? What's that?" not quite believing it was English he had heard.

"I said that no cavalry has passed this way since this afternoon. Are they looking for you, you jail-bird in perspective?"

He was near enough now. "Well, I be dam'!" he cried. "What the devil are you doing here, of all places?"

"I was looking for you," said I, locking my arm in his.

"Everybody has been making that their occupation since I left Austria," cursing lowly. "I never saw such people."

"What have you been doing this time?"

"Nothing; but I want to do something right away. They have been hounding me all over the kingdom. What have I done? Nothing, absolutely nothing. It makes me hot under the collar. These German blockheads! Do they think to find the Princess Hildegarde by following me around? I'd give as much as they to find her."

"So you haven't seen anything of her?"

"Not a sign. I came here first, but not a soul was at the castle. Nobody knows where she is. I came here this time to throw them off the track, but I failed. I had a close shave this noon. I'll light out to-morrow. It isn't safe in these parts. It would be of no use to tell them that I do not know where the princess is. They have connected me with her as they connect one link of a chain to another. You can kill a German, but you can't convince him. How long have you been here?"

I did not reply at once. "About ten days."

"Ten days!" he echoed. "What on earth has kept you in this ruin that long?"

"Rest," said I, glibly. "But I am going away to-morrow. We'll go together. They will not know what to do with two of us."

"Yes, they will. You will be taken for my accomplice. . . . Hark! What's that?" holding his hand to his ear. "Horses. Come, I'm not going to take any risk."

So we made a run for the inn. In the twilight haze we could see two horsemen coming along the highway at a brisk gallop.

"By the Lord Harry!" Hillars cried excitedly; "the very men I have been dodging all day. Hurry! Can you put me somewhere for the time being? The garret; anywhere."

"Come on; there's a place in the garret where they'll never

find you."

I got him upstairs unseen. If no one but I knew him to be at the inn, so much the better.

"O, say! This'll smother me," said Dan, as I pushed him into the little room.

"They'll put you in a smaller place," I said. "Hang it all Jack; I'd rather have it out with them."

"They have their pistols and sabres."

"That's so. In that case, discretion is the better part of valor, and they wouldn't appreciate any coup on my side. Come back and let me out as soon as they go."

I descended into the barroom and found the two officers interrogating the innkeeper. They were the same fellows who had visited the inn earlier in the day. Gretchen was at her place behind the bar. She was paler than usual.

"Ah," said the innkeeper, turning to me, "am I not right in saying that you are the only guest at the inn, and that no American has been here?"

I did not understand his motive, for he knew that I was an American.

"It is perfectly true," said I, "that I am your only guest."

"Ah, the Englishman!" said the lieutenant, suspiciously. "We are looking for a person by the name of Hillars whom we are charged to arrest. Do you know anything about him?"

"It is not probable," said I, nonchalantly.

I glanced at Gretchen. I could fathom nothing there.

"Well," snarled the lieutenant, "I suppose you will not object to my seeing your passports?"

"Not in the least," said I. But I felt a shock. The word "American" was written after the nationality clause in my passports. I was in for some excitement on my own account. If I returned from my rooms saying that I could not find my passports they would undoubtedly hold me till the same were produced. "I'll go and bring them for you," said I. I wanted some time in which to mature a plan of action, if action became necessary.

There was rather a sad expression in Gretchen's eyes. She understood to a fuller extent than I what was likely to follow when it was found that I had misrepresented myself. I cursed the folly which had led me to say that I was English. And I swore at the innkeeper for meddling. As I left the room I smiled at Gretchen, but she did not answer it. Perhaps I was gone five minutes. In that time I made up my mind to show the passports, and trust to luck for the rest. When I came back Gretchen had engrossed their attention. They took no notice of me. I have never understood how it came about, but all at once the lieutenant bent forward and kissed Gretchen on the cheek. She started back with a cry, then looked at me. That swift glance told me what to do. I took the lieutenant by the collar and flung him into the corner. The surprise on his face was not to be equaled. Then, as he rose to his feet, the veins in his neck swelled with rage.

"I'll pay you for that, you meddling beef-eater!" he roared.

"Don't mention it," said I, with an assumption of bland-ness which I did not feel. "That was simply gratuitous. It is a sample of what I shall do to you if you do not immediately ask this lady's pardon for the gross insult you have just offered her."

"Insult! To kiss a common barmaid an insult!" he yelled, now purpling. "Why—why—what is this woman to you—this tavern wench, this—"

"Be careful," I warned.

Gretchen was calmly wiping her cheek; but her eyes were like polished emeralds.

"You came here, I believe," said I, "to see if my passports were proper."

"Damn you and your passports! Are you a gentleman?"

"Would you recognize one if you saw him?" I laughed.

"Can you fight?"

"Certainly," said I, thinking of the weapons nature in her kindness had given to me.

"Good! Otto, have the horses brought around. We will cut for the barracks and get the colonel's weapons—the rapiers."

The word "rapier" sent an icy chill up my spine. A duel!

"The devil!" said I, under my breath. I knew less about fencing than I did about aerial navigation, which was precious little. The fact that Gretchen was now smiling aggravated the situation. I could not help the shudder. Why, the fellow would make a sieve out of me!

"Will you look at my passports now?" I asked. "You may

not have the opportunity again."

"Your passports from now on will be void," was the retort. "But I shall be pleased to give you a passport to the devil. I shall kill you," complacently.

"Think of my family," said I, a strange humor taking possession of me.

"You should have thought of your family before you struck me that blow," he replied.

My laughter was genuine; even Gretchen smuggled a smile. The lieutenant had taken my remark in all seriousness.

"You will not run away?" he asked.

"I shall probably be obliged to run away to-morrow," said I, smoothly. "I should not be able to account for your presence here. But I shall await your return from the barracks, never fear." All this was mere bravado; honestly, I shrunk within my clothes and shivered in my shoes. But I had an unfailing mental nerve. Some call it bluff.

Gretchen had been whispering to the innkeeper. When he moved from her side, she was smiling.

"What the deuce is she smiling about?" I wondered. "Does the woman take me for a modern D'Artagnan?"

"Innkeeper," said the lieutenant, "if this man is not here when I return, I'll take satisfaction out of your hide."

The innkeeper shrugged. "I have never heard of an Englishman running away."

"And I have seen many a German do that," I put in. "How am I to know that your going to the barracks is not a ruse?"

He gasped. The words would not come which would do justice to his feelings. He drew off one of his gloves and threw it into my face. It stung me. I should have knocked him down, but for the innkeeper stepping between.

"No, Herr," he said; "do not disable him."

"You had best go to the barracks at once," said I to the lieutenant. My clothes were too small for me now, and I did not shiver in my shoes. My "Yankee" blood was up. I would have fought him with battle axes.

"Herr," said the innkeeper, when the two had made off for the barracks, "you are a man of courage."

"Thanks," said I.

"Do you know anything about rapiers?" he asked.

"I know the handle from the blade; that's all. But that does not make any difference. I'd fight him with any weapon. He struck me; and then—then, he kissed Gretchen."

"I have wiped it off, Herr," said Gretchen, dryly. Then she passed from the room.

I went upstairs too. I looked out of my window. There was moonlight; possibly the last time I should ever see moonlight in the land of the living. Nothing but a mishap on my opponent's part, and that early in the combat, would save my epidermis. The absurd side of the affair struck me, and I laughed, mirthlessly, but none the less I laughed. If it had been pistols the chances would have been equal. A German does not like pistols as a dueling apparatus. They often miss fire. A sword is a surer weapon. And then, the French use them—the pistols—in their fiascoes. Rapiers? I was as familiar with the rapier as I was with the Zulu assegai. I unstrapped my traveling case and took out Phyllis's photograph. I put it back. If I was to have a last look at any woman it should be at Gretchen. Then I got out my cane and practiced thrusting and parrying. My wrist was strong.

"Well," I mused, "there's consolation in knowing that in two hours I shall be either dead or alive."

I flung the cane into the corner. To pass away the time I paced back and forth. It passed too quickly; and it was not long ere I heard the clatter of the returning cavalrymen. Some one knocked at my door. I swung it open and—was thrown to the floor, bound and gagged in a tenth of a minute.

"Put him on the bed," whispered the leader of my assailants. When this was done the voice added: "Now you can go to the stables and wait there till I call you."

It was the innkeeper. He surveyed me for a moment and scratched his chin.

"Will Herr keep perfectly quiet if I take the handkerchief from his mouth?" he asked.

I nodded, bewildered.

"What in tophet does this mean?" I gasped. I did not say tophet, but it looks better in writing.

"It means nothing and everything," was the answer. "In the first place, Herr will fight no duel. The man with whom you were to fight was sent on an errand to this out-of-the-way place as a punishment for dueling at the capital. I know him by reputation. He is a brawler, but a fair swordsman. He would halve you as I would a chicken. There is another who has a prior claim on him. If there is anything left of Herr Lieutenant at the end of the fray, you are welcome to it. Yes, there will be a duel, but you will not be one of the principals. It is all arranged."

"But I do not understand," I cried.

"It is not necessary that you should." He laughed and rubbed his hands in pleasurable anticipation. "There is a young man downstairs, who arrived a few moments before the lieutenant. He has a special affair. There were words. Herr Lieutenant is mad enough to fight a whole company."

"Then, why in heaven's name am I up here in this condition?" I cried. "Let me go and be the young man's second; though I can't for the life of me see where he has come from so suddenly, and I might say, opportunely. Come, cut me loose."

"It is too late!"

"Too late?"

"Yes. Herr Lieutenant has been informed that you ran away."

"Ran away!" I roared. "You told him that I ran away? Damn your insolence! I'll break every bone in your body for this!" I cried, straining at the ropes.

"The ropes are new," said he; "you'll hurt yourself."

"You told him that I ran away?" This was too much.

"Yes. Ah, but you will be surprised. The duel will last five minutes. Herr Lieutenant will thrust; the thrust will be parried. He will feint; useless. Thrust on thrust; parry on parry. Consternation will take the place of confidence; he will grow nervous; he will try all his little tricks and they will fail. Then his eyes will roll and his breath come in gasps. Suddenly he thinks he sees an opening; he lunges—ach! the fool; it is all over!" The old man's voice quivered with excitement. He had passed his time in the barracks and had seen many a sword skirmish.

"Well, are you going to take off these ropes?"

"No. You would break every bone in my body."

"Damn it, man!" I groaned, in exasperation.

"You will soon be out of breath."

Oh! could I have but loosened those cords!

"Stahlberg, who left the service a year ago, will act in the capacity of second." Stahlberg was at the head of the vineyard. "I shall watch the affair from the window here; the scene of action will take place in the clearing beyond. It will be an affair worth witnessing."

"And where is Gretchen?"

"Where she should be; at the bar, a dutiful bar-maid." Then I heard nothing but the deep cachinations of the innkeeper. There was something in the affair which appealed to his humor. I could not see it. For ten minutes my vocabulary was strictly unprintable.

"Will you kindly tell me what the meaning of all this is?"

"Herr Winthrop, the idyl has come to an end; the epic now begins."

CHAPTER XII

The golden summer moon was far up now, and the yellow light of it came into the window and illumined the grim face of the innkeeper, throwing a grotesque shadow of him onto the floor. The leaves rustled and purred against the eaves. As the branches moved so did the light and darkness move over the innkeeper's visage. He was silent and meditative.

"An epic?" I said.

"An epic."

"Innkeeper," said I, "if I give you my word of honor not to molest you or leave this room, will you let me be a witness?"

He passed into the gloom, then back into the light.

"This is no trick?" suspiciously. "I have a deal of regard for my bones, old as they are."

"On my honor."

"Well, I'll do it. It is in the blood of us all. But a false move on your part, and I promise you that this knife shall find a resting place in you."

He cut the ropes and I was free. But my arms ached.

The two of us took our stand by the window and waited for the principals in the drama about to be enacted in the clearing. I confess that my conscience was ill at ease; why, I knew not. I was dreading something, I knew not what. The inn-keeper's hand trembled on my arm.

"Sh! they come," he whispered.

As I looked beyond his finger I saw four figures advance over the sward. One of them, a slight boyish form, was new to me. The fellow walked briskly along at the side of Stahlberg, who was built on the plan of a Hercules. When they came to the clearing they stopped. The seconds went through the usual formalities of testing the temper of the swords. Somehow, I could not keep my eyes off the youngster, who was going to do battle with the veteran; and I could not help wondering where in the world he had come from, and why in the world he had chosen this place to settle his dispute in. There were plenty of convenient places in the village, in and around the barracks. He took his position, back to me, so I could not tell what he was like. The moon shone squarely in the lieutenant's face, upon which was an expression of contempt mingled with confidence. My heart thumped, for I had never seen a duel before.

"I do not know where you came from," I heard the lieutenant say; "but you managed nicely to pick a quarrel. It is all on your own head. It is too bad that cur of an Englishman had to run away."

The innkeeper's knife was so close that I could feel the point of it against my ribs. So I gave up the wild idea of yelling from the window that I hadn't run away.

The lieutenant's opponent shrugged. He placed himself on guard; that was his reply. Suddenly the two sprang forward, and the clash of swords followed. I could not keep track of the weapons, but I could see that the youngster was holding his own amazingly well. Neither was touched the first bout.

"Two minutes," murmured the old rascal at my side. "It will be over this time."

"You seem to have a good deal of confidence in your young man," said I.

"There is not a finer swords—swordsman in the kingdom, or on the continent, for that matter. There! they are at it again."

Step by step the lieutenant gave ground; the clashing had stopped; it was needle-like work now. Gradually they began to turn around. The blades flashed in the moon-shine like heat lightning. My pulse attuned itself to every stroke. I heard a laugh. It was full of scorn. The laugh—it recalled to me a laugh I had heard before. Evidently the youngster was playing with the veteran. I became fascinated. And while the innkeeper and I watched a curious thing happened. Something seemed to be slipping from the youngster's head; he tried to put up his free hand, but the lieutenant was making furious passes! A flood of something dimly yellow suddenly fell about the lad's shoulders. Oh, then I knew! With a snarl of rage I took the inn-keeper by the throat and hurled him, knife and all, to the floor, dashed from the room, thence to the stairs, down which I leaped four at a time. Quick as I was, I was too late. The lieutenant's sword lay on the grass, and he was clasping his shoulder with the sweat of agony on his brow.

"Damnation!" he groaned; "a woman!" Then he tottered and fell in the arms of his subordinate. He had fainted.

"This will make a pretty story," cried the young officer, as he laid his superior lengthwise, and tried to staunch the flow of blood. "Here's a man who runs away, and lets a woman—God knows what sort—fight his duels for him, the cur!"

I never looked at him, but went straight to Gretchen. Stahlberg gave me a questioning glance, and made a move as though to step between.

"Stand aside, man!" I snapped. "Gretchen, you have dishonored me."

"It were better than to bury you"—lightly. "I assure you he caused me no little exertion."

Yet her voice shook, and she shuddered as she cast aside the sword.

"You have made a laughing stock of me. I am a man, and can fight my own battles," I said, sternly. "My God!" breaking down suddenly, "supposing you had been killed?"

"It was not possible. And the man insulted me, not you. A woman? Very well. I can defend myself against every-thing but calumny. Have I made a laughing stock of you? It is nothing to me. It would not have altered my—"

She was very white, and she stroked her forehead.

"Well?" said I.

"It would not have altered my determination to take the

sword in hand again."

She put her hand to her throat as though something there had tightened.

"Ah, I am a woman, for I believe that I am about to faint! No!" imperiously, as I threw out my arms to catch her. "I can reach the door alone, without assistance."

And so we went along. I did not know what to do, nor yet what to say. A conflict was raging in my heart between shame and love; shame, that a woman had fought for me and won where I should have lost; love, that strove to spring from my lips in exultation. I knew not which would have conquered had I not espied the blood on Gretchen's white hand.

"You are wounded!" I cried.

She gazed at her hand as though she did not understand; then, with a little sob and a little choke she extended her arms toward me and stumbled. Was ever there a woman who could look on blood without fainting? Gretchen had not quite fainted, but the moon had danced, she said, and all had grown dim.

"Gretchen, why did you risk your life? In God's name, what manner of woman are you, and where did you learn to use the sword? Had you no thought of me?" I was somewhat incoherent.

"No thought of you?" She drew the back of her hand over her eyes. "No thought of you? I did it because—because I did not—I could not—you would have been killed!"

I was a man—human. I loved her. I had always loved her; I had never loved any one else. I was a coward to do what

I did, but I could not help it. I crushed her to my breast and kissed her lips, not once, but many times.

"How dare you!" weakly.

"How dare I, Gretchen, dear Gretchen?" I said. "I dare because I love you! I love you! What is it to me that you have dishonored me in the eyes of men? Nothing. I love you! Are you a barmaid? I care not. Are you a conspirator? I know not, nor care. I know but one thing: I love you; I shall always love you! Shall I tell you more? Gretchen, you love me!"

"No, no! it cannot be!" she sobbed, pushing me back. "I am the most wretched woman in the world! Do not follow me, Herr; leave me, I beg you to leave me. I have need of the little strength left. Leave me, leave me!"

And she passed through the doorway into the darkness beyond. I did not move from where I stood. I grew afraid that it was a dream, and that if I moved it would vanish. I could yet feel her lithe, warm body palpitating in my arms; my lips still tingled and burned with the flame of hers. An exultant wave swept over me; she loved me! She had not told me so, but I knew. She had put her heart before mine; my life was dearer to her than her own. I could have laughed for joy. She loved me! My love overwhelmed my shame, engulfed it. Then—

"I know you," said a harsh voice at my elbow. It startled me, and I wheeled swiftly. It was the lieutenant's brother officer. "I thought from what I heard of you that you were a man worth trouble and caution. Ach! you, the man we have scoured the country for? I should not have believed it. To let a woman fight for him! And she—she is more than a woman—she is a goddess!" with enthusiasm. "If I was betrothed to her I'd find her if I had to hunt in heaven and hell for her. And what does she see in you?" He snapped his fingers derisively. "I warn you that your race is run. You cannot leave a railway station within the radius of a hundred miles. The best thing you can do is to swim the river and stop in the middle. The Prince is at the village, and he shall know. Woe to you, you meddler!"

"Young man," said a voice from over my shoulder, from the doorway, "you should by right address those impertinent remarks to me. I am Hillars, the man you seek."

And I had forgotten his very existence! What did he know? What had he seen?

"You may inform Count von Walden," continued Dan, "that I shall await his advent with the greatest of impatience. Now let me add that you are treating this gentleman with much injustice. I'll stake my life on his courage. The Princess Hildegarde is alone responsible for what has just happened."

"The Princess Hildegarde!" I cried.

Hillars went on: "Why she did this is none of your business or mine. Why she substituted herself concerns her and this gentleman only. Now go, and be hanged to you and your Prince and your Count, and your whole stupid country. Come, Jack."

The fellow looked first at me, then at Dan.

"I apologize," he said to Dan, "for mistaking this man for you." He clicked his heels, swung around, and marched off.

"Come," said Dan.

I dumbly followed him up to my room. He struck a match and lit the candle.

"Got any tobacco?" he asked, taking out a black pipe. "I have not had a good smoke in a week. I want to smoke awhile before I talk."

I now knew that he had been a witness to all, or at least to the larger part of it.

"There is some tobacco on the table," I said humbly. I felt that I had wronged him in some manner, though unintentionally. "The Princess Hildegarde!" I murmured.

"The very person," said Hillars. He lit his pipe and sat on the edge of the bed. He puffed and puffed, and I thought he never would begin. Presently he said: "And you never suspected who she was?"

"On my word of honor, I did not, Dan," said I, staring at the faded designs in the carpet. The golden galleon had gone down, and naught but a few bubbles told where she had once so proudly ridden the waters of the sea. The Princess Hildegarde? The dream was gone. Castles, castles! "I am glad you did not know," said Dan, "because I have always believed in your friendship. Yet, it is something we cannot help—this loving a woman. Why, a man will lay down his life for his friend, but he will rob him of the woman he loves. It is life. You love her, of course."

"Yes." I took out my own pipe now. "But what's the use. She is a Princess. Why, I thought her at first a barmaid—a barmaid! Then I thought her to be in some way a lawbreaker, a socialist conspirator. It would be droll if it were not sad. The Princess Hildegarde!" I laughed dismally. "Dan, old man, let's dig out at once, and close the page. We'll talk it over when we are older."

"No, we will face it out. She loves you. Why not? So do I." He got off the bed and came over to me and rested his hands on my shoulders. "Jack, my son, next to her I love you better than anything in the world. We have worked together, starved together, smoked and laughed together. There is a bond between us that no human force can separate. The Princess, if she cannot marry you, shall not marry the Prince. I have a vague idea that it is written. 'The moving finger writes; and, having writ, moves on.' We cannot cancel a line of it."

"Dan, you will do nothing rash or reckless?"

"Sit down, my son; sit down. Premeditation is neither rashness nor recklessness. Jack, life has begun with you; with me it has come to an end. When there is nothing more to live for, it is time to die. But how? That is the question. A war would be a God-send; but these so-called war lords are a lazy lot, or cowardly, or both. Had I a regiment, what a death! Jack, do you not know what it is to fight the invisible death? Imagine yourself on the line, with the enemy thundering toward you, sabres flashing in the sunlight, and lead singing about your ears. It is the only place in the world to die—on a battlefield. Fear passes away as a cloud from the face of the sun. The enemy is bringing you glory—or death. Yes, I would give a good deal for a regiment, and a bad moment for our side. But the regiment non est; still, there is left—"

"Dan, what are you talking about?" I cried.

"Death; grim, gaunt and gray death, whose footstep is as noiseless as the fall of snow; death, the silent one, as the Indian calls him."

He knocked the ash from his pipe and stuffed the briar into his pocket.

"Jack, I am weary of it all. If I cannot die artistically, I wish to die a sudden and awful death. What! Do I look like a man to die in bed, in the inebriates' ward? For surely I shall land there soon! I am going to pieces like a sand house in a wind storm. I suppose I'm talking nonsense. After all, I haven't as much to say as I thought I had. Suppose we turn in? I'm tired. You see, those fellows moved me around to-day."

CHAPTER XIII

Hillars and I stood in the middle of the road. He held the binoculars.

"How many can you make out?" I asked.

"Four; all on horseback. There's a coach of some sort following on behind. But everything is blurred and my hand trembles; the whiskey here is terrible. Here, look for yourself," handing the glasses to me. "Tell me what you see."

"There's one with a white cap—ah, it is Count von Walden! There are two soldiers in the Hohenphalian uniform; cavalry. I do not know who the fourth fellow is."

"Describe him to me," said Hillars, trying to roll a cigarette with his trembling fingers. "Curse it!" throwing away the rice paper, "I've got so bad that I can't roll a cigarette. Well, what's he look like?"

"He's in civilian dress; little black mustache and an imperial."

"Look anything like Napoleon III?"

"You've hit it. Who is he?"

"They say he's Prince Ernst of Wortumborg," said Hillars; "but it is my opinion that he's the devil on a furlough."

"Then he is the man—" I began.

"He is. Your love affair is all over once he gets here; unless—" Dan looked at the sky as though he was undecided about the weather.

"Unless what?" I asked.

"O, just unless," said he. "I'd give 5 pounds for a glass of home-made whiskey."

"You've got a plan of some sort," said I. "Speak it out."

"It wasn't a plan; it was just an idea. It's gone now. Maybe it will come back later. Are you going to stay here, or come with me and tackle a bottle of the innkeeper's Rhine wine? The German vinegar used to make you hilarious."

"What's the coach for?" I asked. "Are they going to carry us off like a couple of chickens?"

"I presume it is for her Serene Highness. I wonder how they found out she was here? Probably the lieutenant you were going to fight, but didn't, informed them. At any rate, the coach will not be for us. The Prince will not bother with you and me while the Princess is here. I don't know what they will do with us; possibly nothing, possibly put us in jail. Come along; I'm thirsty."

It was late in the afternoon of the day following. I had not seen her Serene Highness, the Princess Hildegarde—Gretchen. She had remained in her room, and all efforts of mine to hold communication with her had proved futile. I had stood at her door and supplicated; she had told me to go away. The innkeeper had scowled when I suggested that he carry a note to his mistress. He had refused.

"The Princess receives no notes," he had said. "Gretchen —it was a different matter."

And Hillars had slept till after noon. It had been a bad morning for me. The wounded lieutenant had been carried away the night before, and there had not been anything for me to do but wander about—waiting.

"Will you help me with the Rhine wine?" asked Hillars.

"No. My head is fuddled enough as it is."

"Then you must let me do all the talking."

"And why you?"

"I shall know better how to irritate them," with a laugh. "They will not take any particular interest in you when they set eyes on me. Homo sum! I am the man they are looking for. They will find plenty of me. I shall be a syndicate in myself; where they expect to find one man, they will find a dozen, all alive and kicking. It will be good sport."

"What the devil are you up to?" I demanded.

"Wait and see; wait and see. Come, let us receive them in the hall. The affair must be conducted on the line of court etiquette. First, we shall try to avert hostilities by the aid of diplomacy; if that fails the Princess herself will be made to vindicate us. And why not?"

"You are not going to drag her in!" I exclaimed.

"My dear Jack, of course not. The Prince and the Count will do that for us. You understand that she is concerned in all that is to take place, do you not? Well, then, it will cost her but little."

"But this fellow, the Prince!" I cried. "Let us get out while there is time."

Dan regarded me seriously.

"You aren't afraid of him; what do you want to run away for? My son, there will be some very good sport before this is done. You will miss it by running away."

"It's meeting the man who is to marry her—the woman I love. That is the reason."

"To marry her—the woman I love!" he repeated softly. "Yes, it is hard. But it isn't any worse for you than for me."

"Forgive me, Dan! You know—"

"Yes, yes; I know," crossly. "Hang it! can't I punch it into your head that I am taking all this trouble on your account? If it were not for you, do you suppose I'd wait? The Prince shall never marry the Princess. Will that satisfy you? Now, look pleasant, as the photographer says, for here they are."

The Count entered first, then the Prince, who was followed by two cavalrymen. Hillars and I stood silently by our chairs, and waited. The Prince, a man with a hooked nose, black eyes with half-shut lids, regarded me curiously. He had the air of one amused.

When his eyes grew accustomed to the semi-darkness of

the room, the Count sounded a note of satisfaction.

"Ah! so you are here? You have given me a devil of a chase."

"I return the compliment, Herr General," said Hillars, with a good-humored smile. "But, may I ask, what the devil have you been chasing me for?"

For reply the Count turned to the cavalryman.

"Arrest that man and bind him," he said.

"You might make the order wholesale," said I stepping over to the side of Hillars.

"I told you there would be some sport," whispered Dan. He put his arm across my shoulders.

"And who, in the name of Weimer, are you?" bawled the Count. He scrutinized me intently; then a light of recognition broke over his face. "The other one! A nest of them!"

"Count," interposed the Prince, seating himself at the table, "let me have a short talk with them before you act. There may be extenuating circumstances. Anything of this sort amuses and interests me. Let us use a little diplomacy in the matter."

"Yes," said Hillars; "let us lie a little."

"And who can do it better than a journalist?" the Prince laughed.

"Diplomatists," Hillars sent back.

"What is her Serene Highness to you?" resumed the Prince.

"Nothing—positively nothing."

"Then you are afraid to acknowledge your regard for her?"

"I?" Hillars dropped his arm from my shoulders. "I am not afraid of anything—not even the Count here." Then he laughed. "If her Serene Highness was anything to me, your Highness, I should not be afraid to say so before the King himself."

"You impudent—" But a wave of the Prince's hand silenced the Count.

"Have patience, my friend. This is not impudence; it is courage and prudence. I believe," re-addressing Hillars, "that once you were on the point of eloping with the Princess Hildegarde."

Hillars thrust his hands into his pockets.

"So they say."

"And yet you deny your regard for her!"

"Oh, as to that affair," said Hillars, easily, "it was the adventure more than anything else. It is not every man in my position who has such a chance. And then, perhaps, I saw a good newspaper story." The muscles in his jaws hardened, despite the airy tone he used.

"I see that there is nothing to be gotten from you." Then the Prince directed his glance to me. "And you, sir; what is she to you? What is her Serene Highness to you?"

"She is everything in the world to me," said I.

The consternation which followed cannot be described here. The Count stepped back, dumb-founded. Hillars regarded me as though he thought I had suddenly gone mad. The countenance of the Prince alone remained unruffled.

"Count," he said, laughing, "it seems that the Princess gathers lovers as a woolen coat does teasels. Her lovers—there must now be a legion!"

"You lie!" said Hillars, in an oddly suppressed tone. "You know that you lie."

The Prince's lips drew to a thin line, but that was all.

"Still, who will disprove it?" he asked.

"If you will allow me," said a voice behind us.

We beheld the Princess framed in the doorway. There was a pallor and a look of utter weariness in her face. At the sight of her the Count uncovered and the Prince rose.

"Your arrival is quite timely," said he. "Here are two champions of yours. Come, which do you love?"

A fury sprang to my head, and I said, "You have too much confidence in our patience. I warn you that I have no fear of the sabres back of you."

The same sabres leapt from their scabbards and fell stiffly against their owners' shoulders, instinctively.

"Has it come to this," said the Princess, a superb scorn in her eyes, "that my honor must needs be defended by strangers and aliens?" For the briefest space her glance plunged into my eyes. She moved toward the Prince. "And you, sir, are to be my husband?"

"It is the will of the King," said the Prince, a mocking smile on his lips.

How I lusted for his blood!

"And though my honor is doubtful," went on the woman I loved, "you still would marry me?"

"Your Highness," said the Prince, with a bow which entailed the sweeping of his hands, "I would marry you were your honor as—"

"Hell!" roared Hillars in English.

But he was a moment too late. My hands were around the throat of Prince Ernst of Wortumborg, and I was shaking him till his teeth chattered on each other like castanets. Surely I would have throttled him but for the intervention of the Count and the cavalrymen. The Count swung his arm around my neck, while the cavalrymen, their sabre points at Hillars' breast, wrenched loose my hands. I stood glaring at him, panting and furious. He leaned against the table, gasping and coughing. Finally he recovered his composure.

"Count, I was wrong; you were right. These fellows are dangerous."

"I will fight you on any terms!" I fired back at him.

"I shall send you one of my lackeys," he replied. "Take them away, and shoot them if they resist."

"Liberate the gentlemen," said Gretchen.

The Count gazed at her in amazement.

"Liberate them?" he cried.

"I command it."

"You?" said the Prince.

"Yes. This is my principality; these are my soldiers; I command here."

This was a coup indeed.

"But we represent his Majesty!" cried the Count, still holding me by the throat. I was all but strangled myself.

"I care not whom you represent," said Gretchen. "I am obedient only to the King, not his minions. Release the gentlemen."

The Count's arm slowly unwound. Hillars pressed down the sabre points with his hands and shook off the hand of one of the cavalrymen.

"If it be Your Highness' will," he said, "we will throw these intruders into the road. Might is right," waving his hand to the door which led to the barroom.

The innkeeper and three others filed into the room, grimly and silently. They were armed.

For the first time the Prince lost patience.

"This is all very well, Your Highness," he sneered. "You misunderstand the limits of your power to command."

"Not in any part," said Gretchen. "I am sovereign here, notwithstanding the King's will is paramount to my own. These people are my people; these soldiers are fed of my bounty; this is my country till the King takes it back. You will act further at your peril."

CHAPTER XIV

A bar of sunlight suddenly pervaded the room; red sunlight, lighting in its passing a tableau I shall never forget. Gretchen stood at her full height, her arms held closely to her sides and her hands clenched. On her face there was that half smile called consciousness of triumph. Hillars was gazing at her with his soul swimming in his eyes. And I—I had a wild desire to throw myself at her feet, then and there. Over the hard-set visage of the innkeeper the bar of sunlight traveled; over the scowling countenance of the Prince, over the puzzled brow of the Count, and going, left a golden purple in its wake, which imperceptibly deepened.

The Prince was first to speak. "I protest," said he.

"Against what?" asked Gretchen.

"It is the King's will that you become my wife. He will not tolerate this attitude of yours. Your principality is in jeopardy, let me tell you."

"Does the fact that I have promised the King to become your wife detract from my power? Not a jot. Till you are my husband, I am mistress here—and after."

"As to that, we shall see," said the Prince. "Then you

intend to keep your promise?"

"Is there man or woman who can say that I ever broke one?"

"Your Highness, what are your commands?" It was the innkeeper who spoke. His fingers were twitching about the hammer of his carbine. He nodded approvingly toward me. My assault upon the Prince had brought me again into his good graces.

Gretchen did not answer him, but she smiled kindly.

"Ah, yes!" said the Prince. "This is that Breunner fellow."

The innkeeper made a movement. The Prince saw it, and so did I. Prince Ernst of Wortumborg was never so near death in all his life as at that moment. He knew it, too.

"Your Highness has a very good memory," said the innkeeper, dryly.

"There are some things it were best to forget," replied the Prince.

"I am pleased that Your Highness shares my opinion," returned the old fellow. The muzzle of the carbine was once more pointed at the ceiling.

The rest of us looked on, but we understood nothing of these passes. Even Gretchen was in the dark.

"We met long ago," said the innkeeper.

"Yes; but I have really forgotten what the subject of Our discussion was," said the Prince, regarding the innkeeper through half-closed lids. "Perhaps he can explain."

"It is very kind of Your Highness," said the innkeeper, laughing maliciously. "But I am old, and my memory serves me ill."

The Prince shrugged. "But we have drifted away from the present matter. Your Highness, then, promises to bend to the will of the King?"

"Yes," said Gretchen. "I gave the King my promise because I had wearied of resistance, having no one to turn to—then. I shall marry you, though I detest you; but I shall be your wife only in name, and not in the eyes of God."

"The latter sacrifice was not asked of you," smiled the Prince.

"I shall depart this day for the capital," continued Gretchen. "I warn you not to inflict your presence upon me during the journey. Now go. The air while you remain is somewhat difficult to breathe."

The Prince surveyed the menacing faces which surrounded him, then gathered up his hat and gloves.

"I see that Your Highness will be a dutiful wife," he said, smoothing the silk of his hat with his elbow. He blew into his gloves and carefully drew them over his hands. "A pleasant journey to Your Highness," he added. "Come, Count. And these?" waving his hand toward Hillars and me.

"They have my fullest protection."

He smiled villainously, then walked to the door with a measured tread. At the door he turned. There was a flash of rage in his eyes, but he quickly subdued it.

"Auf wiedersehen!" with a sweeping glance which took in all of us, and particularly me.

He passed out, the Count following him soberly. The two cavalrymen thrust their sabres into the scabbards with a clank, and made as though to follow.

"Wait," said Gretchen. "I shall have need of you. You will escort me to the station. Now you may go."

They saluted gravely. They appreciated the situation. The Princess was their bread and butter.

"Your Highness," said Hillars, "there has been a mistake."

"A mistake?" repeated Gretchen, wonderingly.

"Yes. They have made you a Princess, whereas they should have made you a Queen. Will you forgive me the trouble I have caused?"

"It is I who must ask forgiveness of you," she said, with a sad smile. "You may kiss my hand, sir."

Hillars remained somewhat long over it.

"And how comes it that you gentlemen know each other?" she asked.

"Damon and Pythias, Your Highness," answered Hillars. "We were brought up together, and we have shared our tents and kettles. I recommend Pythias to you as a brave gentleman." Then he came to me. "You are a brave fellow, Jack," grasping my hand. "Good luck to you. I had an idea; it has returned. Now, then, innkeeper, come with me."

"With you, and where?" asked the innkeeper. If there was one thing for which he could not account, it was the presence of Hillars at the inn.

"Never mind where, but come," answered Hillars, gayly. He bent and whispered something into the old fellow's ear. It was something which pleased him, for he screwed his lips into a smile, and took the white hand of the whisperer in his brawny fist and nigh crushed it.

"Well, well! it doesn't matter where you came from. Here, you," to the trio behind him, "go back to the stables." They filed out. Then the innkeeper took Hillars by the arm. "Come along; time passes."

"And where are you going?" I asked anxiously. Hillars should not have passed from my sight but for Gretchen.

"We'll be back shortly," he answered. "You will know all about then, my son."

He stood on the sill of the door, a handsome picture. His gray eyes sparkled, his face was full of excitement and there was a color in his cheeks. There was no sign here of the dissipated man of the night before. It was Hillars as I had seen him in the old days. But for his 19th century garb, he might have just stepped down from a frame—a gallant by Fortuny, who loved the awakened animal in man. The poise was careless, but graceful, and the smile was debonair. His eyes were holding Gretchen's. A moment passed; another and another.

Then: "Long live and God bless her Serene Highness the Princess Hildegarde!" And he was gone.

And as he disappeared a shadow of some sort passed before my eyes, and a something dull and heavy pressed upon my heart. Presently came the sound of beating hoofs, and then all became still.

Gretchen and I were alone.

Gretchen appeared to be studying the blue veins in her hands which she listlessly held before her. An interval of three or four minutes passed, still she remained in that pathetic attitude, silent and motionless.

"Gretchen," said I, "have you nothing to say?"

"Yes." Her eyes raised to the level of mine, and I saw that they were deep in tears. "Herr, I shall say to you that which I have never said to any man, and that which I shall never say to any man again. I may say it now because it is sinless. I love you! I love you, and, loving you, God knows what the future without you shall be. Yes! I love you. Take me once in your arms and kiss me, and let me go—forever."

Then with a smile which partly shielded a sob, her arms went around my neck and her face lay close to mine. Heaven knows which was the greater, the joy or the pain.

"Gretchen, think!" I cried, distractedly. "What is a Prince or a King to you and me, who love?"

"There is honor," gently. She caressed my cheek with her fingers.

"Honor!" I cried, vehemently. "Is it honorable to marry the man you do not love and break the heart of the one you do?"

She did not answer, but her arms fell from my neck, and she approached the window. The passing river was reflected in her eyes. Her reverie was a short one.

"Listen, Herr; I will tell you why it is honorable. The Prince and the King? I fear the one as little as I do the other. It is not the Prince, it is not the King, it is not the principality. Herr, I have come near to being a very wicked woman, who was about to break the most sacred promise a sovereign can make. Before I came here a delegation of my people approached me. On bended knees they asked me not to voluntarily return the principality to the King, who was likely to give them a ruler rapacious or cruel or indifferent. And while they understood what a sacrifice it meant to me, they asked me to bend my will to the King's and wed the Prince, vowing that I alone should be recognized as their sovereign ruler. Since my coronation they said that they had known the first happiness in years. Herr, it was so pathetic! I love my people, who, after all, are not adopted since I was born here. So I gave my promise, and, heaven forgive me, I was about to break it! There are some things, Herr, which the publican does not understand. One of these is the duty a sovereign owes to the people. The woman in me wishes to follow your fortunes, though they carry her to the ends of the world; but the sovereign sees but one path—honor and duty. What is one human heart to a hundred thousand? A grain of sand. Herr, let mine be broken; I shall not murmur. Alas! to be a princess, a puppet in this tinsel show of kings and queens! It is my word and the King's will which have made my happiness an impossibility. Though I love you, I wish never to see you again. I shall be wife but in name, yet I may not have a lover. I am not a woman of the court. I am proud of my honor, though the man who is to be my husband doubts that."

"No, Gretchen," said I, "he does not doubt it, but he wishes me to do so. I believe in your innocence as I believe in your love."

"It is sad, is it not," said she, "that we must go through our days loving each other and all the world standing between? I have never loved a man before; I did not want to love you. I did not know that I loved you till I saw that your life was in danger. Yet I am glad that I have lived for a brief second, for till a woman loves she does not live. I am brave; do you be likewise. I shall go back to the world, and who shall know of the heart of fire beneath the ice! Not even the man I love. Kiss me; it is the last kiss I shall take from the lips of any man."

And it seemed to me that our souls met in that last kiss, melted and became one. Her hands dropped to her side, and swiftly she sped from the room.

She had entered the coach. The cavalrymen were perched upon the box. There was a crack of the lash, and the coach rolled away. I watched it, standing in the road. A cloud of yellow dust partially obscured it from view. Half a mile beyond rose a small hill. This the coach mounted, and the red gold of the smoldering sun engulfed it. Was it a face I saw at the window? Perhaps. Then over the hill all disappeared, and with it the whole world, and I stood in emptiness, alone.

Gretchen had gone.

CHAPTER XV

I was wandering aimlessly through the rose gardens, when the far-off sound of galloping hoofs came on the breeze. Nearer and nearer it drew. I ran out into the highway. I saw a horse come wildly dashing along. It was riderless, and as it came closer I saw the foam of sweat dripping from its flanks and shoulders. As the animal plunged toward me, I made a spring and caught the bridle, hanging on till the brute came to a standstill. It was quivering from fright. There was a gash on its neck, and it was bleeding and turning the white flakes of sweat into a murky crimson.

"Good Lord!" I ejaculated. "It's one of the cavalry horses. Hillars or the innkeeper has been hurt."

I was of the mind to mount the animal and go in search of them, when Stahlberg, who had come to my assistance, said that I had best wait. A quarter of an hour passed. Then we could see another horse, perhaps half a mile away, coming toward the inn at a canter. From what I could see in the pale light, the horse carried a double burden. A sheet of ice seemed to fall on my heart. What had happened? Had Dan and the Prince come to blows? Alas, I could have cried out in anguish at the sight which finally met my gaze. The innkeeper held the reins, and, propped up in front of him, was Hillars, to all appearances dead.

"Gott!" cried the innkeeper, discovering me, "but I am glad to see you, Herr. Your friend has been hurt, badly, badly."

"My God!" I cried. The hand and wrist of the innkeeper which encircled Hillars were drenched in blood.

"Yes. A bullet somewhere in his chest. Help me down with him. He is not dead yet. I'll tell you the story when we have made it comfortable for him."

Tenderly we carried the inanimate form of poor Hillars into the inn and laid it on the sofa. I tore back his blood-wet shirt. The wound was slightly below the right lung. The bullet had severed an artery, for I could see that the blood gushed. We worked over him for a few moments, and then he opened his eyes. He saw me and smiled.

"There wasn't any regiment, old man, but this will suffice. My hand trembled. But he'll never use his right arm again, curse him!"

"Dan, Dan!" I cried, "what made you do it?"

"When I am a man's friend, it is in life and death. He was in the way. He may thank liquor that he lives." The lids of his eyes contracted. "Hurts a little, but it will not be for long, my son. I am bleeding to death inside. Jack, the woman loves you, and in God's eyes, Princess or not, she belongs to you. You and I cannot understand these things which make it impossible for a man and a woman who love each other to wed. Let me hold your hand. I feel like an old woman. Give me a mouthful of brandy. Ah, that's better! Innkeeper, your courage is not to be doubted, but your judgment of liquor is. Any way, Jack, I suppose you will not forget me in a week or so, eh?"

"Dan!" was all I could say, bending over his hand to hide my tears.

"Jack, you are not sorry?"

"Dan, you are more to me than any woman in the world."

"Oh, say! You wouldn't—hold me up a bit higher; that's it—you wouldn't have me hang on now, would you? I haven't anything to live for, no matter how you put it. Home? I never had one. The only regret I have in leaving is that the Prince will not keep me company. Put an obol in my hand, and Charon will see me over the Styx.

"And when, like her, O Saki, you shall pass
Among the guests star-scattered on the grass,
And in your joyous errand, reach the spot
Where I made one—turn down an empty glass!

"Well, hang me, Jack, if you aren't crying! Then you thought more of me than I believed; a man's tears mean more than a woman's. . . . A man must die, and what is a year or two? How much better to fold the tent when living becomes tasteless and the cup is full of lees! . . . The Prince was a trifle cruel; but perhaps his hand trembled, too. Innkeeper, you're a good fellow."

"Herr is a man of heart," said the grizzled veteran, sadly.

"Tell Jack how it happened," said Dan; "it hurts me."

On leaving me, Hillars and the innkeeper, after having taken a pair of pistols, had mounted the cavalry horses despite the protests of the owners, and had galloped away in pursuit of the Prince and Count von Walden. They caught sight of them a mile or so ahead. They were loping along at a fair speed. It took half an hour to bring the two parties within speaking distance. Although the Prince and von Walden heard them, they never turned around, but kept on straight ahead. This made Hillars' choler rise, and he spurred forward.

"One moment, gentlemen," he cried. "I have a word with you."

They galloped on unheeding. When Hillars got in front of them they merely veered to either side.

"Ah!" said Hillars, choking with rage. With a quick movement he bent and caught the bridle of the Prince's horse. The Count, seeing that the Prince was compelled to rein in, did likewise. The Prince looked disdainful.

"Well, what is it?" asked Von Walden. "Speak quickly. Has your scribbling friend run away with Her Highness?"

"My remarks, most noble and puissant Count," said Hillars, bowing, satirically, to the neck of his horse, "I shall confine to the still more noble and puissant Prince of Wortumborg."

"This is an unappreciated honor," sneered the Prince.

"So it is," replied Hillars, lightly. "When an honest man speaks to you he is conferring an honor upon you which you, as you say, cannot appreciate. It appears to me that Your Highness has what we in America call malaria. I propose to put a hole through you and let out this bad substance. Lead, properly used, is a great curative. Sir, your presence on this beautiful world is an eyesore to me."

"One excuse is as good as another," said the Prince. "Did Her Highness delegate you to put me out of the way?"

"Oh, no; but since you have brought her name into it, I confess that it is on her account. Well, sir, no man has ever insulted a woman in my presence and gone unscathed. In English speaking lands we knock him down. This being Rome I shall do as the Romans do. I believe I called you a liar; I will do so again. Is the object of my errand plain?"

"As I said to your friend," smiled the Prince, "I will send a lackey down here to take care of you. Count, we shall hardly get to the station in time to catch the train. Young man, stand aside; you annoy me, I have no time to discuss the Princess or her lovers. Release my horse!"

"What a damned cur you are!" cried Hillars, losing his airy tone. "By God, you will fight me, if I have to knock you down and spit upon you!" Then with full force he flung his hat into the face of the Prince.

"You have written finis to your tale," said the Prince, dismounting.

"Your Highness!" exclaimed the Count, springing to the ground, "this must not be. You shall not risk your life at the hands of this damned adventurer."

"Patience, Count," said the Prince, shaking off the hand which the Count had placed upon his shoulder. "Decidedly, this fellow is worth consideration. Since we have no swords, sir, and they seem to be woman's weapons these days, we will use pistols. Of course, you have come prepared. It is a fine time for shooting. This first light of twilight gives us equal advantage. Will it be at ten or twenty paces? I dare say, if we stand at twenty, in the centre of the road, we shall have a good look at each other before we separate indefinitely."

"Your Highness insists?" murmured the Count.

"I not only insist, I command." The Prince took off his coat and waistcoat and deposited them on the grass at the side of the road. Hillars did likewise. There was a pleased expression on his face. "I do believe, Count," laughed the Prince, "this fellow expects to kill me. Now, the pistols."

"If you will permit me," said the innkeeper, taking an oblong box from under his coat. "These are excellent weapons."

The Prince laughed. "I suppose, innkeeper, if the result is disastrous to me, it will please you?"

The innkeeper was not lacking in courtesy. "It would be a pleasure, I assure you. There are certain reasons why I cannot fight you myself."

"To be sure."

"It would be too much like murder," continued the innkeeper. "Your hand would tremble so that you would miss me at point-blank. There goes the last of the sun. We must hurry."

With a grimace the Count accepted the box and took out the pistols.

"They are old-fashioned," he said.

"A deal like the innkeeper's morals," supplemented the Prince.

"But effective," said the innkeeper.

The Count scowled at the old fellow, who met the look with phlegm. As an innkeeper he might be an inferior, but as a second at a duel he was an equal. It was altogether a different matter.

The Count carefully loaded the weapons, the innkeeper watching him attentively. In his turn he examined them.

"Very good," he said.

The paces were then measured out. During this labor the Prince gazed indifferently toward the west. The aftermath of the sun glowed on the horizon. The Prince shaded his eyes for a spell.

"Gentlemen," he said, "I believe the Princess is approaching. At any rate here comes the coach. Let us suspend hostilities till she has passed."

A few minutes later the coach came rumbling along in a whirlwind of dust. The stoical cavalrymen kept on without so much as a glance at the quartet standing at the side of the road. Hillars looked after the vehicle till it was obscured from view. Then he shook himself out of the dream into which he had fallen. He was pale now, and his eyebrows were drawn together as the Count held out the pistol.

"Ah, yes!" he said, as though he had forgotten. "There goes the woman who will never become your wife."

"That shall be decided at once," was the retort of the Prince.

"She will marry the gentleman back at the inn."

"A fine husband he will make, truly!" replied the Prince. "He not only deserts her but forsakes her champion. But, that is neither here nor there. We shall not go through any polite formalities," his eyes snapping viciously.

The two combatants took their places in the centre of the road. The pistol arm of each hung at the side of the body.

"Are you ready, gentlemen?" asked the Count, the barest tremor in his voice.

"Yes," said the Prince.

Hillars simply nodded.

"When I have counted three you will be at liberty to fire. One!"

The arms raised slowly till the pistols were on the level of the eyes.

"Two!"

The innkeeper saw Hillars move his lips. That was the only sign.

"Three!"

The pistols exploded simultaneously. The right arm of the Prince swung back violently, the smoking pistol flying from his hand. Suddenly one of the horses gave a snort of pain and terror, and bolted down the road. No attention was given to the horse. The others were watching Hillars. He stood perfectly motionless. All at once the pistol fell from his hand; then both hands flew instinctively to his breast. There was an expression of surprise on his face. His eyes closed, his knees bent forward, and he sank into the road a huddled heap. The Prince shrugged, a sigh of relief fell from the Count's half-parted lips, while the innkeeper ran toward the fallen man.

"Are you hurt, Prince?" asked the Count.

"The damned fool has blown off my elbow!" was the answer. "Bind it up with your handkerchief, and help me on with my coat. There is nothing more to do; if he is not dead he soon will be, so it's all the same."

When the Prince's arm was sufficiently bandaged so as to stop the flow of blood, the Count assisted him to mount, jumped on his own horse, and the two cantered off, leaving the innkeeper, Hillars' head propped up on his knee, staring after them with a dull rage in his faded blue eyes. The remaining horse was grazing a short distance away. Now and then he lifted his head and gazed inquiringly at the two figures in the road.

"Is it bad, Herr?" the innkeeper asked.

"Very. Get back to the inn. I don't want to peter out here." Then he fainted.

It required some time and all the innkeeper's strength to put Hillars on the horse. When this was accomplished he turned the horse's head toward the inn. And that was all.

"Dan?" said I.

The lids of his eyes rolled wearily back.

"Is there anything I can do for you?"

"Bury me."

It was very sad. "Where?" I asked.

"Did you see the little cemetery on the hill, across the valley? Put me there. It is a wild, forgotten place. 'Tis only my body. Who cares what becomes of that? As for the other, the soul, who can say? I have never been a good man; still, I believe in God. I am tired, tired and cold. What fancies a man has in death! A moment back I saw my father. There was a wan, sweet-faced woman standing close beside him; perhaps my mother. I never saw her before. Ah, me! these chimeras we set our hearts upon, these worldly hopes! Well, Jack, it's curtain and no encore. But I am not afraid to die. I have wronged no man or woman; I have been my own enemy. What shall I say, Jack? Ah, yes! God have mercy on my soul. And this sudden coldness, this sudden ease from pain—is death!"

There was a flutter of the eyelids, a sigh, and this poor flotsam, this drift-wood which had never known a harbor in all its years, this friend of mine, this inseparable comrade—passed out. He knew all about it now.

There were hot tears in my eyes as I stood up and gazed down at this mystery called death. And while I did so, a hand, horny and hard, closed over mine. The innkeeper, with blinking eyes, stood at my side.

"Ah, Herr," he said, "who would not die like that?"

And we buried him on the hillside, just as the sun swept aside the rosy curtain of dawn. The wind, laden with fresh morning perfumes, blew up joyously from the river. From where I stood I could see the drab walls of the barracks. The windows sparkled and flashed as the gray mists sailed heavenward and vanished. The hill with its long grasses resembled a green sea. The thick forests across the river, almost black at the water's edge, turned a fainter and more delicate hue as they receded, till, far away, they looked like mottled glass. Only yesterday he had laughed with me, talked and smoked with me, and now he was dead. A rage pervaded me. We are puny things, we, who strut the highways of the world, parading a so-called wisdom. There is only one philosophy; it is to learn to die.

"Come," said I to the innkeeper; and we went down the hill.

"When does the Herr leave?"

"At once. There will be no questions?" I asked, pointing to the village.

"None. Who knows?"

"Then, remember that Herr Hillars was taken suddenly ill and died, and that he desired to be buried here. I dare say the Prince will find some excuse for his arm, knowing the King's will in regard to dueling. Do you understand me?"

"Yes."

I did not speak to him again, and he strode along at my heels with an air of preoccupation. We reached the inn in silence.

"What do you know about her Serene Highness the Princess Hildegarde?" I asked abruptly.

"What does Herr wish to know?" shifting his eyes from my gaze.

"All you can tell me."

"I was formerly in her father's service. My wife—" He

hesitated, and the expression on his face was a sour one.

"Go on."

"Ah, but it is unpleasant, Herr. You see, my wife and I were not on the best of terms. She was handsome . . . a cousin of the late Prince. . . . She left me more than twenty years ago. I have never seen her since, and I trust that she is dead. She was her late Highness's hair-dresser."

"And the Princess Hildegarde?"

"She is a woman for whom I would gladly lay down my life."

"Yes, yes!" I said impatiently. "Who made her the woman she is? Who taught her to shoot and fence?"

"It was I."

"You?"

"Yes. From childhood she has been under my care. Her mother did so desire. She is all I have in the world to love. And she loves me, Herr; for in all her trials I have been her only friend. But why do you ask these questions?" a sudden suspicion lighting his eyes.

"I love her."

He took me by the shoulders and squared me in front of him.

"How do you love her?" a glint of anger mingling with the suspicion.

"I love her as a man who wishes to make her his wife."

His hands trailed down my sleeves till they met and joined mine.

"I will tell you all there is to be told. Herr, there was once a happy family in the palace of the Hohenphalians. The Prince was rather wild, but he loved his wife. One day his cousin came to visit him. He was a fascinating man in those days, and few women were there who would not give an ear to his flatteries. He was often with the Princess, but she hated him. One day an abominable thing happened. This cousin loved the Princess. She scorned him. As the Prince was entering the boudoir this cousin, making out that he was unconscious of the husband's approach, took the Princess in his arms and kissed her. The Prince was too far away to see the horror in his wife's face. He believed her to be acquiescent. That night he accused her. Her denials were in vain. He confronted her with his cousin, who swore before the immortal God himself that the Princess had lain willing in his arms. From that time on the Prince changed. He became reckless; he fell in with evil company; he grew to be a shameless ruffian, a man who brought his women into his wife's presence, and struck her while they were there. And in his passions he called her terrible names. He made a vow that when children came he would make them things of scorn. In her great trouble, the Princess came to my inn, where the Princess Hildegarde was born. The Prince refused to believe that the child was his. My mistress finally sickened and died—broken-hearted. The Prince died in a gambling den. The King became the guardian of the lonely child. He knows but little, or he would not ask Her Highness—" He stopped.

"He would not ask her what?"

"To wed the man who caused all this trouble."

"What! Prince Ernst?"

"Yes. I prayed to God, Herr, that your friend's bullet would carry death. But it was not to be."

"I am going back to London," said I. "When I have settled up my affairs there I shall return."

"And then?"

"Perhaps I shall complete what my friend began."

I climbed into the ramshackle conveyance and was driven away. Once I looked back. The innkeeper could be seen on the porch, then he became lost to view behind the trees. Far away to my left the stones in the little cemetery on the hillside shone with brilliant whiteness.

CHAPTER XVI

There were intervals during the three months which
followed when I believed that I was walking in a dream,
and waking would find me grubbing at my desk in New
York. It was so unreal for these days; mosaic romance in
the heart of prosaic fact! Was there ever the like? It was
real enough, however, in the daytime, when the roar of
London hammered at my ears, but when I sat alone in my
room it assumed the hazy garments of a dream. Sometimes I caught myself listening for Hillars: a footstep in
the corridor, and I would take my pipe from my mouth
and wait expectantly. But the door never opened and the
footsteps always passed on. Often in my dreams I stood
by the river again. There is solace in these deep, wide
streams. We come and go, our hopes, our loves, our
ambitions. Nature alone remains. Should I ever behold
Gretchen again? Perhaps. Yet, there was no thrill at the
thought. If ever I beheld her again it would be when she
was placed beyond the glance of my eye, the touch of my
hand. She was mine, aye, as a dream might be; something
I possessed but could not hold. Heigho! the faces that peer
at us from the firelight shadows! They troop along in a
ghostly cavalcade, and the winds that creep over the
window sill and under the door—who can say that they
are not the echoes of voices we once heard in the past?

I was often on the verge of sending in my resignation, but

I would remember in time that work meant bread and butter—and forgetfulness. When I returned to the office few questions were asked, though my assistant looked many of them reproachfully. I told him that Hillars had died abroad, and that he had been buried on the continent at his request; all of which was the truth, but only half of it. I did my best to keep the duel a secret, but it finally came out. It was the topic in the clubs, for Hillars had been well known in political and literary circles. But in a month or so the affair, subsided. The world never stops very long, even when it loses one of its best friends.

One late October morning I received a note which read:

"JOHN WINTHROP:

"Dear Sir—I am in London for a few days, homeward bound from a trip to Egypt, and as we are cousins and 'orphans too,' I should like the pleasure of making your acquaintance. Trusting that I shall find you at leisure, I am,

"Your humble servant,

"PHILIP PEMBROKE."

"Ah," said I; "that Louisianian cousin of mine, who may or may not live the year out," recalling the old lawyer's words. "He seems to hang on pretty well. I hope he'll be interesting; few rich men are. He writes like a polite creditor. What did the old fellow say was the matter with him? heart trouble, or consumption? I can't remember." I threw the note aside and touched up some of my dispatches.

Precisely at ten o'clock the door opened and a man came in. He was fashionably dressed, a mixture of Piccadilly and Broadway in taste. He was tall, slender, but well-formed; and his blonde mustache shone out distinctly against a background of tanned skin. He had fine blue eyes.

"Have I the pleasure of speaking to John Winthrop of New York?" he began, taking off his hat.

I rose. "I am the man."

He presented his card, and on it I read, "Philip Pembroke."

"Philip Pembroke!" I exclaimed.

"Evidently you are surprised?" showing a set of strong white teeth.

"Truthfully, I am," I said, taking his hand. "You see," I added, apologetically, "your family lawyer—that is—he gave me the—er—impression that you were a sickly fellow—one foot in the grave, or something like. I was not expecting a man of your build."

The smile broadened into a deep laugh, and a merry one, I thought, enviously. It was so long since I had laughed.

"That was a hobby of the old fellow," he replied. "When I was a boy I had the palpitation of the heart. He never got rid of the idea that I might die at any moment. He was always warning me about violent exercises, the good old soul. Peace to his ashes!"

"He is dead?"

"Yes. When I took to traveling he all but had nervous prostration. I suppose he told you about that will I made in your favor. It was done to please him. Still," he added soberly, "it stands. I travel a deal, and no one knows what may happen. And so you are the John Winthrop my dad treated so shabbily? Oh, don't protest, he did. I should have hunted you up long ago, and given you a solid bank account, only I knew that the son of my aunt must necessarily be a gentleman, and, therefore, would not look favorably upon such a proceeding."

"Thank you," said I. The fellow pleased me.

"And then, I did not know but what you cared nothing for money."

"True. A journalist doesn't care anything about money; the life is too easy and pleasant, and most of the things he needs are thrown in, as they say."

This bit of sarcasm did not pass; my cousin laughed again that merry laugh of his.

"I think we shall become great friends," he said. "I like frankness."

"My remark in its literal sense was the antithesis of frankness."

"Ah, you said too much not to be frank. Frankness is one of the reasons why I do not get on well with the women. I can't lie in the right place, and when I do it is generally ten times worse than the plain truth."

"You're a man of the world, I see."

"No, merely a spectator."

"Well, you have the price of admission; with me it's a free

pass. Some day we will compare notes."

"Who is your banker?"

"Banker? I have none. I distrust banks. They take your mite and invest it in what-nots, and sometimes when you go for it, it is not there."

"And then again it multiplies so quickly that you have more than you know what to do with; eh?"

"As to that I cannot say. It is hearsay, rumor; so far as I know it may be so. Experience has any number of teachers; the trouble is, we cannot study under them all. Necessity has been my principal instructor. Sometimes she has larruped me soundly, though I was a model scholar. You will go to luncheon with me?"

"If you will promise to dine with me this evening?" And I promised.

For an hour or more we chatted upon congenial topics. He was surprisingly well informed. He had seen more of the world than I, though he had not observed it so closely. As we were about to leave, the door opened, and Phyllis, Ethel and her husband, Mr. Holland, entered. For a moment the room was filled with the fragrance of October air and the essence of violets. They had been in town a week. They had been "doing" the Strand, so Ethel said, and thought they would make me a brief visit to see how "it was done," the foreign corresponding. Mr. Wentworth and his wife were already domiciled at B—, and the young people were going over to enjoy the winter festivities. Phyllis was unchanged. How like Gretchen, I thought.

While Ethel was engaging my cousin's attention, I

conducted Phyllis through the office.

"What a place to work in!" said Phyllis, laughing. The laugh awakened a vague thrill. "Dust, dust; everywhere dust. You need a woman to look after you, Jack?"

As I did not reply, she looked quickly at me, and seeing that my face was grave, she flushed.

"Forgive me, Jack," impulsively; "I did not think."

I answered her with a reassuring smile.

"How long are you to remain in town?" I asked, to disembarrass her.

"We leave day after to-morrow, Saturday. A day or two in Paris, and then we go on. Every one in New York is talking about your book. I knew that you were capable."

"I hope every one is buying it," said I, passing over her last observation.

"Was it here that you wrote it?"

"Oh, no; it was written in my rooms, under the most favorable circumstances."

"I thought so. This is a very dreary place."

"Perhaps I like it for that very reason."

Her eyes were two interrogation points, but I pretended not to see.

"What nice eyes your cousin has," she said, side glancing.

With a woman it is always a man's eyes.

"And his father was the man who left you the fortune?"

"Yes," I answered, with a short laugh. Of course, I had never told Phyllis of that thousand-dollar check.

"You must run over this winter and see us," she said. "I anticipate nothing but dinners, balls and diplomatic receptions. I have never been there, it will all be new to me. Think of seeing Egypt, the Holy Lands, Russia, France and Spain, and yet not seeing the very heart of the continent! Thank goodness, I know the language."

"And will she not be a sensation?" joined in Ethel.

"A decided sensation," said I, scrutinizing the beautiful face so near me. What if they met, as probably they would—Phyllis and Gretchen? "Phyllis," said I, suddenly, "where were you born?"

"Where was I born?" with a wondering little laugh; "in America. Where did you suppose?"

"Eden," said I. "I wasn't sure, so I asked."

"I do not know how to take that," she said, with mock severity.

"Oh, I meant Eden when it was Paradise," I hastened to say.

"Yes," put in Pembroke; "please go back, Miss Landors, and begin the world all over again."

"Phyllis," said I, in a whisper, "have you ever met that remarkable affinity of yours?" I regretted the words the moment they had crossed my lips.

"Yes, you are changed, as I said the other night," distrust-fully. "There is something in your voice that is changed. You have grown cynical. But your question was imper-tinent. Have you found yours?"

I was expecting this. "Yes," I said. "Once I thought I had; now I am sure of it. Some day I shall tell you an interesting story."

"We came up to ask you to dine with us this evening," she said, trailing her brown-gloved finger over the dusty desk. "Are you at liberty?"

"No. I have only just met my cousin, and have promised to dine with him."

"If that is all, bring him along. I like his face."

We passed out of the file room.

"Phyllis, we must be going, dear," said Ethel.

I led Phyllis down the narrow stairs. A handsome victoria stood at the curb.

"I shall be pleased to hear your story," said she.

It occurred to me that the tale might not be to her liking. So I said: "But it is one of those disagreeable stories; one where all should end nicely, but doesn't; one which ends, leaving the hero, the heroine, and the reader dissatisfied with the world in general, and the author (who is Fate) in particular."

I knew that she was puzzled. She wasn't quite sure that I

was not referring to the old affair.

"If the story is one I never heard before," suspiciously, "I should like to hear it."

"And does it not occur to you," throwing back the robes so that she might step into the victoria, "that fate has a special grudge against me? Once was not enough, but it must be twice."

"And she does not love you? Are you quite sure? You poor fellow!" She squeezed my hand kindly. "Shall I be candid with you?" with the faintest flicker of coquetry in her smile.

"As in the old days," said I, glancing over my shoulder to see now near the others were. A groom is never to be considered. "Yes, as in the old days."

"Well, I have often regretted that I did not accept you as an experiment."

Then I knew that she did not understand.

"You must not think I am jesting," said I, seriously. "The story is of the bitter-sweet kind. The heroine loves me, but cannot be mine."

"Loves you?" with a slight start. "How do you know?"

"She has told me so," lowering my voice.

Frankness of this sort to a woman who has rejected you has a peculiar effect. The coquetry faded from her smile, and there was a perceptible contraction of the brows. Her eyes, which were looking into mine, shifted to the back of the groom. No, I shall never understand a woman. She should have been the most sympathetic woman in the world, yet she appeared to be annoyed.

"What's all this between you and Phyllis?" asked Ethel, coming up.

"There is nothing between her and me," said I.

"Well, there should be," she retorted. "That is the trouble."

My observation was: "I have always held that immediately a woman gets married she makes it her business to see that all old bachelors are lugged out and disposed of to old maids."

"I shall never forgive that," Phyllis declared; "never."

"Then I shall always have the exquisite pleasure of being a supplicant for your pardon. It is delightful to sue pardon of a beautiful woman."

Phyllis sniffed.

"Forgive him at once," said Ethel, "if only for that pretty speech."

Mr. Holland pulled out his watch suggestively.

"Well," I said, "I see that I am keeping you from your lunch. Good-by, then, till dinner, when I shall continue at length on the evils—"

"William," interrupted Ethel, addressing the groom, "drive on."

And so they left us.

"Shall we go to lunch now?" I asked of Pembroke.

"Yes," rather dreamily I thought. "Do you know," with sudden animation, "she is a remarkably beautiful woman?"

"Yes, she is." After all, the sight of Phyllis had rather upset me.

"I had a glimpse of her in Vienna last winter," went on Pembroke. "I never knew who she was."

"Vienna!" I exclaimed.

"Yes. It was at a concert. Her face was indelibly graven on my memory. I asked a neighbor who she was, but when I went to point her out she was gone. I should like to see more of her."

So Gretchen had been in Vienna, and poor Hillars had never known!

I took Pembroke to the club that afternoon, and we dallied in the billiard room till time to dress for dinner. Dinner came. But Phyllis forgot to ask me about the story, at which I grew puzzled, considering what I know of woman's curiosity. And she devoted most of her time to Pembroke, who did not mind. Later we went to the theatre—some production of Gilbert and Sullivan. Whenever I glanced at Phyllis I fell to wondering how Gretchen would have looked in evening dress. Yes, Phyllis was certainly beautiful, uncommonly. For years I had worshipped at her shrine, and then—how little we know of the heart. I was rather abstracted during the performance, and many of my replies went wide the mark.

As we were leaving the foyer, Phyllis said: "Jack, a man has been staring me out of countenance."

"Pembroke?" I laughed.

"No. And moreover, the stare was accompanied by the most irritating sneer."

"Point him out to me when we reach the street," I said, humoring what I thought to be a fancy, "and I'll put a head on him."

The sneer was probably meant for an ogle. Beauty has its annoyances as well as its compensations. As we came under the glare of the outside lights, Phyllis's hand tightened on my arm.

"Look! there he is, and he is making for us."

At the sight of that face with its hooked nose, its waxed mustache and imperial, I took a deep breath and held it. In the quick glance I saw that his right arm hung stiffly at his side. I attempted to slip into the crowd, but without success. He lifted his hat, smiling into the astonished face of Phyllis.

"The Princess Hildegarde—" But with those three words the sentence on his lips came to an end. Amazement replaced the smile. He stepped back. Phyllis's eyes expressed scornful surprise. What she understood to be rudeness I knew to be a mistake. He had mistaken her to be Gretchen, just as I had mistaken Gretchen to be Phyllis. It was a situation which I enjoyed. All this was but momentary. We passed on.

"Was the man crazy?" asked Phyllis, as we moved toward the carriages, where we saw Pembroke waving his hand.

"Not exactly crazy," I answered.

"The Princess Hildegarde; did he not call me that?"

"He did."

"He must have mistaken me for some one else, then."

"The very thing," said I. "I wonder what he is doing here in London?"

"Mercy! do you know him?"

"Slightly." We were almost at the carriage. "I am sorry to say that he is a great personage in this very court which you are so soon to grace."

"How strange! I'm afraid we shan't get on."

Pembroke and I dismissed our carriage. We were going back to the club. Ethel and her husband were already seated in their carriage.

Said Phyllis as I assisted her to enter; "And who is this Princess Hildegarde?"

"The most beautiful woman in all the world," I answered with enthusiasm. "You will meet her also."

"I do not believe I shall like her either," said Phyllis. "Good night;" and the door swung to.

Pembroke and I made off for the club. . . . Perhaps it was my enthusiasm.

CHAPTER XVII

I had just left the office when I ran into Pembroke, who was in the act of mounting the stairs. It was Saturday morning. Phyllis had left town.

"Hello!" he cried. "A moment more, and I should have missed you, and then you would not have learned a piece of news."

"News?"

"Yes. I have made up my mind not to go home till February."

"What changed your plans so suddenly?" I asked.

"My conscience."

"In heaven's name, what has your conscience to do with your plans?"

"Well, you see, my conscience would not permit me to meet such a remarkable woman as Miss Landors without becoming better acquainted with her." He swung his cane back and forth.

"This is very sudden," said I, lighting a cigar. "When did

it happen?"

"What time did she come into your office the other day?"

"It must have been after eleven."

"Then it happened about eleven-fifteen." Pembroke's eyes were dancing. "Do you—er—think there are any others?"

"Thousands," said I, "only—" I turned the end of my cigar around to see if the light had proved effective.

"Only what?"

"Only she won't have them."

"Then there is really a chance?"

"When a woman is not married there is always a chance," said I, wisely. "But let me tell you, cousin mine, she has a very high ideal. The man who wins her must be little less than a demigod and a little more than a man. Indeed, her ideal is so high that I did not reach it by a good foot."

Pembroke looked surprised. "She—ah—rejected—"

"I did not say that I had proposed to her," said I.

"If you haven't, why haven't you?"

"It is strange." As his face assumed an anxious tinge, I laughed. "My dear relative, go ahead and win her, if you can; you have my best wishes. She is nothing to me. There was a time—ah, well, we all can look back and say that. If it isn't one woman it's another."

Sunshine came into Pembroke's face again. "Ideal or not

ideal, I am going to make the effort."

"Success to you!" patting his shoulder. He was good to look at, and it was my opinion that Phyllis might do worse. We miss a good deal in this world by being over particular.

We were coming into Trafalgar. Nelson stood high up in the yellow fog.

"Nature is less gracious than history sometimes," mused Pembroke, gazing up. "She is doing her best to dull the lustre of the old gentleman. Ah, those were days when they had men."

"We have them still," said I. "It is not the men, but the opportunities, which are lacking."

"Perhaps that is so. Yet, it is the great man who makes them."

I was thinking of Hillars. "I would give a good deal for a regiment and a bad moment for our side." There was no mighty column in his memory, scarcely a roll of earth. "What do you want to do?" I asked. "Shall we hail a cab and drive to the park?"

"Just as you say, if it is not interfering with your work."

"Not at all."

"Have a cigar," said Pembroke, after we had climbed into the cab and arranged our long legs comfortably. The London cab is all very well for a short and thin person. "These came to me directly from Key West."

"That is one of the joys of being rich," said I. "Gold is

Aladdin's lamp. I have to take my chances on getting good tobacco in this country."

"Talking about gold—" he began.

"Don't!" I entreated.

"I was about to say that I drew on my bankers for 20,000 pounds this morning."

"You intend to go in for a figure abroad, then?"

"Oh, no. I deposited the money in another bank—in your name."

"Mine? Deposited 20,000 pounds in my name?" I gasped.

"Just so."

"I understood you to say, because you thought me to be a gentleman, that you weren't going to do anything like this? Have I done something to change your opinion?"

"Of course not. And I never said that I should not do it. You may or may not use it, that is as you please. But so far as I am concerned, it will stay there and accumulate interest till the crack of doom. It isn't mine any more. If I were not almost your brother, I dare say you might justly take offense at the action. As it is," complacently, "you will not only accept the gift, but thank me for it."

"How old are you?" I asked.

"Exactly twenty-five."

"I thought that you could not be older than that. Aren't you afraid to be so far away from home?"

Pembroke lay back and laughed. "You haven't thanked me yet."

"I must get a new tailor," said I. "What! shall I pay a tailor to make a well-dressed man out of me, and then become an object of charity? Do I look, then, like a man who is desperately in need of money?"

"No, you don't look it. That's because you are clever. But what is your salary to a man of your brains?"

"It is bread and butter and lodging."

He laughed again. To laugh seemed to be a part of his business. "Jack, I haven't a soul in the world but you. I have only known you three days, but it seems that I have known you all my life. I have so much money that I cannot even fritter away the income."

"It must be a sad life," said I.

"And if you do not accept the sum in the spirit it is given, I'll double it, and then you'll have trouble. You will be a rich man, then, with all a rich man's cares and worries."

"You ought to have a trustee to take care of your money."

"It would be a small matter to bribe him off, Jack, of course, you do not need the money now, but that is no sign you may not in the days to come. I have known many journalists; they were ever improvident. I want to make an exception in your case. You understand; the money is for your old age."

"Let me tell you why a newspaper man is improvident. He earns money only to spend it. He has a fine scorn for money as money. He cares more for what a dollar spent has bought than what five saved might buy."

"Poor creditors!" was the melancholy interpolation.

I passed over this, and went on: "It is the work which absorbs his whole attention. He begins at the bottom of the ladder, which is in the garret. First, he is running about the streets at two and three in the morning, in rain and snow and fog. The contact with the lower classes teaches him many things. He becomes the friend of the policeman and the vagabond. And as his mind grows broader his heart grows in proportion. It is the comparing of the great and small which makes us impartial and philosophical. Well, soon the reporter gets better assignments and shorter hours. He meets the noted men and women of the city. Suddenly from the city editor's desk his ambition turns to Washington. He succeeds there. He now comes into the presence of distinguished ambassadors, ministers and diplomatists. He acquires a polish and a smattering of the languages. His work becomes a feature of his paper. The president chooses him for a friend; he comes and goes as he wills. Presently his eye furtively wanders to Europe. The highest ambition of a journalist, next to being a war correspondent, is to have a foreign post. In this capacity he meets the notable men and women of all countries; he speaks to princes and grand dukes and crowned heads. In a way he becomes a personage himself, a man whom great men seek. And he speaks of the world as the poet did of the fall of Pompeii, 'Part of which I was and all of which I saw.' Ah," as my mind ran back over my own experiences, "what man with this to gain would care for money; a thing which would dull his imagination and take away the keen edge of ambition, and make him play a useless part in this kingly drama of life!"

"I like your frankness," said Pembroke. "I have no doubt

that journalism is the most fascinating profession there is. Yet, you must not accuse the rich of being ambitionless. I have known of rich men losing their all to make papers for men who are ambitious to be foreign correspondents." The young fellow was brimming with raillery. "I have never tried to run a newspaper, but I am, notwithstanding your tirade, ambitious. I am desirous to wed Miss Landors."

The cab was now rolling along the row.

"A truly great ambition," I admitted. "After all, what greater ambition is there than to marry the woman you love? Philip, I will accept your gift in the spirit it is given, and I'll make use of it in the days to come, when I am old and rusted. I understand your motive. You are happy and wish every one to be."

"That's the idea," said he, leaning back and spreading an arm behind my shoulders.

"But not all the money in the world, nor all the fame for that matter, would make me happy." Gretchen was so far away! "Very well; we'll go to Paris together; that is as far as I go. To follow her you will have to go alone."

"And why can't you go the rest of the way?"

"Work. I must be back in town in three days. You must not forget that I have had my vacation; there is plenty to be done."

"Now that you are comparatively wealthy, why not give up the grind, as you call it?"

"The truth is, I must work. When a man works he forgets."

"Then you have something to forget?"

"Every man who has reached the age of thirty has something to forget," said I.

I was gloomy. In my pocket I had the only letter I had ever received from Gretchen. Every hour fate outdoes the romancer. The story she had written for me was a puzzling one. And the finis? Who could say? Fate is more capricious than the novelist; sometimes you can guess what he intends for an end; what fate has in store, never. Gretchen's letter did not begin as letters usually do. It began with "I love you" and ended with the same sentence. "In November my marriage will take place. Do not come abroad. I am growing strong now; if I should see you alas, what would become of that thin ice covering the heart of fire; we have nothing to return, you and I. I long to see you; I dare not tell you how much. Who knows what the world holds hidden? While we live there is always a perhaps. Remember that I love you!"

"Perhaps," I mused absently.

"Perhaps what?" asked Pembroke.

"What?" I had forgotten him. "Oh, it was merely a slip of the tongue." I poked the matting with my cane. "It is high noon; we had best hunt up a lunch. I have an engagement with the American military attache at two, so you will have to take care of yourself till dinner."

Let me tell you what happened in the military club that night. I was waiting for Col. J—of the Queen's Light, who was to give me the plan of the fall maneuvers in Africa. Pembroke was in the billiard room showing what he knew about caroms and brandy smashes to a trio of tanned Indian campaigners. I was in the reading room perusing the evening papers. All at once I became aware of a man standing before me. He remained in that position so long that I glanced over the top of my paper.

It was Prince Ernst of Wortumborg. He bowed.

"May I claim your attention for a moment?" he asked.

Had I been in any other place but the club I should have ignored him. I possessed the liveliest hatred for the man.

"If you will be brief."

"As brief as possible," dropping into the nearest chair. "It has become necessary to ask you a few questions. The matter concerns me."

"Whatever concerns you is nothing to me," I replied coldly.

He smiled. "Are you quite sure?"

I had turned the sword on myself, so it seemed. But I said: "I answered some of your questions once; I believe I was explicit."

"As to that I can say you were; startlingly explicit. It is a delicate matter to profess one's regard for a woman before total strangers. It is not impossible that she would have done the same thing in your place. Her regard for you—"

I interrupted him with a menacing gesture. "I am extremely irritable," I said. "I should regret to lose control of myself in a place like this."

"To be sure!" he said. "This is England, where they knock one another down."

"We do not murder on this side of the channel," I retorted.

"That is unkind. Your friend was a very good shot," with a significant glance at his useless arm. "But for my arm, and his nerves, which were not of the best order, I had not lived to speak to you to-night."

"So much the worse for the world," said I. "Your questions?"

"Ah! Who was that remarkably beautiful woman under your distinguished care Thursday evening?"

"I see that our conversation is to be of the shortest duration. Who she was is none of your business," rudely. I unfolded my paper and began reading.

"Perhaps, after all," not the least perturbed by my insolence, "it were best to state on paper what I have to say. I can readily appreciate that the encounter is disagreeable. To meet one who has made a thing impossible to you sets the nerves on edge." He caught up his opera hat, his cane and gloves. He raised the lapel of his coat and sniffed at the orchid in the buttonhole.

Some occult force bade me say, "Why do you wish to know who she was?"

He sat down again. "I shall be pleased to explain. That I mistook her for another who I supposed was on the other side of the channel was a natural mistake, as you will agree. Is it not strange that I should mistake another to be the woman who is so soon to be my wife? Is there not something behind this remarkable, unusual likeness? Since when are two surpassingly beautiful women, born in different lands, of different parents, the exact likeness of each other?"

Now as this was a thing which had occupied my mind more than once, I immediately put aside the personal affair. That could wait. I threw my paper onto the table.

"Do you know, sir," said I, "that thought echoes my own?"

"Let us for the moment put ourselves into the back-ground," said the Prince. "What do you know about her Serene Highness the Princess Hildegarde; her history?"

"Very little; proceed."

"But tell me what you know."

"I know that her father was driven to a gambler's grave and that her mother died of a broken heart, and that the man who caused all this wishes to break the heart of the daughter, too."

"Scandal, all scandal," said the Prince. "Who ever heard of a broken heart outside of a romantic novel? I see that the innkeeper has been holding your ear. Ah, that inn-keeper, that innkeeper! Certainly some day there will come a reckoning."

"Yes, indeed," said I. "Beware of him."

"It was twenty years ago," said the Prince. "It is beyond the recall. But let me proceed. Not many years ago there was a Prince, a very bad fellow."

"Most of them are."

"He married a woman too good for him," went on the Prince, as though he had not heard.

"And another is about to do likewise."

"There was some scandal. When the Princess was born, her father refused to believe her to be his child. Now, it came to pass, as they say in the Bible, which I assure you is a very interesting book, that there were vague rumors immediately after the birth of Princess Hildegarde that another child had been born."

"What!" I was half out of my chair. "Another child?"

"Another child. The fact that the Prince swore that when children came he would make them counterparts of their kind and loving father, lent color to the rumor that the Princess had had one spirited away to escape this threatened contamination. And one of the nurses was missing. Whither had she gone remained a mystery, and is still a mystery, for she never has returned. Did she spirit away the other child, the other girl? I say girl advisedly; if there had been a son, the mother would have retained him. Two years after this interesting episode, the Princess died, and dying, confessed the deception. But the curious thing is, nobody believed her. Her mind was not strong, and it was thought to be a hallucination, this second child. Now let me come to the present time. Twins are generally alike; one mirrors the other; when they mature, then comes the deviation, perhaps in the color of the hair and the eyes. Behold! here are two women, but for their hair and eyes were one. Tell me what you know of the other." He bent forward with subdued eagerness.

"Do you think it possible?" I cried excitedly.

"Not only possible, but probable. She is a Princess; at least she should be."

Then I told him what I knew about Phyllis.

"America! Born in America! It cannot be." He was baffled.

"I have known her for eight years," said I. "She was born in America as certainly as I was."

"But this likeness? This rumor of another daughter? Ah, there is something here I do not understand. And this uncle of hers, this Wentworth; who is he?"

"A retired banker, very wealthy, and at present with the American ministry at your own capital."

"To him we must go, then." He rose and walked the length of the room, stopped a moment at the chess table in the corner, then resumed his chair. "You are wondering, no doubt, what it is to me, all this?"

"I confess you have read my mind correctly."

"Then listen. I am a Prince without a principality; a Prince by courtesy, my brother ruling the principality of Wortumborg. Thus being without a principality, I am necessarily without revenues. I must replenish my very low exchequer by a marriage, a marriage not so distasteful as it might be." He met my darkening eyes with serenity. "Since Thursday night I have not been so certain of my wife's dowry. If there are two Princesses, twins, they must govern jointly, or one may abdicate in favor of the other. Her Serene Highness the Princess Hildegarde is the one who will be most likely to relinquish her claims to Hohenphalia. If your friend is proved to be her sister—" He stroked the orchid reflectively.

"Well?" I cried, my pulse quickening.

"I shall withdraw my claim to the hand of the Princess

Hildegarde. I do not care to rule half a principality or share half its revenues. There are better things left than that. It is my hope, however, that no proofs can be found, and that your banker-diplomatist will show conclusively that his niece was born in America. Until this question is definitely settled, my fortunes shall not undergo any risks. This is what I wanted to say to you, why I wanted to know who your friend was. Will you help me to get at the bottom of things? We are both concerned; the result will mean all or nothing to you and me. Ah, believe me, but you are a favored mortal. The friendship of the one, and the love of the other! No; do not look angry. With all my sins, it cannot be said that I lack frankness and truthfulness. You love the Princess Hildegarde; I offer you an equal chance to win her. Is not that remarkable good nature? Till the affair is settled my marriage is postponed. Now, to our personal affair. You cannot blame me if I give you all my honest hatred. I am at your service, after, of course, the respective positions of the Princesses are assured. I should take more pleasure in shooting you, or running a sword through your body, than I took in the affair with your friend. His courage was truly admirable. I had nothing against him. But you have grievously wounded my self-love; we forgive all wrongs but that. I warn you that the affair will not be conducted after the French mode. You have perhaps a fortnight in which to improve your markmanship. The matter which shall carry us abroad will conclude within that time. I shoot and fence with my left hand as well as I did with my right."

"I shall be only too happy to meet you," I replied. "I prefer the pistol, there is less exertion, and it is quicker."

"You shall have every advantage," said the Prince. "You will have that to nerve your arm which I shall not have—a woman's love." With a bow which was not without a

Harold MacGrath

certain dignity and grace, he walked from the room.

Phyllis a Princess? Gretchen free? I sent for my coat and hat and went out. I forgot all about my appointment with Col. J— of the Queen's light and that I had left Pembroke playing billiards in a strange club, where I myself had been but a guest. The crisp October air blew in my face as I rapidly walked up the mall, and it cooled the fever in my veins. But my mind ran on rather wildly. Gretchen free? Phyllis a Princess? Gretchen's little word, "perhaps," came back and sang into my ears. Yet, win or lose, I was to meet the Prince in mortal combat. If Phyllis was not proven Gretchen's twin sister, I should care but little for the Prince's bullet. On the other hand—Well, I should trust to luck. Before I was aware of my destination, I stood fumbling the key in the door of my apartment. I wanted my pipe. At eleven by the clock, Pembroke came in.

"Hang your apologies!" he said.

CHAPTER XVIII

"Phyllis," said I, "do you remember the day we first met?"

We were in the morning room of the Wentworth mansion at B—. Phyllis, Pembroke and I sat before the warm grate, while Mrs. Wentworth and Ethel stood by one of the windows, comparing some shades of ribbon. My presence at B—was due to a wire I had sent to New York, which informed headquarters that I was on the track of a great sensation. The return wire had said, "Keep on it."

"When first we met?" echoed Phyllis. "Why, it was at Block Island."

"Oh," said I, "I do not refer to the time when you had shouldered the responsibilities of a society bud. I mean the time when the introduction was most informal. You were at the time selling lemonade without license and with very little lemon."

"Selling lemonade?" cried Pembroke.

"Never mind him, Mr. Pembroke," laughed Phyllis.

"It was a long time ago," I went on. "I was a new reporter. Mr. Wentworth had to be interviewed. It was one of those hot days in May. The servant at the door said that Mr.

Harold MacGrath

Wentworth was in the back yard—he called it the garden—where I soon found myself. You had a small table, a glass and a pitcher. I suppose every time your uncle got thirsty you sold him a glass. You wore short dresses—"

"Terrible!" cried Phyllis, shielding her face with the handscreen.

"And looked as cool as the ice in the pitcher, and as fresh as the flowers which lined the walls. I thought that if I bought a glass of you I might make my approach to your uncle an easier task. So I looked at you and smiled, and you giggled."

"Giggled!" cried Phyllis, indignantly.

Pembroke was laughing.

"Yes, actually giggled," I went on. "I laid down a twenty-five-cent piece, and you poured but some water which had had nothing more than a mild flirtation with a lemon, and I gulped it down. I held out my hand, and you said that there wasn't any change. I smiled a false smile. Let me make a confession."

"Well?" mockingly from Phyllis.

"It was my last quarter. It was very pathetic. I had to walk four miles down town. I did not know your uncle well enough or I should have borrowed carfare from him."

"And I took your last penny?" said Phyllis, gently. "Why did you not tell me then?"

"I was twenty-two and proud," said I. "Where are you going?" for she had risen.

"I'll be back in a moment," she said, as she left the room. When she returned she put out her hand. On the palm lay two bright American dimes.

"What's this?" I asked.

"The change."

"Very good!" laughed Pembroke.

I said nothing, but took out my wallet. In opening it to put in the dimes, something fell to the floor. It was Gretchen's rose.

"What is that?" asked Phyllis, as I stooped to pick it up.

"It is the end of a story," I answered. I busied myself with the fire till the poker grew too hot.

"How many romances commonplace wallets contain?" said Pembroke, sententiously.

"I have two in mine," said I.

Pembroke looked at Phyllis, but the fire seemed to be claiming her attention. Then he looked at me, but I was gazing at Phyllis. He was in a puzzle.

"Do you know, Miss Landors," he said, "that I never dreamed to meet you again when I saw you in Vienna last year?"

"Vienna?" said she. "I have never been to Vienna."

I suddenly brought down my heel on Pembroke's toes.

"Ah, a curious mistake on my part. I suppose the ball at

the ministry to-night will be your first on the continent?"

I gazed admiringly at him. He had not even looked at me. He was certainly clever.

"Yes," said Phyllis, "and already I believe I am going to have what they call stage fright, though I cannot understand why I should feel that way."

"Possibly it's a premonition," said I, absently.

"And of what?" asked Phyllis.

"How should I know?" said I, mysteriously.

"What in the world is going on?" she demanded. "You step on Mr. Pembroke's toes, you prophesy, and then you grow mysterious."

My glance and Pembroke's met. He burst out laughing. A possible contretemps was averted by the approach of Mrs. Wentworth, who asked us to have a cup of chocolate before we went out into the chill air. Finally we rose to make our departure. While Pembroke was bidding Ethel a good morning, Phyllis spoke to me.

"The last flowers you sent me were roses," she said softly.

"Were they?" said I. "I had forgotten. Shall I send you some for this evening?"

It was something in her eyes that I did not understand.

"Thank you, but Mr. Pembroke has promised to do that." And then she added: "So you have really had two romances?"

"Yes," said I; "and both ended badly."

"Let us hope that the third will be of happier termination," she smiled. The smile caused me some uneasiness.

"There never will be a third," I said. "It is strange, is it not, when you think that there might have been—but one? You will give me a waltz to-night?"

"With pleasure. Good morning."

Pembroke and I passed down the broad stairs. On the street we walked a block or so in silence.

Finally Pembroke said: "What the deuce made you step on my foot? And why does she not want me to know that she was in Vienna last winter?"

"Because," said I, "Miss Landors never was in Vienna."

"But, man, my eyes!"

"I do not care anything about your eyes."

"What makes you so positive?"

"Knowledge."

"Do you love her?" bluntly.

"No."

"Because—?"

"There is another. Pembroke, to-night will be pregnant with possibilities. You will see the woman you love and the woman I love."

Harold MacGrath

"What do you mean?"

"Have you ever heard of her Serene Highness the Princess Hildegarde of Hohenphalia?"

"So high?"

"Yes."

"Then the woman I saw in Vienna—"

"Was the Princess."

"But this remarkable likeness?"

"Perhaps I had best tell you all." And when I had done, his astonishment knew no bounds.

"Great George, that makes Miss Landors a Princess, too!"

"It does, truly. Herein lies the evil of loving above one's station. In our country love is like all things, free to obtain. We are in a country which is not free. Here, those who appear to have the greatest liberty have the least."

"And she knows nothing about it?"

"Nothing."

"Why tell her?" he asked, fearful of his own love affair now.

"It is a duty. Some day she might learn too late. This afternoon I shall visit the Chancellor and place the matter before him and ask his assistance. He must aid me to find the proofs."

Pembroke began kicking the snow with his toes.

"I wish you had not told me, Jack."

"It is for the best. You and I are in the same boat; we ride or sink together."

At luncheon his mind was absent and he ate but little. And I ate less than he. It was going to be very hard for me to meet Gretchen.

The Chancellor waved his hand toward a chair. We were very good friends.

"What is it now?" he asked, smiling. "I dare not stir up the antagonists against the government to give you a story, and aside from the antagonists it is dull."

"I will find the story in the present instance," said I. And in the fewest words possible I laid before him the object of my visit.

"This is a very strange story," he said, making a pyramid of his fingers and contemplating the task with a careful air. "Are you not letting your imagination run away with you?"

"Not for a moment. I ask you to attend the ball at the American ministry this evening, and if the likeness between the two women does not convince you, the matter shall drop, so far as I am concerned."

"Has Herr Wentworth any idea of the affair?"

"It is not possible. What would be his object in keeping it a secret?"

Harold MacGrath

"Still, it is a grave matter, and without precedent. We must move carefully. You understand that there was no knowledge of another child, only rumor; and then it was believed to be an hallucination of the mother, whose mind was not very strong."

"Do you believe," I asked, "that two persons born of different parentage, in different lands, may resemble each other as these two do?"

"No. I shall let you know what stand I'll take when I have seen them together. And what will His Majesty say?" he mused. "I'm afraid the matter will assume many complications. And I might add that you seem particularly interested."

A slight warmth came into my cheeks.

"Your Excellency understands that a journalist always takes great interest in affairs of this sort," was my rejoinder.

"Yes, yes!" pleasantly. "But this so-called sister; has she not lived most of her life in America, your own country?"

"Your Excellency," said I, honestly, "whether she regains her own or not is immaterial to me, from a personal standpoint."

"Well, one way or the other, I shall decide what to do to-night. But, mind you, there must be proofs. Though they may look enough alike to be two peas in a pod, that will give your friend nothing you claim for her. The fate of your Princess rests in the hands of Herr Wentworth. Have the two met?"

"No; but during the short time they have been in the city

they have been mistaken for each other. And why do you call her my Princess?"

"She is not ours yet. It was a strange story, as I remember it. In those days we had our doubts, as we still have, of another child. By the way, who suggested the matter to you?"

I recounted my interview with the Prince.

"Ah," said the Chancellor; "so it was he? He is a greedy fellow and careful. I can readily understand his object. He wants all or nothing. I shall help you all I can," he concluded, as I reached for my hat.

"I ask nothing more," I replied; and then I passed from the cabinet into the crowded anteroom. It was filled with diplomats and soldiers, each waiting for an audience. They eyed me curiously and perhaps enviously as I made my way to the street. "Yes, indeed, what will the King say?" I mused on the way back to my rooms. What could he say?

That night Pembroke and I arrived at the ministry a little after ten. I was in a state of extreme nervousness.

"I'm in a regular funk," said Pembroke. "Supposing your Princess does not come?"

"It is written that she will come."

"Well, I'm glad that I looked you up in London. I would not have missed this adventure."

We found Phyllis in a nook under the grand staircase. I gave a slight exclamation as I saw her. I had never seen her looking so beautiful.

Harold MacGrath

"Come and sit down," said she, making room for us. "I have had a curious adventure."

"Tell us all about it," said Pembroke.

"I have had the honor of being mistaken for a Princess," triumphantly.

"Who could doubt it!" said I, with a glance I could not help, which made her lower her eyes.

"Moreover," she continued, this time looking at Pembroke, "the gentleman who committed the error was the Austrian Ambassador. What a compliment to take home!"

"And who was the Princess?" I felt compelled to ask, though I knew perfectly well.

"The Princess Hildegarde. Do you recall the night in London," to me, "when the same thing occurred? I am very anxious to meet this Princess who looks so like me."

"You will have that pleasure immediately after the opera," said I.

Pembroke's eyes said something to me then, and I rose.

"There is Mr. Wentworth. I wish to speak to him. Will you excuse me?"

"With pleasure!" laughed Pembroke.

I threaded my way through the gathering throng to the side of Mr. Wentworth.

"How d'y' do, Winthrop?" he said, taking me by the arm.

"Come into the conservatory. I want you to see some of the finest orchids that ever came from South America. The girls are looking well to-night. I suppose you noticed."

"Especially Phyllis." Our eyes met.

When we entered the conservatory, he suddenly forgot all about the orchids.

"Jack, I'm worried about her—Phyllis. You see, she is not my niece. There's a long story, This morning a gentleman visited my department. He was Prince Ernst of Wortumborg. He began by asking me if Phyllis was my niece. That started the business. He proceeded to prove to me, as far as possible, that Phyllis was a Princess. I could not say that it was all nonsense, because I did not know. Some twenty years ago, a strange thing happened. I occupied the same residence as to-day. It was near midnight, and snowing fiercely. I was looking over some documents, when the footman came in and announced the presence of a strange woman in the hall, who demanded to see me. The woman was young and handsome, and in her arms she carried a child. Would I, for humanity's sake, give a roof to the child till the morrow? The woman said that she was looking for her relatives, but as yet had not found them, and that the night was too cold for the child to be carried around. She was a nurse. The child was not hers, but belonged to a wealthy family of the south, who were to have arrived that day, but had not. The thing seemed so irregular that I at once consented, thinking to scan the papers the next day for an account of a lost or stolen child. She also carried a box which contained, she said, the child's identity. Now, as I am a living man, there was nothing in that box to show who the child was; nothing but clothes, not a jewel or a trinket. I looked through the papers in vain. And the woman never appeared again. Much against my will I was forced to keep the child. I am glad I did, for I have grown to love her as one of my own. I had a married sister who died in Carolina, so I felt secure in stating that Phyllis was her daughter, therefore my niece. And that is positively all I know. And here comes a fellow who says he knows who she is, and, moreover, that she is a Princess. What do you say to that?"

"What he said was true," gloomily. Without proofs Gretchen remained as far away as ever. I told him what I knew.

"I must see this Princess before I move. If they look alike, why, let things take their course. As a matter of fact, Phyllis is to share equally with Ethel. So, whether or not she proves to be a Princess, it will not interfere with her material welfare. And, by the way, Jack, isn't there a coldness of some sort between you and Phyllis?"

"Not a coldness," said I; "merely an understanding. Let us be getting back to the ballroom. I am anxious to see the two when they meet."

I left him in the reception room. As I was in the act of crossing the hall which led to the ballroom, I was stopped. It was the Prince.

"Well," he said, smiling ironically, "the matter is, sadly for you, definitely settled. Your friend may in truth be a Princess, but there are no proofs. In the eyes of men they are sisters; in the eyes of the law they are total strangers. I shall not ask you to congratulate me upon my success. I shall now wed the Princess Hildegarde with a sense of security. Come—have you seen her yet? She does not know that you are here. It will be a surprise and a pleasure. As to that other matter, I shall send a gentleman around to your rooms in the morning to arrange the affair."

I shivered. I had forgotten that I had accepted a challenge.

"Take me to her," said I. "She will be happy indeed to see me, as you know." I laughed in his face. "How convenient it would be for both of us—her and me—should my bullet speed to the proper place! Believe me, I shall be most happy to kill you. There are many things on the slate to wipe out."

"I see that you are a gentleman of spirit," said he, smoothing the scowl from his brow. "Ah, there she stands. Look well, my friend; look at her well. This is probably the last night you will see her, save as my wife."

The sight of that dear face took the nerves from me, and left me trembling. Even in the momentary glance I detected a melancholy cast to her features. She was surrounded by several men, who wore various decorations.

"Your Highness," said the Prince, mockery predominating his tones, "permit me to present to you an old friend."

Was it because her soul instinctively became conscious of my presence and nerved her for the ordeal, that she turned and smiled on me? The Prince appeared for a moment crestfallen. Perhaps the scene lacked a denouement. Oh, I was sure that implacable hate burned under that smile of his, just as I knew that beneath the rise and fall of Gretchen's bosom the steady fire of immutable love burned, burned as it burned in my own heart. It was a defeat for the Prince, a triumph for Gretchen and me. The greeting took but a moment. I stepped back, strong and hopeful. She loved me. I knew that her heart was singing the same joyous song as my own.

"Ah, here you are!" said a voice behind me, giving me an indescribable start. "I have been looking high and low for you. You have forgotten this dance."

It was Phyllis.

And then a sudden hush fell upon the circle. The two women stood face to face, looking with strange wonder into each other's eyes.

CHAPTER XIX

Phyllis and I were sitting in one of the numerous cozy corners. I had danced badly and out of time. The music and the babel of tongues had become murmurous and indistinct.

"And so that is the Princess Hildegarde?" she said, after a spell.

"Yes; she is your double. Is she not beautiful?"

"Is that a left-handed compliment to me?" Phyllis was smiling, but she was colorless.

"No," said I. "I could never give you a left-handed compliment."

"How strange and incomprehensible!" said she, opening her fan.

"What?—that I have never, and could never, give you a—"

"No, no! I was thinking of the likeness. It rather unnerved me. It seemed as though I was looking into a mirror."

"What do you think of her?" suppressing the eagerness in

Harold MacGrath

my voice.

"She is to be envied," softly.

And I grew puzzled.

"Jack, for a man who has associated with the first diplomatists of the world, who has learned to read the world as another might read a book, you are surprisingly unadept in the art of dissimulation."

"That is a very long sentence," said I, in order to gain time enough to fathom what she meant. I could not. So I said: "What do you mean?"

"Your whole face was saying to the Princess, 'I love you!' A glance told me all. I was glad for your sake that no other woman saw you at that moment. But I suppose it would not have mattered to you."

"Not if all the world had seen the look," moodily.

"Poor Jack, you are very unlucky!" Her voice was full of pity. "I feel so sorry for you, it is all so impossible. And she loves you, too!"

"How do you know?"

"I looked at her while she was looking at you."

"You have wonderful eyes."

"So I have been told. I wonder why she gave you that withered and worm-eaten rose?"

"A whim," I said, staring at the rug. I wondered how she came to surmise that it was Gretchen's rose?

Intuition, perhaps.

"Do you love her well enough," asked Phyllis, plucking the lace on her fan, "to sacrifice all the world for her, to give up all your own happiness that she might become happy?"

"She never can be happy without me—if she loves me as I believe." I admit that this was a selfish thought to express.

"Then, why is it impossible—your love and hers? If her love for you is as great as you say it is, what is a King, a Prince, or a principality to her?"

"It is none of those. It is because she has given her word, the word of a Princess. What would you do in her place?" suddenly.

"I?" Phyllis leaned back among the cushions her eyes half-closed and a smile on her lips. "I am afraid that if I loved you I should follow you to the end of the world. Honor is a fine thing, but in her case it is an empty word. If she broke this word for you, who would be wronged? No one, since the Prince covets only her dowry and the King desires only his will obeyed. Perhaps I do not understand what social obligation means to these people who are born in purple."

"Perhaps that is it. Phyllis, listen, and I will tell you a romance which has not yet been drawn to its end. Once upon a time—let me call it a fairy story," said I, drawing down a palm leaf as if to read the tale from its blades. "Once upon a time, in a country far from ours, there lived a Prince and a Princess. The Prince was rather a bad fellow. His faith in his wife was not the best. And he made a vow that if ever children came he would make them as evil as himself. Not long after the good fairy

Harold MacGrath

brought two children to her godchild, the Princess. Remembering the vow made by the Prince, the good fairy carried away one of the children, and no one knew anything about it save the Princess and the fairy. When the remaining child was two years old the Princess died. The child from then on grew like a wild flower. The Prince did his best to spoil her, but the good fairy watched over her, just as carefully as she watched over the child she had hidden away. By and by the wicked Prince died. The child reached womanhood. The good fairy went away and left her; perhaps she now gave her whole attention to the other." I let the palm leaf slip back, and drew down a fresh one, Phyllis watching me with interest. "The child the fairy left was still a child, for all her womanhood. She was willful and capricious; she rode, she fenced, she hunted; she was as unlike other women as could be. At last the King, who was her guardian, grew weary of her caprices. So he commanded that she marry. But what had the fairy done with the other child, the twin sister of this wild Princess? Perhaps in this instance the good fairy died and left her work unfinished, to be taken up and pursued by a conventional newspaper reporter. Now this pro tem fairy, who was anything but good, as the word goes, made some curious discoveries. It seems that the good fairy had left the lost Princess in the care of one of a foreign race. Having a wife and daughter of his own, he brought the Princess up as his niece, not knowing himself who she really was. She became wise, respected, and beautiful in mind and form. Fate, who governs all fairy stories, first brought the newspaper reporter into the presence of the lost Princess. She was a mere girl then, and was selling lemonade at—at twenty-five cents a glass. She—"

"Jack," came in wondering tones, "for mercy's sake, what are you telling me?"

"Phyllis, can you not look back, perhaps as in a dream, to

an old inn, where soldiers and ministers in a hurry and confusion moved to and fro? No; I dare say you were too young. The Princess Hildegarde of Hohenphalia is your sister." I rose and bowed to her respectfully.

"My sister?—the Princess?—I, a Princess? Jack," indignantly, "you are mocking me! It is not fair!"

"Phyllis, as sure as I stand before you, all I have said is true. And now let me be the first to do homage to Your Serene Highness," taking her hand despite her efforts to withdraw it, and kissing it.

"It is unreal! Impossible! Absurd!" she cried.

"Let me repeat the words of the French philosopher, who said, 'As nothing is impossible, let us believe in the absurd,'" said I.

"But why has Uncle Bob kept me in ignorance all these years?" unconvinced.

"Because, as I have said before, he knew nothing till to-day. I have even spoken to the Chancellor, who has promised to aid in recovering your rights."

"And does she know—the Princess Hildegarde? My sister? How strange the word feels on my tongue."

"No; she does not know, but presently she will."

Then Phyllis asked in an altered tone, "And what is all this to you that you thrust this greatness upon me?—a greatness, I assure you, for which I do not care?"

I regarded her vaguely. I saw a precipice at my feet. I could not tell her that in making her a Princess I was making Gretchen free. I could not confess that my motive was purely a selfish one.

"It was a duty," said I, evasively.

"And in what way will it concern the Princess Hildegarde's affairs—and yours?" She was rather merciless.

"Why should it concern any affair of mine?" I asked.

"You love her, and she loves you; may she not abdicate in my favor?"

"And if she should?" with an accent of impatience.

Phyllis grew silent. "Forgive me, Jack!" impulsively. "But all this is scarcely to be believed. And then you say there are no proofs."

"Not in the eyes of the law," I replied; "but nature has written it in your faces." I was wondering why she had not gone into raptures at the prospect of becoming a Princess.

"It is a great honor," she said, after some meditation, "and it is very kind of you. But I care as little for the title as I do for this rose." And she cast away one of Pembroke's roses. It boded ill for my cousin's cause.

Presently we saw the giver of the rose loom up in the doorway. He was smiling as usual.

"It is supper, Jack," he said; "I'm afraid you'll have to go."

"Does he know?" whispered Phyllis as we rose.

"Yes."

She frowned. And as they went away I mused upon the uncertainty of placing valuable things in woman's hands.

The next person I saw was the Chancellor.

"Well?" I interrogated.

"There can be no doubt," he said, "but—" with an expressive shrug.

"Life would run smoother if it had fewer 'buts' and 'its' and 'perhapses.' What you would say," said I, "is that there are no proofs. Certainly they must be somewhere."

"But to find them!" cried he.

"I shall make the effort; the pursuit is interesting."

The expression in his eyes told me that he had formed an opinion in regard to my part. "Ah, these journalists!" as he passed on.

Everything seemed so near and yet so far. Proofs? Where could they be found if Wentworth had them not? If only there had been a trinket, a kerchief, even, with the Hohenphalian crest upon it! I shook my fists in despair. Gretchen was so far away, so far!

I went in search of her. She was still surrounded by men. The women were not as friendly toward her as they might have been. The Prince was standing near. Seeing me approach, his teeth gleamed for an instant.

"Ah," said Gretchen, "here is Herr Winthrop, who is to take me in to supper."

It was cleverly done, I thought. Even the Prince was of

the same mind. He appreciated all these phases. As we left them and passed in toward the supper room, I whispered:

"I love you!"

CHAPTER XX

When I whispered these words I expected a gentle pressure from Gretchen's fingers, which rested lightly on my arm. But there was no sign, and I grew troubled. The blue-green eyes sparkled, and the white teeth shone between the red lips. Yet something was lacking.

"Let us go into the conservatory," she said. "It was merely a ruse of mine. I want no supper. I have much to say to you."

Altogether, I had dreamed of a different reception. When I entered the doorway, and she first saw me, it was Gretchen; but now it was distinctly a Princess, a woman of the world, full of those devices which humble and confuse us men.

Somehow we selected, by mutual accord, a seat among the roses. There was a small fountain, and the waters sang in a murmurous music. It seemed too early for words, so we drew our thoughts from the marble and the water. As for me, I looked at, but did not see, the fountain. It was another scene. There was a garden, in which the roses grew in beautiful disorder. The sunbeams straggled through the chestnuts. Near by a wide river moved slowly, and with a certain majesty. There was a man and a woman in the garden. She was culling roses, while the

Harold MacGrath

man looked on with admiring eyes.

"Yes," said the Princess, "all that was a pretty dream. Gretchen was a fairy; and now she has gone from your life and mine—forever. My dear friend, it is a prosaic age we live in. Sometimes we forget and dream; but dreams are unreal. Perhaps a flash of it comes back in after days, that is all; and we remember that it was a dream, and nothing more. It is true that God designs us, but the world molds us and fate puts on the finishing touches." She was smiling into my wonder-struck face. "We all have duties to perform while passing. Some of us are born with destinies mapped out by human hands; some of us are free to make life what we will. I am of the first order, and you are of the second. It is as impossible to join the one with the other as it is to make diamonds out of charcoal and water. Between Gretchen and the Princess Hildegarde of Hohenphalia there is as much difference as there is between—what simile shall I use?—the possible and the impossible?"

"Gretchen—" I began.

"Gretchen?" The Princess laughed amusedly. "She is flown. I beg you not to waste a thought on her memory."

Things were going badly for me. I did not understand the mood. It brought to mind the woman poor Hillars had described to me in his rooms that night in London. I saw that I was losing something, so I made what I thought a bold stroke. I took from my pocket a withered rose. I turned it from one hand to the other.

"It appears that when Gretchen gave me this it was as an emblem of her love. Still, I gave her all my heart."

"If that be the emblem of her love, Herr, throw it away; it

is not worth the keeping."

"And Gretchen sent me a letter once," I went on.

"Ah, what indiscretion!"

"It began with 'I love you,' and ended with that sentence. I have worn the writing away with my kisses."

"How some men waste their energies!"

"Your Highness," said I, putting the rose back into my pocket, "did Gretchen ever tell you how she fought a duel for me because her life was less to her than mine?"

The Princess Hildegarde's smile stiffened and her eyes closed for the briefest instant.

"Ah, shall I ever forget that night!" said I. "I held her to my heart and kissed her on the lips. I was supremely happy. Your Highness has never known what a thing of joy it is to kiss the one you love. It is one of those things which are denied to people who have their destinies mapped out by human hands."

The Princess opened her fan and hid her lips.

"And do you know," I continued, "when Gretchen went away I had a wonderful dream?"

"A dream? What was it?" The fan was waving to and fro.

"I dreamed that a Princess came in Gretchen's place, and she threw her arms around my neck and kissed me of her own free will."

"And what did she say, Herr?" Certainly the voice was

Harold MacGrath

growing more like Gretchen's.

I hesitated. To tell her what the dream Princess had said would undo all I had thus far accomplished, which was too little.

"It will not interest Your Highness," said I.

"Tell me what she said; I command it!" And now I was sure that there was a falter in her voice.

"She said—she said that she loved me."

"Continue."

"And that, as she was a Princess and—and honor bound, it could never be." I had to say it.

"That is it; that is it. It could never be. Gretchen is no more. The Princess who, you say, came to you in a dream was then but a woman—"

"Aye, and such a woman!" I interrupted. "As God hears me, I would give ten years of my life to hold her again in my arms, to kiss her lips, to hear her say that she loved me. But, pardon me, what were you going to say?"

"Your dream Princess was but a woman—ah, well; this is Tuesday; Thursday at noon she will wed the Prince. It is written."

"The devil!" I let slip. I was at the start again.

"Sir, you do him injustice."

"Who?—the Prince?" savagely.

"No; the—the devil!" She had fully recovered, and I had no weapon left.

"Gretchen, did you really ever love me?"

There was no answer.

"No; I do not believe you did. If you had loved me, what to you would have been a King, a Prince, a principality? If you broke that promise who would be wronged? Not the King, not the Prince."

"No, I should not have wronged them, but," said the Princess rising, "I should have wronged my people whom I have sworn to protect; I should have wronged my own sense of honor; I should have broken those ties which I have sworn to hold dear and precious as my life; I should have forsaken a sacred duty for something I was not sure of—a man's love!"

"Gretchen!"

"Am I cruel? Look!" Phyllis stood at the other end of the conservatory. "Does not there recur to you some other woman you have loved? You start. Come; was not your love for Gretchen pique? Who is she who thus mirrors my own likeness? Whoever she is, she loves you! Let us return; I shall be missed." It was not the woman but the Princess who spoke.

"You are breaking two hearts!" I cried, my voice full of disappointment, passion and anger.

"Two? Perhaps; but yours will not be counted."

"You are—"

"Pray, do not lose your temper," icily; and she swept toward the entrance.

I had lost.

As the Princess drew near to Phyllis the brown eyes of the one met the blue-green eyes of the other. There was almost an exclamation on Phyllis's lips; there was almost a question on Gretchen's; both paled. Phyllis understood, but Gretchen did not, why the impulse to speak came. Then the brown eyes of Phyllis turned their penetrating gaze to my own eyes, which I was compelled to shift. I bowed, and the Princess and I passed on.

By the grand staircase we ran into the Prince. His face wore a dissatisfied air.

"I was looking for Your Highness," he said to Gretchen. "Your carriage is at the curb. Permit me to assist you. Ah, yes," in English, "it is Herr Winthrop. I regret that the interview of to-morrow will have to be postponed till Monday."

"Any time," said I, watching Gretchen whose eyes widened, "will be agreeable to me."

Gretchen made as though to speak, but the Prince anticipated her.

"It is merely a little discussion, Your Highness," he said, "which Herr Winthrop and I left unfinished earlier in the evening. Good night."

On the way to the cloak room it kept running through my mind that I had lost. Thursday?—she said Thursday was the day of her wedding? It would be an evil day for me.

Pembroke was in the cloak room.

"Going?" he asked.

"Yes."

"Well, let us go together. Where shall it be—Egypt or the steppes of Siberia?"

"Home first," said I; "then we shall decide."

When we got into the carriage we lit cigars. For some reason Pembroke was less talkative than usual. Suddenly he pulled down the window, and a gust of snow blew in. Then up went the window again, but the cigar was gone.

"Has anything gone wrong?" I asked.

"'One more unfortunate. . . . Make no deep scrutiny!'" he quoted. "Jack, she wouldn't think of it, not for a moment. Perhaps I was a trifle too soon. Yes, she is a Princess, indeed. As for me, I shall go back to elephants and tigers; it's safer."

"'The Bridge of Sighs,'" said I. "Let us cross it for good and all."

"And let it now read 'Sighs Abridged.'"

He asked me no questions, and I silently thanked him. Once in our rooms, he drank a little more brandy than I thought good for one "who may or may not live the year out." I told him so. He laughed. And then I laughed. Both of us did it theatrically; it was laughter, but it was not mirth.

"Cousin," said I, "that's the idea; let us laugh. Love may

sit on the windowsill and shiver to death."

"That fellow Anacreon was a fool," said Pembroke. "If the child of Venus had been left then and there, what a lot of trouble might have been averted! What do you say to this proposition; the north, the bears and the wolves? I've a friend who owns a shooting box a few miles across the border. There's bears and gray wolves galore. Eh?"

"I must get back to work," said I, but half-heartedly.

"To the devil with your work! Throw it over. You've got money; your book is gaining you fame. What's a hundred dollars a week to you, and jumping from one end of the continent to the other with only an hour's notice?"

"I'll sleep on it."

"Good. I'll go to bed now, and you can have the hearth and the tobacco to yourself."

"Good night," said I.

Yes, I wanted to be alone. But I did not smoke. I sat and stared into the flickering flames in the grate. I had lost Gretchen. . . . To hold a woman in your arms, the woman you love, to kiss her lips, and then to lose her! Oh, I knew that she loved me, but she was a Princess, and her word was given, and it could not be. The wind sang mournfully over the sills of the window; thick snow whitened the panes; there was a humming in the chimneys. . . . She was jealous of Phyllis; that was why I knew that she loved me. . . . And the subtle change in Phyllis's demeanor towards me; what did it signify? . . . Gretchen was to be married Thursday because there were no proofs that Phyllis was her sister. . . . What if Gretchen had been Phyllis, and Phyllis had been Gretchen. . . . Heigho! I threw some more coals on the fire. The candle sank in the socket. There are some things we men cannot understand; the sea, the heavens and woman. . . . Suddenly I brought both hands down on my knees. The innkeeper! The innkeeper! He knew! In a moment I was rummaging through the stack of time tables. The next south-bound train left at 3:20. I looked at the clock; 2:20. My dress suit began to fly around on various chairs. Yes; how simple it was! The innkeeper knew; he had known it all these years. I threw my white cravat onto the table and picked up the most convenient tie. In ten minutes from the time the idea came to me I was completely dressed in traveling garments. I had a day and a half. It would take twenty hours to fetch the innkeeper. I refused to entertain the possibility of not finding him at the inn. I swore to heaven that the nuptials of the Princess Hildegarde of Hohenphalia and the Prince Ernst of Wortumborg should not be celebrated at noon, Thursday. I went into the bedroom.

"Pembroke?"

"What is it?" came drowsily.

"I am going on a journey."

"One of those cursed orders you get every other day?" he asked.

"No. It's one on my own account this time. I shall be back in twenty-four hours. Goodby!" And I left him there, blinking in the dim light of the candle.

I rushed into the street and looked up and down it. Not a vehicle in sight. I must run for it. The railway station was a long way off. A fine snow pelted my face. I stopped at the first lamp and pulled out my watch. It was twenty minutes to three. What if the time-tables had been changed? A prayer rose to my lips; there was so much in the balance. Down this street I ran, rounding this corner and that. I knocked down a drunken student, who cursed me as he rolled into the gutter. I never turned, but kept on. One of the mounted police saw me rushing along. He shaded his eyes for a moment, then called to me to stop. I swore under my breath.

"Where are you going at such a pace and at this time of morning?" he demanded.

"To the station. I beg of you not to delay me. I am in a great hurry to catch the 3:20 south-bound train. If you doubt me, come to the station with me." An inspiration came to me. "Please see," I added impressively, "that no one hinders me. I am on the King's business."

"His Majesty's business? Ach! since when has His Majesty chosen an Englishman to dispatch his affairs? I will proceed with you to the station."

And he kept his word. When he saw the gateman examine my ticket and passports and smile pleasantly, he turned on his heel, convinced that there was nothing dangerous about me. He climbed on his horse and galloped away. He might have caused me no end of delay, and time meant everything in a case like mine. Scarcely had I secured a compartment in a first-class carriage than the wheels groaned and the train rolled out of the station. My brow was damp; my hands trembled like an excited woman's. Should I win? I had a broken cigar in my pocket. I lit the preserved end at the top of the feeble carriage lamp. I had the compartment alone. Sleep! Not I. Who could sleep when the car wheels and the rattling windows kept saying, "The innkeeper knows! The innkeeper knows!" Every stop was a heartache. Ah, those eight hours were eight separate centuries to me. I looked careworn and haggard enough the next morning when I stepped on the station platform. I wanted nothing to eat; not even a cup of coffee to drink.

To find conveyance to the inn was not an easy task. No one wanted to take the drive. Finally I secured a horse. There was no haggling over the price. And soon I was loping through the snowdrifts in the direction of the old inn. The snow whirled and eddied over the stubble fields; the winds sang past my ears; the trees creaked and the river flowed on, black and sluggish. It was a dreary scene. It was bitter cold, but I had no mind for that. On, on I went. Two miles were left in the rear. The horse was beginning to breathe hard. Sometimes the snow was up to his knees. What if the old man was not there? The blood sank upon my heart. Once the horse struck a slippery place and nearly fell, but I caught him in time. I could now see the inn, perhaps a mile away, through the leafless trees. It looked dismal enough. The vines hung dead about it, the hedges were wild and scrawny, the roses I knew to be no more, and the squirrel had left his summer home for a warmer nest in the forest. A wave of joy swept over me as I saw a thin stream of smoke winding above the chimney. Some one was there. On, on; presently I flew up the roadway. A man stood on the porch. It was Stahlberg. When I pushed down my collar his jaw dropped. I flung the reins to him.

"Where is the innkeeper?" I cried with my first breath.

"In the hall, Herr. But—"

I was past him and going through the rooms. Yes, thank God, there he was, sitting before the huge fireplace, where the logs crackled and seethed, his grizzled head sunk between his shoulders, lost in some dream. I tramped in noisily. He started out of his dream and looked around.

"Gott!" he cried. He wiped his eyes and looked again. "Is it a dream or is it you?"

"Flesh and blood!" I cried. "Flesh and blood!"

I closed the door and bolted it. He followed my movements with a mixture of astonishment and curiosity in his eyes.

"Now," I began, "what have you done with the proofs which you took from your wife—the proofs of the existence of a twin sister of the Princess Hildegarde of Hohenphalia?"

CHAPTER XXI

The suddenness of this demand overwhelmed him, and he fell back into the chair, his eyes bulging and his mouth agape.

"Do you hear me?" I cried. "The proofs!" going up to him with clenched fists. "What have you done with those proofs? If you have destroyed them I'll kill you."

Then, as a bulldog shakes himself loose, the old fellow got up and squared his shoulders and faced me, his lips compressed and his jaws knotted. I could see by his eyes that I must fight for it.

"Herr Winthrop has gone mad," said he. "The Princess Hildegarde never had a sister."

"You lie!" My hands were at his throat.

"I am an old man," he said.

I let my hands drop and stepped back.

"That is better," he said, with a grim smile. "Who told you this impossible tale, and what has brought you here?"

"It is not impossible. The sister has been found."

Harold MacGrath

"Found!" I had him this time. "Found!" he repeated. "Oh, this is not credible!"

"It is true. And to-morrow at noon the woman you profess to love will become the wife of the man she abhors. Why? Because you, you refuse to save her!"

"I? How in God's name can I save her?" the perspiration beginning to stand out on his brow.

"How? I will tell you how. Prince Ernst marries Gretchen for her dowry alone. If the woman I believe to be her sister can be proved so, the Prince will withdraw his claims to Gretchen's hand. Do you understand? He will not marry for half the revenues of Hohenphalia. It is all or nothing. Now, will you produce those proofs? Will you help me?" The minute hand of the clock was moving around with deadly precision.

"Are you lying to me?" he asked, breathing hard.

"You fool! can't you see that it means everything to Gretchen if you have those proofs? She will be free, free! Will you get those proofs, or shall your god-child live to curse you?"

This was the most powerful weapon I had yet used.

"Live to curse me?" he said, not speaking to me, but to the thought. He sat down again and covered his face with his hands. The minute which passed seemed very long. He flung away his hands from his eyes with a movement which expressed despair and resignation. "Yes, I will get them. It is years and years ago," he mused absently; "so long ago that I had thought it gone and forgotten. But it was not to be. I will get the proofs," turning to me as he left the chair. "Wait here." He unbolted the door and passed forth. . . . It was a full confession of the deception, written by the mother herself, and witnessed by her physician, the innkeeper and his wife. Not even the King could contest its genuineness.

"Where is this Dr. Salzberg?"

The innkeeper leaned against the side of the fireplace, staring into the flames.

"He is dead," briefly.

"Who was he?"

"Her late Highness's court-physician. Oh, have no fear, Herr; this new-found Princess of yours will come into her own," with a bitter smile.

"And why have you kept silent all these years?" I asked.

"Why?" He raised his arms, then let them fall dejectedly. "I loved the Princess Hildegarde. I was jealous that any should share her greatness. I have kept silent because I carried her in my arms till she could walk. Because her father cursed her, and refused to believe her his own. Because she grew around my heart as a vine grows around a rugged oak. And the other? She was nothing to me. I had never seen her. My wife spirited her away when it was night and dark. I took the proofs of her existence as a punishment to my wife, who, without them, would never dare to return to this country again. Herr, when a man loads you with ignominy and contempt and ridicule for something you are not to blame, what do you seek? Revenge. The Prince tried to crush this lonely child of his. It was I who brought her up. It was I who taught her to say her prayers. It was I who made her what she is to-day, a noble woman, with a soul as spotless as yonder snowdrift. That was my revenge."

"Who are you?" I cried. For this innkeeper's affection and eloquence seemed out of place.

"Who am I?" The smile which lit his face was wistful and sad. "The law of man disavows me—the bar sinister. In the eyes of God, who is accountable for our being, I am Gretchen's uncle, her father's brother."

"You?" I was astounded.

"And who knows of this?"

"The King, the Prince—and you."

I thrust a hand toward him. "You are a man."

"Wait. Swear to God that Her Highness shall never know."

"On my honor."

Then he accepted my clasp and looked straight into my eyes.

"And all this to you?"

"I love her."

"And she?"

"It is mutual. Do you suppose she would have put her life before mine if not? She knew that the lieutenant would have killed me."

"Ach! It never occurred to me in that light. I understood it to be a frolic of hers. Will you make her happy?"

"If an honest man's love can do it," said I. "Now, get on your hat and coat. You must go to the capital with me. The King would send for you in any case. The next train leaves at five, and to save Gretchen, these proofs must be in the Chancellor's hands to-morrow morning."

"Yes, my presence will be necessary. Perhaps I have committed a crime; who knows?" His head fell in meditation. "Herr, and this other sister, has she been happy?"

"Happier than ever Gretchen."

He had the sleigh brought around. Stahlberg was to ride my horse back to the village and return with the sleigh. We climbed into the seat, there was a crunching of snow, a jangle of bells, and we were gliding over the white highway. As I lay back among the robes, I tried to imagine that it was a dream, that I was still in New York, grinding away in my den, and not enacting one of the principal roles in a court drama; that I was not in love with a woman who spoke familiarly to kings and grand dukes and princes, that I was not about to create a Princess of whom few had vaguely heard and of whom but one had really known; that Phyllis and I were once more on the old friendly grounds, and that I was to go on loving her till the end of time—till the end of time.

"You have known this sister?" asked the innkeeper.

"For many years," said I.

And those were the only words which passed between us during that five-mile drive. At the station I at once wired the Chancellor that the proofs had been found, and requested him to inform the King and Prince Ernst. And

Harold MacGrath

then another eight hours dragged themselves out of existence. But Gretchen was mine!

The King was dressed in a military blouse, and, save for the small cross suspended from his neck by a chain of gold, there was nothing about him to distinguish his rank. He strode back and forth, sometimes going the whole length of the white room. The Chancellor sat at a long mahogany table, and the Prince and Mr. Wentworth were seated at either side of him. The innkeeper stood before the Chancellor, at the opposite side of the table. His face might have been cut from granite, it was so set and impressive. I leaned over the back of a chair in the rear of the room. The King came close to me once and fixed his keen blue eyes on mine.

"Was this the fellow, Prince," he asked, "who caused you all the trouble and anxiety?"

I felt uneasy. My experience with Kings was not large.

"No, Your Majesty," answered the Prince. "The gentleman to whom you refer has departed the scene." The Prince caught the fire in my eye, and laughed softly.

"Ah," said the King, carelessly. "It is a strange story. Proceed," with a nod to the Chancellor.

"What is your name?" the Chancellor asked, directing his glance at the innkeeper.

The innkeeper gazed at the King for a space. The Prince was watching him with a mocking smile.

"Hermann Breunner, Your Excellency."

The King stood still. He had forgotten the man, but not

the name.

"Hermann Breunner," he mused.

"Yes, Your Majesty," said the innkeeper.

"The keeper of the feudal inn," supplemented the Prince.

The glance the innkeeper shot him was swift. The Prince suddenly busied himself with the papers.

"Are you aware," went on the Chancellor, who had not touched the undercurrent, "that you are guilty of a grave crime?"

"Yes, Your Excellency."

"Which is punishable by long imprisonment?"

The innkeeper bent his head.

"What have you to say in your defense?"

"Nothing," tranquilly meeting the frowning eyes of the King.

"What was your object in defrauding the Princess—" the Chancellor opened one of the documents which lay before him—"the Princess Elizabeth of her rights?"

"I desired the Princess Hildegarde to possess all," was the answer. It was also a challenge to the Prince to refute the answer if he dared. "I acknowledge that I have committed a crime. I submit to His Majesty's will," bowing reverentially.

The King was stroking his chin, a sign of deep meditation

Harold MacGrath

in him.

"Let Their Highnesses be brought in," he said at last.

The Chancellor rose and passed into the anteroom. Shortly he returned, followed by Gretchen. I could see by the expression in her face that she was mystified by the proceeding.

"Her Highness the Princess Elizabeth is just leaving the carriage," announced the Chancellor, retiring again.

Gretchen looked first at the King, then at the Prince. As she saw the innkeeper, a wave of astonishment rippled over her face.

"Be seated, Your Highness," said the King, kindly.

She knew that I was in the room, but her eyes never left the King.

The Prince was plucking at his imperial. The innkeeper's eyes were riveted on the door. He was waiting for the appearance of her whom he had wronged. Presently Phyllis came in. Her cheeks were red, and her eyes sparkled with excitement. Wentworth nodded reassuringly. The innkeeper was like one stricken dumb. He stared at Phyllis till I thought his eyes would start from their sockets.

"Your Majesty has summoned me?" said Gretchen.

"Yes. Explain," said the King to the Chancellor.

"Your Highness," began the Chancellor, "it has been proved by these papers here and by that man there," pointing to the innkeeper, "that your mother of lamented memory gave birth to twins. One is yourself; the other was spirited away at the request of your mother. We shall pass over her reasons. It was all due to the efforts of this clever journalist here—" Gretchen was compelled to look at me now, while the King frowned and the Prince smiled—"that your sister has been found."

Gretchen gave a cry and started to go to Phyllis with outstretched arms; but as Phyllis stood motionless she stopped, and her arms fell.

"Your Highness," said the King to Phyllis, "it is your sister, the Princess Hildegarde. Embrace her, I beg you."

The King willed it. But it occurred to me that there was a warmth lacking in the embrace. Gretchen lightly brushed with her lips the cheek of her sister, and the kiss was as lightly returned. There was something about it all we men failed to understand.

"Moreover," said the King, "she desires you to remain the sovereign Princess of Hohenphalia."

"Nay, Your Majesty," said Gretchen, "it is I who will relinquish my claims. Your Majesty is aware that I have many caprices."

"Indeed, yes," said the King. "And I can assure you that they have caused me no small anxiety. But let us come to an understanding, once and for all. Do you wish to abdicate in favor of your sister?"

Gretchen gave me the briefest notice.

"Yes, Your Majesty."

Phyllis was regarding me steadfastly.

"This is final?" said the King.

"It is."

"And what is your will?" to Phyllis. "Yes, the likeness is truly remarkable," communing aloud to his thought.

I could not suppress the appeal in my eyes.

"Your Majesty," said Phyllis, "if my sister will teach me how to become a Princess, I promise to accept the responsibility."

"You will not need much teaching," replied the King, admiringly.

"You will do this?—you, my sister?" asked Gretchen eagerly.

"Yes." There was no color now in Phyllis's cheeks; they were as white as the marble faun on the mantel.

"Remember, Your Highness," said the King, speaking to Gretchen, "there shall be no recall."

"Sire," said the Prince, rising, "I request a favor."

"And it shall be granted," said the King, "this being your wedding day."

It was Gretchen who now paled; the hands of the innkeeper closed; I clutched the chair, for my legs trembled. To lose, after all!

"Ah," said the Prince, "I thank Your Majesty. The favor I ask is that you will postpone this marriage—indefinitely."

"What!" cried the King. He was amazed. "Have I heard you aright, or do my ears play me false?"

"It is true. I thank Your Majesty again," said the Prince, bowing.

"But this is beyond belief," cried the King in anger. "I do not understand. This marriage was at your own request, and now you withdraw. Since when," proudly, "was the hand of the Princess Hildegarde to be ignored?"

"It is a delicate matter," said the Prince, turning the ring on his finger. "It would be impolite to state my reasons before Her Highness. Your Highness, are you not of my opinion, that, as matters now stand, a marriage between us would be rather absurd?"

"Now, as at all times," retorted Gretchen, scornfully. "It has never been my will," a furtive glance at the King.

"But—" began the King. He was wrathful.

"Your Majesty," said the innkeeper, "you are a great King; be a generous one."

All looked at him as though they expected to see the King fly at him and demolish him—all but I. The King walked up to the bold speaker, took his measure, then, with his hands clasped behind his back, resumed his pacing. After a while he came to a standstill.

"Your Highness," he said to Phyllis, "what shall I do with this man who has so grossly wronged you?"

"Forgive him."

The King passed on. I was not looking at him, but at the

Harold MacGrath

innkeeper. I saw his lip tremble and his eyes fill. Suddenly he fell upon his knees before Phyllis and raised her hand to his lips.

"Will Your Highness forgive a sinner who only now realizes the wrong he has done to you?"

"Yes, I forgive you," said Phyllis. "The only wrong you have done to me is to have made me a Princess. Your Majesty will forgive me, but it is all so strange to me who have grown up in a foreign land which is dearer to my heart than the land in which I was born."

I felt a thrill of pride, and I saw that Mr. Wentworth's lips had formed into a "God bless her!"

"It is a question now," said the King, "only of duty."

"And Your Majesty's will regarding my marriage?" put in the Prince, holding his watch in his hand. It was ten o'clock.

"Well, well! It shall be as you desire." Then to me: "I thank you in the name of Their Highnesses for your services. And you, Mr. Wentworth, shall always have the good will of the King for presenting to his court so accomplished and beautiful a woman as Her Highness the Princess Elizabeth. Hermann Breunner, return to your inn and remain there; your countenance brings back disagreeable recollections. I shall expect Your Highnesses at dinner this evening. Prince, I leave to you the pleasant task of annulling your nuptial preparations. Good morning. Ah! these women!" as he passed from the room. "They are our mothers, so we must suffer their caprices."

And as we men followed him we saw Gretchen weeping silently on Phyllis's shoulder.

The innkeeper touched the Prince.

"I give you fair warning," he said. "If our paths cross again, one of us shall go on alone."

"I should be very lonely without you," laughed the Prince. "However, rest yourself. As the King remarked, your face recalls unpleasant memories. Our paths shall not cross again."

When the innkeeper and the Chancellor were out of earshot, I said: "She is mine!"

"Not yet," the Prince said softly. "On Tuesday morn I shall kill you."

CHAPTER XXII

The affair caused considerable stir. The wise men of diplomacy shook their heads over it and predicted grave things in store for Hohenphalia. Things were bad enough as they were, but to have a woman with American ideas at the head—well, it was too dreadful to think of. And the correspondents created a hubbub. The news was flashed to Paris, to London, thence to New York, where the illustrated weeklies printed full-page pictures of the new Princess who had but a few months since been one of the society belles. And everybody was wondering who the "journalist" in the case was. The Chancellor smiled and said nothing. Mr. Wentworth said nothing and smiled. A cablegram from New York alarmed me. It said: "Was it you?" I answered, "Await letter." The letter contained my resignation, to take effect the moment my name became connected with the finding of the Princess Elizabeth. A week or so later I received another cablegram, "Accept resignation. Temptation too great." In some manner they secured a photograph of mine, and I became known as "The reporter who made a Princess;" and for many days the raillery at the clubs was simply unbearable. But I am skipping the intermediate events, those which followed the scene in the King's palace.

I was very unhappy. Three days passed, and I saw neither Phyllis nor Gretchen. The city was still talking about the dramatic ending of Prince Ernst's engagement to the Princess Hildegarde, Twice I had called at the Hohenphalian residence to pay my respects. Once I was told that Their Highnesses were at the palace. The second time I was informed that Their Highnesses were indisposed. I became gloomy and disheartened. I could not understand. Gretchen had not even thanked me for my efforts in saving her the unhappiness of marrying the Prince. And Phyllis, she who had called me "Jack," she whom I had watched grow from girlhood to womanhood, she, too, had forsaken me. I do not know what would have become of me but for Pembroke's cheerfulness.

Monday night I was sitting before the grate, reading for the hundredth time Gretchen's only letter. Pembroke was buried behind the covers of a magazine. Suddenly a yellow flame leaped from a pine log, and in it I seemed to read all. Gretchen was proud and jealous. She believed that I loved Phyllis and had made her a Princess because I loved her. It was the first time I had laughed in many an hour. Pembroke looked over his magazine.

"That sounds good. What caused it?"

"A story," I answered. "Some day I shall tell you all about it. Have you noticed how badly I have gone about lately?"

"Have I!" he echoed. "If I haven't had a time of it, I should like to know!"

"Well, it is all over," said I, placing a hand on his shoulder and smiling into his questioning eyes. "Now if you will excuse me, cousin mine, I'll make a call on her Serene Highness the Princess Hildegarde."

Just then the door opened and Pembroke's valet came in. He handed a card to me, and I read upon it, "Count von

Walden." I cast it into Pembroke's lap.

"That's the man. He is the inseparable of the Prince of Wortumborg." Then to the valet, "Show him up."

"What's it all about?" asked Pembroke.

"Honestly, I should like to run away," I said musingly. The snow on the housetops across the way sparkled in the early moonshine. "It's about a woman. If I live—ah!" I went to the door and swung it open. The Count gravely passed over the threshold.

"Good evening," he said, with a look of inquiry at Pembroke.

"This gentleman," said I, as I introduced him, "will second me in the affair to-morrow morning. I suppose you have come to make the final arrangements?"

"Pardon me," began Pembroke, "but I do not understand—"

"Oh, I forgot. You are," I responded, "to be my second in a duel to-morrow morning. Should anything happen to me, it were well to have a friend near by, better still a relative. Well, Count?"

"The Prince desires me to inform you that he has selected pistols at your request, and despite the fact that he has only the use of his left hand, he permits you to use either of yours. There will be one shot each, the firing to be drawn for on the grounds. The time is six, the place one mile out on the north road, in the rear of the Strasburg inn. I trust this is entirely satisfactory to you?"

"It is," I answered.

"Then allow me to bid you good night." He bowed and backed toward the door. He remained a moment with his hand on the knob, gazing into my eyes. I read in his a mixture of amusement and curiosity. "Good night," and he was gone.

Pembroke stared at me in bewilderment. "What the devil—"

"It is a matter of long standing," said I.

"But a duel!" he cried, impatiently. "Hang me if I'll be your second or let you fight. These are not the days of Richelieu. It is pure murder. It is against the law."

"But I cannot draw back honorably," I said. "I cannot."

"I'll notify the police and have them stop it," he said with determination.

"And have us all arrested and laughed at from one end of the continent to the other. My dear cousin, that man shot the dearest friend I had in the world. I am going to try to kill him at the risk of getting killed myself. He has also insulted the noblest woman that ever lived. If I backed down, I should be called a coward; the people who respect me now would close their doors in my face."

"But you have everything to lose, and he has nothing to gain."

"It cannot be helped," said I. "The woman I love once fought a duel for me; I cannot do less for her. You will be my second?"

"Yes. But if he wounds you, woe to him."

"Very well, I'll leave you," said I.

It was not far to the residence of Their Highnesses, so I walked. It was a fine night, and the frost sang beneath my heels. I had never fought a duel. This time no one would stand between. I was glad of this. I wanted Gretchen to know that I, too, was brave, but hitherto had lacked the opportunity to show it. It was really for her sake, after all, even though it would be something to avenge poor Hillars. And I wondered, as I walked along, would Gretchen and Phyllis love each other? It was difficult to guess, since, though sisters, they were utter strangers in lives and beliefs. Soon my journey came to an end, and I found myself mounting the broad marble steps of the Hohenphalian mansion. My heart beat swiftly and I had some difficulty in finding the bell.

The liveried footman took my card.

"Present it to her Highness the Princess Hildegarde," I said, as I passed into the hall.

"Her Serene Highness has left town, I believe, Your Excellency. Her Serene Highness the Princess Elizabeth is dining at the palace."

"Gone?" said I.

"Yes, Your Excellency." He examined my card closely. "Ah, allow me to deliver this note to you which Her Serene Highness directed me to do should you call."

My hands shook as I accepted the missive, and the lights began to waver. I passed out into the cold air. Gone? And why? I walked back to the rooms in feverish haste. Pembroke was still at his reading.

"Hello! What brings you back so soon?"

"She was not at home," I answered. I threw my coat and hat on the sofa. I balanced the envelope in my hand. For some moments I hesitated to open it. Something was wrong; if all had been well Gretchen would not have left the city. I glanced at Pembroke. He went on with his reading, unconcerned. Well, the sooner it was over, the better. I drew forth the contents and read it.

"Herr Winthrop—Forgive the indiscretion of a Princess. On my honor, I am sorry for having made you believe that you inspired me with the grand passion. Folly finds plenty to do with idle minds. It was a caprice of mine which I heartily regret. There is nothing to forgive; there is much to forget. However, I am under great obligations to you. I am positive that I shall love my sister as I have never loved a human being before. She is adorable, and I can well comprehend why you should love her deeply. Forgive me for playing with what the French call your summer affections. I am about to leave for Hohenphalia to prepare the way for the new sovereign. Will you kindly destroy that one indiscreet letter which I, in the spirit of mischief, wrote you last autumn?

"The Princess Hildegarde."

The envelope reminded me of a rusty scabbard; there was a very keen weapon within. I lit my pipe and puffed for a while.

"Cousin," said I, "I have a premonition that I shall not kill Prince Ernst of Wortumborg at six o'clock to-morrow morning."

"What put that into your head? You are not going to back down, after all, are you?"

"Decidedly not. Something strikes me that I shall miss fire."

"Pshaw!" exclaimed Pembroke. "I have been thinking it over, and I've come to the conclusion that it would not be a bad plan to rid this world of a man like your Prince. It'll all come out right in the end. You will wed the Princess Hildegarde just as sure as—as I will not wed her sister." He spoke the last words rapidly, as though afraid of them.

"I shall never marry the Princess Hildegarde," said I. "She has gone."

"Gone? Where?"

"It matters not where. Suffice it is that she has gone. Pembroke, you and I were very unfortunate fellows. What earthly use have Princesses for you and me? The little knowledge of court we have was gotten out of cheap books and newspaper articles. To talk with Kings and Princesses it requires an innate etiquette which commoners cannot learn. We are not to the manner born. These Princesses are but candles; and now that we have singed our mothy wings, and are crippled so that we may not fly again, let us beware. This may or may not be my last night on earth. . . . Let us go to the opera. Let us be original in all things. I shall pay a prima donna to sing my requiem from the footlights—before I am dead."

"Jack!" cried Pembroke, anxiously.

"Oh, do not worry," said I. "I am only trying to laugh—but I can't!"

"Are you truly serious about going to the opera?" he asked.

"Yes. Hurry and dress," said I.

I leaned against the mantel and stared into the flickering tongues of flame. A caprice? I read the letter again, then threw it into the grate and watched the little darts of light devour it. Now and then a word stood out boldly. Finally the wind carried the brown ashes up the chimney, I would keep the other letter—the one she had asked for—and the withered rose till the earth passed over me. She was a Princess; I was truly an adventurer, a feeble pawn on the chess-board. What had I to do with Kings and bishops and knights? The comedy was about to end—perhaps with a tragedy. I had spoken my few lines and was going behind the scenes out of which I had come. As I waited for Pembroke the past two years went by as in a panorama. I thought of the old lawyer and the thousand-dollar check; the night at the opera with Phyllis; the meeting of Hillars and his story. "When there is nothing more to live for, it is time to die." If there was such a place as Elysium in the nether world, Hillars and I should talk it all over there. It is pleasant to contemplate the fact that when we are dead we shall know "the reason why."

"Come along," said Pembroke, entering.

So we went to the opera. They are full of wonderful scenes, these continental opera houses. Here and there one sees the brilliant uniforms, blue and scarlet and brown, glittering with insignias and softened by furs. Old men with sashes crossing the white bosoms of their linen dominate the boxes, and the beauty of woman is often lost in the sparkle of jewels. And hovering over all is an oppressive fragrance. Pembroke's glasses were roving about. Presently he touched my arm.

"In the upper proscenium," he said.

It was Phyllis. The Chancellor and the Grand Duke of S—
were with her.

"We shall visit her during the first intermission," said I.

"You had better go alone," replied Pembroke. "I haven't
the courage."

The moment the curtain dropped I left the stall. I passed
along the corridor and soon stood outside the box in
which Phyllis sat. I knocked gently.

"Enter!" said a soft voice.

"Ah," said the Chancellor, smiling as he saw me. "Duke, I
believe their Majesties are looking this way. Let us go to
them. I am pleased to see you, Herr Winthrop. Duke, this
is the gentleman who has turned us all upside down."

The Duke bowed, and the two left me alone with Phyllis.

There was an embarrassing silence, but she surmounted it.

"Why have you not been to see me?" she asked. "Are you
done with me now that you have made me a Princess?"

"I did call, but was told that you were indisposed," said I.

"It was because I did not see your card. I shall never be
indisposed to my friends—the old ones. However, they
will be crowding in here shortly. Will you come and see
me at four to-morrow afternoon?"

"Is it important?" I was thinking of the duel when I said
this.

"Very—to you. You have a strange funereal expression

for a man who is about to wed the woman he loves."

"Your sister has left town?" not knowing what else to say.

"Only for a few days; at least so she told me. Have you seen her?"

"No, I have not. A Princess!" dropping into a lighter tone. "You carry your honors well. It was to be expected of you. I might have made you a Queen, but that would not have changed you any."

"Thank you. Do you know, a title is a most wonderful drawing apparatus? Since Thursday it has been a continued performance of presentations. And I care absolutely nothing for it all. Indeed, it rests heavily upon me. I am no longer free. Ah, Jack, and to think that I must blame you! I have been longing all the evening for the little garden at home. Yes, it will always be home to me. I am almost an alien. I would rather sell lemonade to poor reporters who had only twenty-five-cent pieces in their pockets than queen it over a people that do not interest me and with whom I have nothing in common." She smiled, rather sadly, I thought, at the remembrance of that garden scene so long ago.

"Time has a cruel way of moving us around," said I, snapping the clasps on my gloves, and pulling the fingers and looking everywhere but at her. I was wondering if I should ever see her again. "When is the coronation to take place?"

"In June. The King does not wish to hurry me. You see, I must learn to be a Princess first. It was kind of him. And you will be at Hohenphalia to witness the event?"

"If nothing happens. We live in a continual uncertainty."

She regarded me somewhat strangely.

"Is there a significance in that last sentence?"

"No," I answered. I felt compelled to add something. "But here come some of your new admirers. Their glittering medals will make me feel out of place if I remain. I shall do my best to accept your invitation."

"Jack, you are hiding something from me. Are you going to leave the city to search for her?"

"No," said I. "The truth is," with a miserable attempt to smile, "I have an engagement to-morrow morning, and it is impossible to tell how long it will last. Good night."

Fate played loose with me that night. As I was turning down the corridor I ran into the Prince. He was accompanied by Von Walden and an attache whom I knew.

"Good evening," said the Prince. "Do you not prefer the French opera, after all?"

"All good music is the same to me," I answered, calmly returning his amused look with a contemptuous one. "Wagner, Verdi, Gounod, or Bizet, it matters not."

The attache passed some cigarettes. Only the Prince refused.

"No thanks. I am not that kind of a villain." He laughed as he uttered these words, and looked at me.

I would have given much to possess that man's coolness.

"Till we meet again," he said, as I continued on. "Shall I add pleasant dreams?"

"I am obliged to you," I answered over my shoulder, "but I never have them. I sleep too soundly."

"Cousin," said I, later, "what was that opera?"

"I forgot to bring along a program," said Pembroke.

CHAPTER XXIII

When Pembroke and I arrived at the Strasburg inn, on the north road, neither the Prince nor Von Walden were in evidence. I stepped from our carriage and gazed interestedly around me. The scene was a picturesque one. The sun, but half risen, was of a rusty brass, and all east was mottled with purple and salmon hues. The clearing, a quarter of a mile away, where the Prince and I were to settle our dispute, was hidden under a fine white snow; and the barren trees which encircled it stood out blackly. Pembroke looked at his watch.

"They ought to be along soon; it's five after six. How do you feel?" regarding me seriously.

"As nerveless as a rod of steel," I answered. "Let us go in and order a small breakfast. I'm a bit cold."

"Better let it go at a cup of coffee," he suggested.

"It will be more consistent, that is true," I said. "Coffee and pistols for two."

"I'm glad to see that you are bright," said Pembroke. "Hold out your hand."

I did so.

"Good. So long as it doesn't tremble, I have confidence of the end."

We had scarcely finished our coffee when the Prince, followed by Von Walden, entered.

"Pardon me," he said, "for having made you wait."

"Permit me," said I, rising, "to present my second; Mr. Pembroke, His Highness Prince Ernst of Wortumborg."

The two looked into each other's eyes for a space, and the Prince nodded approvingly.

"I have heard of Your Highness," said my cousin, with a peculiar smile.

"Some evil report, I presume?" laughed the Prince.

"Many of them," was the answer.

The Prince showed his teeth. "Count, these Americans are a positive refreshment. I have yet to meet one who is not frankness itself. At your pleasure!"

And the four of us left the inn and crossed the field. The first shot fell to me. Pembroke's eyes beamed with exultant light. Von Walden's face was without expression. As for the Prince, he still wore that bantering smile. He was confident of the end. He knew that I was a tyro, whereas he had faced death many times. I sighed. I knew that I should not aim to take his life. I was absolutely without emotion; there was not the slightest tremble in my hand as I accepted the pistol. There is nothing like set purpose to still the tremors of a man's nerves. I thought of Hillars, and for a moment my arm stiffened; then I recalled Gretchen's last letter. . . . I fell to wondering where the bullet would hit me. I prayed that his aim might be sure.

"Many persons think that I am a man without compassion," said the Prince, as we were about to step to our places. "I have an abundance of it. You have everything to lose, and I have nothing to gain. If it is your desire, I shall be happy to explain that you wish to withdraw. But say the word."

He knew what my reply would be. "Withdraw," said I, "and have you laugh at me and tell your friends that I acted the poltroon? Really, you do me injustice."

"And do you hate me so very much?" mockery in his eyes.

"Not now. I did hate you, but hatred is a thing we should not waste any more than love. I have taken the bird and the nest from your hands; that is more than enough. You are merely an object for scorn and contempt and indifference now. No; I have no wish to withdraw."

"You read between the lines," he said. "Indeed, I should like nothing better than to have the privilege of calling you a poltroon and a coward and to tell your Princess of it." He sauntered back to his place leisurely.

"Aim the slightest to the left," whispered Pembroke; "the wind will carry it home."

I pressed his hand. A moment later I stood facing the Prince. I lifted the pistol and fired. Had the Prince been ten feet to the right he must have been hit. I threw the smoking pistol aside, let my arms fall and waited. I could see that Pembroke was biting his lip to hide his anxiety and disappointment. Slowly the Prince leveled the weapon at my breast. Naturally I shut my eyes. Perhaps there was a prayer on my lips. God! how long that wait seemed to me. It became so tedious that I opened my eyes again. The pistol arm of the Prince appeared to have frozen in the air.

"It is getting cold," I cried. "Shoot, for God's sake shoot, and end it!"

In reply the Prince fired into the air, took the pistol by the barrel and flung it at my feet. The rest of us looked on dumfounded.

"They are all of the same kidney, Count, these Americans," said he. "They would be dangerous as a nation were it not for their love of money." Then to me: "Go tell your Princess that I have given your life to you."

"The devil take you!" I cried. The strain had been terrible.

"All in good time," retorted the Prince, getting into his coat and furs. "Yesterday morning I had every intention of killing you; this morning it was farthest from my thoughts, though I did hope to see you waver. You are a man of courage. So was your friend. It is to be regretted that we were on different sides. Devil take the women; good morning!"

After the Count had gathered up the pistols, the two walked toward the inn. Pembroke and I followed them at a distance.

"I wonder if he had any idea of what a poor shot you were?" mused Pembroke. "It was a very good farce."

"I aimed ten feet to the right," said I.

Harold MacGrath

"What?"

"Yes."

"Then you knew—"

"Pembroke," said I, "I had no intention of killing him, or even wounding him. And I never expected to leave this place alive. Something has occurred during the last twenty-four hours which we do not understand."

"He was taking great risks."

"It shows the man he is," said I; and the remainder of the distance was gone in silence.

The carriages were in the road, a short way from the inn. Pembroke and I got into ours. As the Prince placed a foot on the step of his he turned once more to me.

"Pardon me," he said, "but I came near forgetting to tell you why I did not kill you this morning. In some way your Princess came into the knowledge that we were going to fight it out as they did in the old days. She came to my rooms, and there begged me to spare your life. There was a condition. It was that she get down on her knees to sue—down on her knees. Ah, what was your life compared to the joy of her humiliation! Not in the figure of speech—on her living, mortal knees, my friend—her living knees!" The carriage door banged behind him.

It was only because Pembroke threw his arms around me that I did not leap out of the carriage.

"Sit still, Jack, sit still! If she begged your life, it was because she loves you."

And, full of rage, I saw the carriage of the Prince vanish. As the carriage vanished, so vanished the Prince from the scene of my adventures. It was but recently that I read of his marriage to the daughter of a millionaire money lender; and, unlike the villain in the drama, pursues the even tenor of his way, seemingly forgotten by retribution, which often hangs fire while we live.

"There are some curious people in this world," said Pembroke, when he had succeeded in quieting me.

I had no argument to offer. After a time I said: "To-morrow, cousin, we shall return to America, our native land. When we are older it will be pleasant to recount our adventures."

Arriving at our rooms, we found them in possession of a lieutenant of the guard hussars. He was drumming on the hearthstone with the end of his sword scabbard. As we entered he rose and briefly saluted us.

"Which of you two gentlemen is Herr Winthrop?" he asked.

"I am he," said I.

"His Majesty commands your immediate presence at the palace."

"The King?"

"Yes."

"Have you any idea what his desires are?"

"A soldier never presumes to know His Majesty's desires, only his commands. Let us begone at once, sir. I have been waiting for an hour. His Majesty likes dispatch."

"It cannot be anything serious," said I to Pembroke, who wore a worried frown.

Perhaps the King had heard of the duel. I was in a mood to care but little what the King had heard, or what he was going to do. The thing uppermost in my mind was that Gretchen had begged my life of the Prince—and then run away!

At the palace the Chancellor met me in the anteroom. His face was grave almost to gloominess.

"Have you ever seen a King angry?" he asked. "Ah, it is not a pleasant sight, on my word; least of all, to the one who has caused a King's anger."

"You alarm me," I said. "Have I done aught to bring the anger of the King upon my head?"

"Ah, but you have! The King is like a bear in his den. He walks back and forth, waving his hands, pulling his mustache and muttering dire threats."

"Might I not take to my legs?" I asked. After all, I cared more than I thought I should in regard to what the King might do to me.

The Chancellor gave my back a sounding thump, and roared with laughter.

"Cheerful, my son; be cheerful! You are a favorite already."

"You bewilder me."

"You have powerful friends; and if the King is angry you need have no fear."

"I should like to know—" I began.

"Ah!" interrupted the Chancellor, "the audience is ended; it is our turn. The Austrian Ambassador," he whispered as a gray-haired man passed us, bowing. There was an exchange of courtesies, and once more I stood before the King.

"I believe you have kept me waiting," said the King, "as Louis once said." He gazed at me from under knotted eyebrows. "I wish," petulantly, "that you had remained in your own country."

"So do I, Your Majesty," I replied honestly. The Chancellor shook with laughter, and the King glared at him furiously.

"What is your name?" asked the King in a milder tone. He was holding a missive in his hand.

"John Winthrop," I answered. I was wondering what it was all about.

"Were you born in America?"

"Yes, Your Majesty."

"Is your family an honored one in your country?"

"It is," I answered proudly.

"Then, why in heaven's name do you scribble?" cried the King.

"In my country one may have an honored name and still be compelled to earn a competence."

"Ah, yes! After all, scribbling is better than owning a shop." This is the usual argument of Kings. "Can you trace your pedigree very far back?" the King proceeded.

"My ancestors came over in the Mayflower," said I.

"The Mayflower?" said the King, puzzled.

"All the Americans," explained the Chancellor, "went over in the Mayflower. The ark and the Mayflower were the largest ships ever put to sea, Your Majesty." To hide his smile, the Chancellor passed over to the window and began drawing pictures on the frosted panes.

Continued the King: "If you loved one of my country-women, would you be willing to sacrifice your own country? I mean, would you be willing to adopt mine, to become a naturalized citizen, to uphold its laws, to obey the will of its sovereign, and to take up arms in its defense?"

My knees began to knock together. "I should be willing," I answered, "if I should never be called upon to bear arms against the country in which I was born."

"I should never ask you to do that," replied the King.

"No; His Majesty has too wholesome a respect for America," the Chancellor interpolated.

"Prince," said the King, "go and finish your window panes."

The Chancellor meekly obeyed.

"This is your answer?" said the King to me.

"Yes, Your Majesty."

"Then marry the Princess Elizabeth," he said, tossing the missive to me.

"Yes, marry her," said the irrepressible Chancellor; "and some day the King will put a medal on your breast and make you a baron of the realm. Your Majesty, come and help me with this last pane."

The Princess Elizabeth? I glanced at the writing on the envelope. It was Gretchen's. "And, Your Majesty," I read, "it is true that they love each other. Permit them to be happy. I ask your forgiveness for all the trouble I have caused you. I promise that from now on I shall be the most obedient subject in all your kingdom. Hildegarde." I dropped the letter on the table.

"Your Majesty," I began nervously, "there is some mistake. I do not love Her Highness the Princess Elizabeth."

The King and his Chancellor whirled around. The decorations on the panes remained unfinished. The King regarded me with true anger, and the Chancellor with dismay.

"I love the Princess Hildegarde," I went on in a hollow voice.

"Is this a jest?" demanded the King.

"No; on my honor." For once I forgot court etiquette, and left off "Your Majesty."

"Let me see the letter," said the Chancellor, with a pacific purpose. "There is some misunderstanding here." He read the letter and replaced it on the table—and went back to his window.

"Well?" cried the King, impatiently.

"I forgot, Your Majesty," said the Chancellor.

"Forgot what?"

"The letter was written by a woman. I remember when I was a boy," went on the Chancellor tranquilly, "I used to take great pleasure in drawing pictures on frosted window panes. Women always disturbed me."

"Perhaps, Your Majesty," said I, "it is possible that Her Highness . . . the likeness between her and her sister . . . perhaps, knowing that I have known Her Highness Phyllis . . . that is, the Princess Elizabeth . . . she may believe that I . . ." It was very embarrassing.

"Continue," said the King. "And please make your sentences intelligible."

"What I meant to say was that Her Highness the Princess Hildegarde, believes that I love her sister instead of herself . . . I thought . . . she has written otherwise . . ." And then I foundered again.

"Prince," said the King, laughing in spite of his efforts to appear angry, "for pity's sake, tell me what this man is talking about!"

"A woman," said the Chancellor. "Perhaps Her Highness the Princess Hildegarde. . . . That is, I believe. . . . She may love this man . . . perhaps thinking he loves the other. . ." He was mocking me, and my face burned.

"Prince, do not confuse the man; he is bad enough as it is." The King smoothed away the remnant of the smile.

"Your Majesty is right," said I, desperately. "I am confused. I know not what to say."

"What would you do in my place?" asked the King of the Chancellor.

"I should say in an ominous voice, 'Young man, you may go; but if you ever enter our presence again without either one or the other of the Hohenphalian Princesses as your wife, we shall confiscate your property and put you in a dungeon for the remainder of your natural days.' I put in the confiscation clause as a matter of form. Have you any property?"

"What I have," I answered, my confidence returning, "I can put in my pockets."

"Good," said the King. "What the Chancellor says is but just. See to it that his directions are followed."

"Now, my King," concluded the Chancellor, "put a medal on him and let him go."

"In time," replied the King. "You may go, Herr Winthrop."

"Go and scribble no more," added the Chancellor.

I could hear them laughing as I made my escape from the room. It could not be expected of me to join them. And Gretchen was as far away as ever. Phyllis love me? It was absurd. Gretchen had played me the fool. She had been laughing at me all the time. Yet, she had begged my life of the Prince, and on her knees. Or, was it a lie of his? Oh, it seemed to me that my brain would never become clear again.

In the afternoon at four I was ushered into the boudoir of Her Highness the Princess Elizabeth. It was Phyllis no longer; Phyllis had passed; and I became conscious of a vague regret.

"I am glad," she said, "that you were able to come. I wanted to speak to you about—about my sister."

"Your Highness—"

She laughed. "Our interview shall end at once if you call me by that title. Sir," with a gaiety which struck me as unnatural, "you are witnessing the passing of Phyllis. It will not be long before she shall pass away and never more return, and the name shall fade till it becomes naught but a dear memory. Phyllis has left the green pastures for the city, and Corydon followeth not."

"Phyllis," said I, "you are cutting me to the heart."

"But to the matter at hand," she said quickly. "There is a misunderstanding between you and my sister Hildegarde. She sent me this letter. Read it."

It differed but little from the one I had read in the King's chamber that morning. I gave it back to her.

"Do you understand?"

"I confess that I do not. It seems that I am never going to understand anything again."

Phyllis balanced the letter on the palm of her hand. "You are so very blind, my dear friend. Did you not tell her that there had been another affair? Do you not believe she thinks your regard for her merely a matter of pique, of consolation? It was very kind of her to sacrifice herself for me. Some women are willing to give up all to see the man they love made happy. My sister is one of those. But I shall refuse the gift. Jack, can you not see that the poor woman thinks that you love me?" Phyllis was looking at me with the greatest possible kindness.

"I know not what she thinks. I only know that she has written me that she is sorry for having played with my affections. Phyllis, if she loved me she would not leave me as she has done."

"Oh, these doubting Thomases!" exclaimed Phyllis. "How do you know that she does not love you? Have you one true proof that she does not? No; but you have a hundred that she does."

"But—"

"Do you love her?" demanded Phyllis, stamping her foot with impatience.

"Love her? Have I not told you that I do?" gloomily.

"And will you give her up because she writes you a letter? What has ink to do with love and a woman? If you do not set out at once to find her, I shall never forgive you. She is my sister, and by that I know that you cannot win her by sitting still. Go find her and tell her that you will never leave her till she is your wife. I do not mean to infer," with a smile, "that you will leave her after. Go to her as a master; that is the way a woman loves to be wooed. Marry her and be happy; and I shall come and say, 'Heaven bless you, my children.' I have accepted the renunciation of her claims so that she may be free to wed you. If you do not find her, I will. Since I have her promise to teach me the lesson of being a Princess, she cannot have gone far. And when you are married you will promise to visit me often? I shall be very lonely now; I shall be far away from my friends; I shall be in a prison, and men call it a palace."

"I will promise you anything you may ask," I said eagerly. A new hope and a new confidence had risen in my heart. I wonder where man got the idea that he is lord of creation when he depends so much upon woman? "And you will really be my sister, too!" taking her hands and kissing them. "And you will think of me a little, will you not?"

"Yes." She slowly withdrew her hands. "If you do not find her, write to me."

"Your Highness, it is my hope that some day you will meet a Prince who will be worthy of you, who will respect and honor you as I do."

"Who can say? You have promised the King to become a subject of Hohenphalia."

"Yes."

"Then you will be a subject of mine. It is my will—I am in a sovereign mood—that you at once proceed to find Hildegarde, and I will give her to you."

We had arrived at the head of the stairs. The departing light of the smoldering sun poured through the stained windows. The strands of her hair were like a thousand flames, and her eyes had turned to gold, and there was a smile on her lips which filled me with strange uneasiness. I kissed her hands again, then went down the stairs. At the foot I turned.

"Auf wiedersehen!"

"Good-by!"

My ear detected the barest falter in her voice, and something glistened on her eyelashes. . . . Ah! why could not the veil have remained before my eyes and let me gone in darkness? Suddenly I was looking across the chasm of years. There was a young girl in white, a table upon which stood a pitcher. It was a garden scene, and the air was rich with perfumes. The girl's hair and eyes were brown, and there were promises of great beauty. Then, as swiftly as it came, the vision vanished.

On reaching the street I was aware that my sight had grown dim and that things at a distance were blurred. Perhaps it was the cold air.

Harold MacGrath

CHAPTER XXIV

Immediately Pembroke and I journeyed to the feudal inn. When we arrived a mixture of rain and snow was falling. But I laughed at that. What if I were drenched to the skin with chill rain and snow, my heart was warm, warmer than it had been in many a day. Woman is infallible when she reads the heart of another. Phyllis said that Gretchen loved me; it only remained for me to find her. Pembroke began to grumble.

"I am wet through," he said, as our steaming horses plodded along in the melting snow. "You might have waited till the rain let up."

"I'm just as wet as you are," I replied, "but I do not care."

"I'm hungry and cold, too," he went on.

"I'm not, so it doesn't matter."

"Of course not!" he cried. "What are my troubles to you?"

"Nothing!" I laughed and shook the flakes from my sleeves. "Cousin, I am the happiest man in the world."

"And I'm the most dismal," said he. "I wish you had brought along an umbrella."

"What! Ride a horse with an umbrella over you? Where is your sense of romance?"

"Romance is all well enough," said he, "when your stomach is full and your hide is dry. If you can call this romance, this five-mile ride through rain and snow, you are gifted with a wonderful imagination."

"It is beautiful here in the summer," defensively.

"I wish you had waited till then, or brought a mackintosh. Your Princess would have kept." He shoved his head deeper into his collar, and began to laugh. "This is the discomfort man will go through for love. If she is a true woman she will feed you first and explain afterward. But, supposing she is not here?"

"Where else can she be?" I asked.

"The world is very large—when a woman runs away from you."

This set me thinking. If she shouldn't be there! I set my teeth and gave the horse a cut, sending him into a gallop, which I forced him to maintain till the end. At length we turned into the roadway. A man I had never seen before came out.

"Where is the innkeeper?" I asked, my heart sinking.

"He is not here," was the answer,

"Is Her Highness the Princess Hildegarde—"

"Her Highness?" he cried, in astonishment. "She has never been here. This is an inn; the castle is in the village."

"How long have you been here?" asked Pembroke.

"Two weeks, Your Highness." Doubtless he thought us to be high personages to be inquiring for the Princess.

"Is Stahlberg here?" I asked.

"He is visiting relatives in Coberg," was the answer.

"Do you know where Her Highness is?"

"No." It occurred to me that his voice had taken to sullen tones.

"When will the innkeeper be back?"

The fellow shrugged his shoulders. "I cannot say, Your Highness. The inn is not open for guests till March."

"Jack," said Pembroke in English, "it is evident that this fellow has been instructed to be close-lipped. Let us return to the village. The castle is left." He threw some coins to the servant and they rattled along the porch. "Come." And we wheeled and trotted away.

I cannot tell how great was my disappointment, nor what I did or said. The ride back to the village was a dreary affair so far as conversation went. At the castle we found not a soul.

"It is as I expected," said Pembroke. "Remember that Her Highness is accustomed to luxury, and that it is not likely for her to spend her winter in such a deserted place. You're a newspaper man; you ought to be full of resources. Why don't you telegraph to all the news agencies and make inquiries? She is a personage, and it will not be difficult to find her if you go at it the right way."

I followed his advice, and the first return brought me news. Gretchen was at present in Vienna. So we journeyed to Vienna, futilely. Then commenced a dogged, persistent search. I dragged my cousin hither and thither about the kingdom; from village to train, from train to city, till his life became a burden to him and his patience threadbare. At Hohenphalia, the capital, we were treated coldly; we were not known; they were preparing the palace for the coronation of Her Serene Highness the Princess Elizabeth; the Princess Hildegarde might be in Brussels. At Brussels Her Highness was in Munich, at Munich she was in Heidelberg, and so on and so on. It was truly discouraging. The vaguest rumor brought me to the railway, Pembroke, laughing and grumbling, always at my heels. At last I wrote to Phyllis; it was the one hope left. Her reply was to the effect that she, too, did not know where her sister was, that she was becoming a puzzle to her, and concluded with the advice to wait till the coronation, when Gretchen would put in appearance, her presence being imperative. So weeks multiplied and became months, winter passed, the snows fell from the mountains, the floods rose and subsided, summer was at hand with her white boughs and green grasses. May was blooming into June. Still Gretchen remained in obscurity. Sometimes in my despair I regretted having loved her, and half resolved to return to Phyllis, where (and I flushed at the thought!) I could find comfort and consolation. And yet—and yet!

"I shall be a physical wreck," said Pembroke, when we finally returned to B—, "if you keep this up much longer."

"Look at me!" was my gloomy rejoinder.

"Well, you have that interesting pallor," he admitted, "which women ascribe to lovers."

Thrusting my elbows on the table, I buried my chin in my hands and stared. After a while I said: "I do not believe she wants to be found."

"That has been my idea this long while," he replied, "only I did not wish to make you more despondent than you were."

So I became resigned—as an animal becomes resigned to its cage. I resolved to tear her image from my heart, to go with Pembroke to the jungles and shoot tigers; to return in some dim future bronzed, gray-haired and noted. For above all things I intended to get at my books again, to make romances instead of living them.

There were times when I longed to go to Phyllis and confide my troubles to her, but a certain knowledge held me back.

One morning, when I had grown outwardly calm, I said to Pembroke: "Philip, I shall go with you to India."

"Here is a letter for you," he replied; "it may change your plans."

My mail, since leaving the journalistic field, had become so small that to receive a letter was an event. As I stretched forth a hand for the letter my outward calm passed swiftly, and my heart spoke in a voice of thunder. I could not recall the chirography on the envelope. The hand, I judged, which had held the pen was more familiar with flays and scythes. Inside of the envelope I discovered only six words, but they meant all the world to me. "She is here at the inn." It was unsigned. I waved the slip of paper before Pembroke's eyes.

"She is found!" I cried.

"Then go in search of her," he said.

"And you will go with me?"

"Not I! I prefer tigers to princesses. By the way, here is an article in the Zeitung on the coming coronation of Her Serene Highness the Princess Elizabeth of Hohenphalia. I'm afraid that I shan't be present to witness the event." He thrust the paper into my hands and approached the window, out of which he leaned and stared at the garden flowers below. . . . "When I asked her why it could not be, she answered that she had no love to give in return for mine." Presently he rapped his pipe on the sill and drew in his head. His brow was wrinkled and his lips were drawn down at the corners. With some shame I remembered that I had thought only of myself during the past few months. "Jack," he said, "I have gone around with you for the excitement of it, for the temporary forgetfulness, and because I wanted to see you well cared for before I left you. The excitement took my mind from my own malady, but it has returned to-day with all its old violence. There is the same blood in our veins. We must have one woman or none. I must get away from all this. We are at the parting of the ways, old man. To-night I leave for India. The jungle is a great place. I am glad for your sake that you are not to go with me. Sometimes one gets lost."

"She may change her mind," I said, putting a hand on his. "Most women do."

"Most admit of exceptions," he replied, regarding me with earnest eyes as if to read what was going on behind mine. "There are some women who never change. Her Highness

Harold MacGrath

is one of these. As I remarked before, she has no love to give me; it is gone, and as it is gone without reward, she will make no attempt to recall it to give to another. I love her all the more for that. The game fate plays with our hearts is a cruel one. For one affinity there are ten unfinished lives. Her Highness loves a good man."

My hand fell from his, and I went over to the window. This was the first intimation he had given to me that he knew the secret, the secret which had made me so sad, the secret which I tried not to believe.

"You are determined to go to India?" I said, without turning my head. I could find no other words.

"Yes. It will be the best thing in the world."

"You will promise to write?"

"Whenever I strike the post. Marry and be happy; it is the lot of the few."

That night he started for Bombay, by the way of England, and the next morning I put out for the feudal inn.

CHAPTER XXV

I was passing along the highway, a pipe between my teeth. It was the beginning of twilight, that trysting hour of all our reveries, when the old days come back with a perfume as sweet and vague as that which hovers over a jar of spiced rose leaves. I was thinking of the year which was gone; how I first came to the inn; of the hour when I first held her in my arms and kissed her, and vowed my love to her; of the parting, when she of her own will had thrown her arms about my neck and confessed. The shadows were thickening on the ground, and the voices of the forests were hushed. I glanced at the western sky. It was like a frame of tarnished gold, waiting for night with her diadem of stars to step within. The purple hills were wrapping themselves in robes of pearly mists; the flowing river was tinted with dun and vermilion; and one by one the brilliant planets burst through the darkening blues of the heavens. The inn loomed up against the sky, gray and lonely. Behind me, far away down the river, I could catch occasional glimpses of the lamps of the village. Presently there came a faint yellow glow in the east, and I knew that Diana was approaching.

> She tosses loose her locks upon the night,
> And, through the dim wood Dian threads her way.

A wild sweetness filled the air. I was quite half a mile

Harold MacGrath

from the inn, yet I could smell the odor of her roses, Gretchen's roses. It was a long and weary year which had intervened. And now she was there, only a short way from my arms. But she did not know that I was coming. A million diamonds sprang into the air whenever I struck the lush grasses with my cane. Everywhere I breathed the perfume of her roses. They seemed to hide along the hedges, to lurk among the bushes, red roses and white. On the hill, across the valley, I saw the little cemetery with its white stones. I arrested my steps and took off my hat. The dust of Hillars lay there. I stood motionless for some time. I had loved the man as it is possible for one man to love another. I had not thought of him much of late; but in this life we cannot always stand by the grave of those who have gone before. He had loved Gretchen with a love perhaps less selfish than mine, for he had sacrificed his life uselessly for her that she might—be mine! Mine! I thought. And who was I that she should love me instead of him? All the years I had known him I had known but little of him. God only knows the hearts of these men who rove or drift, who, anchorless and rudderless, beat upon the ragged reels of life till the breath leaves them and they pass through the mystic channel into the serene harbor of eternity. A sudden wave of dissatisfaction swept over me. What had I done in the world to merit attention? What had I done that I, and not he, should know the love of woman? Why should I live to-day and not he? From out the silence there came no answer; and I continued on. It was life. It was immutable, and there was no key.

The lights of the inn cheered me and lifted the gloom. Should I enter by stealth or boldly? I chose the second method. Gretchen and the innkeeper were in the old hall. I entered and threw my traps into a corner. As they turned and saw me consternation was written on their faces.

"I have found you at last," I said, holding out a hand to

each of them. The innkeeper thrust his hands behind his back and sauntered leisurely toward the window. Gretchen showed signs of embarrassment, and her eyes were studiously fixed on the cracks which yawned here and there in the floor. My hands fell unnoticed.

"You have been looking for us?" she asked in even tones. "Why have you?"

Vaguely I gazed at her, at the innkeeper, then at my traps in the corner. It was apparent that I was an intruder. I struck my forehead in anger and despair. Triple fool that I was! I was nothing to her. She had told me so, and I had not believed.

"Yes; why?" asked the innkeeper, turning around.

"I believe," said I, my voice trembling, "that I am an unwelcome guest. Is it not so?"

"Oh, as for that," said the innkeeper, observing Gretchen, "this is a public inn, on the highway. All wayfarers are of necessity welcome."

"Go, then, and prepare me a supper," said I. "I am indeed hungry, having journeyed far." I wanted him out of the room.

The innkeeper appeared not to have the slightest intention of leaving the room to do my bidding.

"Yes, Hermann," said Gretchen, coloring, "go and prepare Herr Winthrop's supper."

"Thank you," said I, with a dismal effort to be ironical.

The innkeeper, a puzzling smile on his lips, passed out.

"Gretchen," I burst forth, "in heaven's name what does this mean? I have hunted for you day after day, week after week, month after month. I have traveled the four ends of the continent. I have lived—Oh, I do not know how I have lived! And when I do find you, it is for this!" My voice broke, and I was positively on the verge of tears.

"And was all this fair to her?" asked Gretchen, coldly.

"To her? I do not understand."

"I mean, was all this fair to my sister?"

"Gretchen," a light piercing the darkness, "has she not written to you?"

"A long time ago. She wanted to see me on an important matter, but I could not change my plans at the time. I shall see her at the palace next week. Ought you not to be with her instead of here?"

"Why should I be with her?"

Gretchen laughed, but the key was false.

"Are you not going to marry her? Surely, it is easy after the King has given his permission. Have you already fallen out of love with her, after all your efforts to make her a Princess? Truly, man is as unstable as sand and water! Ah, but you fooled us all to the top of our bent. You knew from the first that she was a Princess; but you could not find the proofs. Hermann and I were the means to the end. But who shall blame you? Not I! I am very grateful to you for having given to me a sister. And if you fooled me, I returned measure for measure. It is game and quit. Time hung heavy on my hands, and the victory, however short, was amusing."

"I never loved her!" I cried. Where were the words I needed?

"So much the worse for you," disdainfully. "But here comes Hermann to announce your supper."

"I shall not break the bread of inhospitality," said I, in the bitterness of my despair. I gathered up my traps—and then I let them tumble back. The needed words came with a rush to my lips. I went close to her. "Why did you humiliate yourself in begging my life of the Prince? Why, if my life was nothing to you? Answer. Why did you stoop to your knees to that man if I was worthless to you? Why?"

Her cheeks grew red, then white; her lips formed words which she could not speak.

"Herr Winthrop's supper is ready," announced the innkeeper.

"Go and eat it!" I said childishly.

"Your appetite is gone then?" imperturbably.

"Yes, and get you gone with it!"

The innkeeper surveyed me for a space. "Will you kindly tell me from whom you received the information that Her Highness was at the inn?"

I produced the unsigned letter. He read it carefully, while Gretchen looked on nervously.

"Ach!" said the innkeeper, "that Stahlberg! He shall be dismissed."

Unhappily for him, that individual was just passing along the corridor. The innkeeper signaled him to approach.

"How dared you?" began the innkeeper, thrusting the letter under Stahlberg's nose.

"Dare?—I?—Herr," said the big fellow, "I do not understand. What is it you accuse me of?"

"This," cried the innkeeper: "You have written to Herr Winthrop and told him that Her Highness was at the inn. And you were expressly forbidden to do so."

Stahlberg looked around blankly. "I swear to heaven, Herr—"

"Do not prevaricate!" the innkeeper interrupted. "You know that you wrote this."

"Stahlberg," I cried excitedly; "tell me why you wrote this note to me and I'll see that you are taken care of the rest of your days."

"I forbid him!" commanded Gretchen in alarm.

"As God hears me, Herr," said Stahlberg stoutly. "I wrote not a line to you or to any one."

"Oh!" cried the innkeeper, stamping. "And you deny that you have written here that you saw Her Highness in the garden three nights ago?"

Gretchen was beginning to grow terrified for some reason. I myself was filled with wonder, knowing well enough that nothing about a garden had been written in the note I had received.

"Do you dare deny," went on the implacable old man, "that you have written here that you saw Her Highness in the garden, and that she was weeping and murmuring this man's name?"

"Oh!" cried Gretchen, gazing wildly at the door.

The innkeeper suddenly took the bewildered giant by the shoulders and pushed him from the room, following him swiftly; and the door closed noisily behind them.

My heart was in flames. I understood all now, though I dare say Gretchen didn't. All at once, her head fell on the back of the chair from which she had but lately risen. She was weeping silently and deeply. I did not move, but stood watching her, drinking in with exultation the loveliness of a woman in tears. She was mine, mine, mine! The innkeeper had not really known her heart till the night in the garden to which he so adroitly referred; then he had made up his mind that things were not as they should be, and had sent me that anonymous note. Mine at last, I thought. Somehow, for the first time in my life I felt what is called masterful; that is to say, not all heaven and earth should take her away from me now. Softly I passed over to her side and knelt at her feet. I lifted the hem of her gown and pressed it to my lips.

"My Princess!" I murmured, "all mine." I kissed her unresisting hand. Then I rose and put my arms around her. She trembled but made no effort to withdraw. "I swear to you, Gretchen, that I will never leave you again, not if the King should send an army against me, which he will never do, since he has commanded that I marry you. Beware! It is a dangerous thing to trifle with a King's will. And then, even if the King should change his mind, I should not. You are mine. I should like to know if I haven't won you! Oh, they do well to call you Princess

Harold MacGrath

Caprice. Oh, Gretchen," falling back to humble tones, "what a weary year has been wasted. You know that I love you; you have never really doubted it; you know that you have not. Had you gone to your sister when she wrote to you, she would have told you that it was for you alone that I made her a Princess; that all my efforts were to make you free to wed. Gretchen, you will not send me away this time, will you? You will be kind and bid me to stay?"

"She loves you," whispered Gretchen.

This admitted no reply. I simply pressed my lips to her hair. The sobs were growing audibly less.

"I read it in her eyes," persisted Gretchen.

"Gretchen, answer me: do you love me?"

"Yes."

I placed my hands against her temples, and turned her head around so that those blue-green eyes, humid and tearful, looked into mine.

"Oh, I cannot deny it. If I wrong her in accepting your love, it is because I cannot help it. I love you better than all the world; so well do I love you that—" Her head sank on my heart, and her sobs began afresh.

"That what, Gretchen?" I asked.

"Nothing." By and by she said; "Keep faith with me, and I promise to love as few women can."

Then I kissed her lips. "Gretchen?"

"What is it?"

"I have an idea that we shall be very happy. Now let us go and make terms of peace with the innkeeper."

We found him alone in the barroom.

"Gretchen," said I, "read this note."

As her eyes ran over those six words, she blushed.

"Hermann," she said, "you have betrayed me."

"And when will Your Highness order me out to be shot?" asked he, smiling.

"At sunrise; but I shall blindfold the soldiers and take the charges from their guns. I forgive you."

"Now, Hermann," said I, "fill me up a stein." I held it high above my head. "A health! Long live the King! Long live Her Serene Highness the Princess—"

"Elizabeth," said Gretchen, gently. "I fear she has lost something which is never to be found again."

I drained the stein, and as I set it down I thought: Phyllis is so far away and Gretchen is so near!

"Let us go into the garden," said I.

For a long time we wandered here and there, saying nothing. I was thinking that I had found a castle at last which neither tides nor winds nor sudden awakenings could tumble down.

"Gretchen, you must never take up the sword again."

Harold MacGrath

"Only in my lord's defence." From the movement of her arm, which clung to mine, I knew that she was laughing.

The moon had risen, the round and mellow moon of summer. The silver mists of night wavered and sailed through the aisles of the forests, and from the river came the cool fresh perfume of the river rush.

"And so you really love me?" I asked.

"I do."

"Why do you love me?"

"Because," said Gretchen.

ABOUT THE AUTHOR

Harold MacGrath (September 4, 1871 - October 30, 1932) was a bestselling American novelist, short story writer, and screenwriter.

Also known occasionally as Harold McGrath, he was born in Syracuse, New York. As a young man, he worked as a reporter and columnist on the Syracuse Herald newspaper until the late 1890s when he published his first novel, a romance titled "Arms and the Woman." According to the New York Times, his next book, "The Puppet Crown," was the No.7 bestselling book in the United States for all of 1901. From that point on, MacGrath never looked back, writing novels for the mass market about love, adventure, mystery, spies, and the like at an average rate of more than one a year. He would have three more of his books that were among the top ten bestselling books of the year. At the same time, he penned a number of short stories for major American magazines such as The Saturday Evening Post, Ladies Home Journal, and Red Book magazine. Several of MacGrath's novels were serialized in these magazines and contributing to them was something he would continue to do until his death in 1932.

In 1912, Harold MacGrath became one of the first nationally-known authors to write directly for the movies when he was hired by the American Film Company to do the screenplay for a short film in the Western genre titled "The Vengeance That Failed."

Choose from Thousands of 1stWorldLibrary Classics By

A. M. Barnard
Ada Leverson
Adolphus William Ward
Aesop
Agatha Christie
Alexander Aaronsohn
Alexander Kielland
Alexandre Dumas
Alfred Gatty
Alfred Ollivant
Alice Duer Miller
Alice Turner Curtis
Alice Dunbar
Allen Chapman
Alleyne Ireland
Ambrose Bierce
Amelia E. Barr
Amory H. Bradford
Andrew Lang
Andrew McFarland Davis
Andy Adams
Angela Brazil
Anna Alice Chapin
Anna Sewell
Annie Besant
Annie Hamilton Donnell
Annie Payson Call
Annie Roe Carr
Annonaymous
Anton Chekhov
Archibald Lee Fletcher
Arnold Bennett
Arthur C. Benson
Arthur Conan Doyle
Arthur M. Winfield
Arthur Ransome
Arthur Schnitzler
Arthur Train
Atticus
B.H. Baden-Powell
B. M. Bower
B. C. Chatterjee
Baroness Emmuska Orczy
Baroness Orczy
Basil King
Bayard Taylor
Ben Macomber
Bertha Muzzy Bower
Bjornstjerne Bjornson

Booth Tarkington
Boyd Cable
Bram Stoker
C. Collodi
C. E. Orr
C. M. Ingleby
Carolyn Wells
Catherine Parr Traill
Charles A. Eastman
Charles Amory Beach
Charles Dickens
Charles Dudley Warner
Charles Farrar Browne
Charles Ives
Charles Kingsley
Charles Klein
Charles Hanson Towne
Charles Lathrop Pack
Charles Romyn Dake
Charles Whibley
Charles Willing Beale
Charlotte M. Braeme
Charlotte M. Yonge
Charlotte Perkins Stetson
Clair W. Hayes
Clarence Day Jr.
Clarence E. Mulford
Clemence Housman
Confucius
Coningsby Dawson
Cornelis DeWitt Wilcox
Cyril Burleigh
D. H. Lawrence
Daniel Defoe
David Garnett
Dinah Craik
Don Carlos Janes
Donald Keyhoe
Dorothy Kilner
Dougan Clark
Douglas Fairbanks
E. Nesbit
E. P. Roe
E. Phillips Oppenheim
E. S. Brooks
Earl Barnes
Edgar Rice Burroughs
Edith Van Dyne
Edith Wharton

Edward Everett Hale
Edward J. O'Biren
Edward S. Ellis
Edwin L. Arnold
Eleanor Atkins
Eleanor Hallowell Abbott
Eliot Gregory
Elizabeth Gaskell
Elizabeth McCracken
Elizabeth Von Arnim
Ellem Key
Emerson Hough
Emilie F. Carlen
Emily Bronte
Emily Dickinson
Enid Bagnold
Enilor Macartney Lane
Erasmus W. Jones
Ernie Howard Pie
Ethel May Dell
Ethel Turner
Ethel Watts Mumford
Eugene Sue
Eugenie Foa
Eugene Wood
Eustace Hale Ball
Evelyn Everett-green
Everard Cotes
F. H. Cheley
F. J. Cross
F. Marion Crawford
Fannie E. Newberry
Federick Austin Ogg
Ferdinand Ossendowski
Fergus Hume
Florence A. Kilpatrick
Fremont B. Deering
Francis Bacon
Francis Darwin
Frances Hodgson Burnett
Frances Parkinson Keyes
Frank Gee Patchin
Frank Harris
Frank Jewett Mather
Frank L. Packard
Frank V. Webster
Frederic Stewart Isham
Frederick Trevor Hill
Frederick Winslow Taylor

Friedrich Kerst
Friedrich Nietzsche
Fyodor Dostoyevsky
G.A. Henty
G.K. Chesterton
Gabrielle E. Jackson
Garrett P. Serviss
Gaston Leroux
George A. Warren
George Ade
Geroge Bernard Shaw
George Cary Eggleston
George Durston
George Ebers
George Eliot
George Gissing
George MacDonald
George Meredith
George Orwell
George Sylvester Viereck
George Tucker
George W. Cable
George Wharton James
Gertrude Atherton
Gordon Casserly
Grace E. King
Grace Gallatin
Grace Greenwood
Grant Allen
Guillermo A. Sherwell
Gulielma Zollinger
Gustav Flaubert
H. A. Cody
H. B. Irving
H.C. Bailey
H. G. Wells
H. H. Munro
H. Irving Hancock
H. R. Naylor
H. Rider Haggard
H. W. C. Davis
Haldeman Julius
Hall Caine
Hamilton Wright Mabie
Hans Christian Andersen
Harold Avery
Harold McGrath
Harriet Beecher Stowe
Harry Castlemon
Harry Coghill
Harry Houidini

Hayden Carruth
Helent Hunt Jackson
Helen Nicolay
Hendrik Conscience
Hendy David Thoreau
Henri Barbusse
Henrik Ibsen
Henry Adams
Henry Ford
Henry Frost
Henry James
Henry Jones Ford
Henry Seton Merriman
Henry W Longfellow
Herbert A. Giles
Herbert Carter
Herbert N. Casson
Herman Hesse
Hildegard G. Frey
Homer
Honore De Balzac
Horace B. Day
Horace Walpole
Horatio Alger Jr.
Howard Pyle
Howard R. Garis
Hugh Lofting
Hugh Walpole
Humphry Ward
Ian Maclaren
Inez Haynes Gillmore
Irving Bacheller
Isabel Cecilia Williams
Isabel Hornibrook
Israel Abrahams
Ivan Turgenev
J.G.Austin
J. Henri Fabre
J. M. Barrie
J. M. Walsh
J. Macdonald Oxley
J. R. Miller
J. S. Fletcher
J. S. Knowles
J. Storer Clouston
J. W. Duffield
Jack London
Jacob Abbott
James Allen
James Andrews
James Baldwin

James Branch Cabell
James DeMille
James Joyce
James Lane Allen
James Lane Allen
James Oliver Curwood
James Oppenheim
James Otis
James R. Driscoll
Jane Abbott
Jane Austen
Jane L. Stewart
Janet Aldridge
Jens Peter Jacobsen
Jerome K. Jerome
Jessie Graham Flower
John Buchan
John Burroughs
John Cournos
John F. Kennedy
John Gay
John Glasworthy
John Habberton
John Joy Bell
John Kendrick Bangs
John Milton
John Philip Sousa
John Taintor Foote
Jonas Lauritz Idemil Lie
Jonathan Swift
Joseph A. Altsheler
Joseph Carey
Joseph Conrad
Joseph E. Badger Jr
Joseph Hergesheimer
Joseph Jacobs
Jules Vernes
Julian Hawthrone
Julie A Lippmann
Justin Huntly McCarthy
Kakuzo Okakura
Karle Wilson Baker
Kate Chopin
Kenneth Grahame
Kenneth McGaffey
Kate Langley Bosher
Kate Langley Bosher
Katherine Cecil Thurston
Katherine Stokes
L. A. Abbot
L. T. Meade

L. Frank Baum
Latta Griswold
Laura Dent Crane
Laura Lee Hope
Laurence Housman
Lawrence Beasley
Leo Tolstoy
Leonid Andreyev
Lewis Carroll
Lewis Sperry Chafer
Lilian Bell
Lloyd Osbourne
Louis Hughes
Louis Joseph Vance
Louis Tracy
Louisa May Alcott
Lucy Fitch Perkins
Lucy Maud Montgomery
Luther Benson
Lydia Miller Middleton
Lyndon Orr
M. Corvus
M. H. Adams
Margaret E. Sangster
Margret Howth
Margaret Vandercook
Margaret W. Hungerford
Margret Penrose
Maria Edgeworth
Maria Thompson Daviess
Mariano Azuela
Marion Polk Angellotti
Mark Overton
Mark Twain
Mary Austin
Mary Catherine Crowley
Mary Cole
Mary Hastings Bradley
Mary Roberts Rinehart
Mary Rowlandson
M. Wollstonecraft Shelley
Maud Lindsay
Max Beerbohm
Myra Kelly
Nathaniel Hawthrone
Nicolo Machiavelli
O. F. Walton
Oscar Wilde

Owen Johnson
P.G. Wodehouse
Paul and Mabel Thorne
Paul G. Tomlinson
Paul Severing
Percy Brebner
Percy Keese Fitzhugh
Peter B. Kyne
Plato
Quincy Allen
R. Derby Holmes
R. L. Stevenson
R. S. Ball
Rabindranath Tagore
Rahul Alvares
Ralph Bonehill
Ralph Henry Barbour
Ralph Victor
Ralph Waldo Emmerson
Rene Descartes
Ray Cummings
Rex Beach
Rex E. Beach
Richard Harding Davis
Richard Jefferies
Richard Le Gallienne
Robert Barr
Robert Frost
Robert Gordon Anderson
Robert L. Drake
Robert Lansing
Robert Lynd
Robert Michael Ballantyne
Robert W. Chambers
Rosa Nouchette Carey
Rudyard Kipling
Saint Augustine
Samuel B. Allison
Samuel Hopkins Adams
Sarah Bernhardt
Sarah C. Hallowell
Selma Lagerlof
Sherwood Anderson
Sigmund Freud
Standish O'Grady
Stanley Weyman
Stella Benson
Stella M. Francis

Stephen Crane
Stewart Edward White
Stijn Streuvels
Swami Abhedananda
Swami Parmananda
T. S. Ackland
T. S. Arthur
The Princess Der Ling
Thomas A. Janvier
Thomas A Kempis
Thomas Anderton
Thomas Bailey Aldrich
Thomas Bulfinch
Thomas De Quincey
Thomas Dixon
Thomas H. Huxley
Thomas Hardy
Thomas More
Thornton W. Burgess
U. S. Grant
Upton Sinclair
Valentine Williams
Various Authors
Vaughan Kester
Victor Appleton
Victor G. Durham
Victoria Cross
Virginia Woolf
Wadsworth Camp
Walter Camp
Walter Scott
Washington Irving
Wilbur Lawton
Wilkie Collins
Willa Cather
Willard F. Baker
William Dean Howells
William le Queux
W. Makepeace Thackeray
William W. Walter
William Shakespeare
Winston Churchill
Yei Theodora Ozaki
Yogi Ramacharaka
Young E. Allison
Zane Grey

www.ingramcontent.com/pod-product-compliance
Lightning Source LLC
Chambersburg PA
CBHW020438270626
47155CB00022B/619